Suzanne,

Sleep with the lights on!

[illegible]

#RARE2014

Also by Karina Halle

The Experiment in Terror Series

Darkhouse (EIT #1)
Red Fox (EIT #2)
The Benson (EIT #2.5)
Dead Sky Morning (EIT #3)
Lying Season (EIT #4)
On Demon Wings (EIT #5)
Old Blood (EIT #5.5)
The Dex-Files (EIT #5.7)
Into the Hollow (EIT #6)
And With Madness Comes the Light (EIT #6.5)
Come Alive (EIT #7)
Ashes to Ashes (EIT #8)
Dust to Dust (EIT #9) – May 2014

Novels by Karina Halle

The Devil's Metal (Devils #1)
The Devil's Reprise (Devils #2)
Sins and Needles (The Artists Trilogy #1)
On Every Street (An Artists Trilogy Novella #0.5)
Shooting Scars (The Artists Trilogy #2)
Bold Tricks (The Artists Trilogy #3)

Coming Soon

Donners of the Dead
Love, in English

ASHES TO ASHES

An Experiment in Terror Novel #8

∞Karina Halle∞

\m/ Metal Blonde Books \m/

First edition published by
Metal Blonde Books December 2013

Publisher's Note: This is a work of fiction. Names, characters, places, and incidents either are the product of the author's imagination or are used fictitiously. Any resemblance to actual events, locales, or persons, living or dead, is entirely coincidental.

Cover design by Najla Qamber
Edited by Kara Malinczak

ISBN-13: 978-1494414542

Metal Blonde Books
P.O. Box 845
Point Roberts, WA
98281 USA

Manufactured in the USA

For more information about the series and author visit: http://khalle.wordpress.com/

For the GoGs and all their inappropriate help with this

CHAPTER ONE

It's been two months since I first told Dex Foray that I loved him. Two months since we've lived together, as an actual couple, in his Seattle apartment. And two months since Rebecca Sims joined us as our welcomed third wheel in the *Experiment in Terror* show. It goes without saying that they've been the best two months of my life.

But, like most things, it hasn't been perfect. My relationship with my family is now awkward as all hell—I mean more so than it used to be, and that says a lot. I'll talk to my mom and dad maybe every two weeks, and it's just one of those *please shoot me in the head* kind of moments where you're grasping for shit to say and your mouth is moving and suddenly you're talking about the weather or the latest celebrity scandal or things you can't even remember just to keep the conversation going, just so it doesn't lag and you don't have to address the giant flaming pink rollerblading elephant in the room.

Yeah ... about that giant flaming pink rollerblading elephant. That would be that I left my parent's house, where I had spent most of my twenty-three years, and decided to move in with my partner. Dex. The guy that my parents absolutely hated because I had an ill-timed fling with him back when he had a girlfriend (no judging), and he turned into a dick right after I slept with him (please no judging), and I ended up miscarrying his baby (okay, the judging is inevitable). I'm not saying any of that lightly because it pretty much ruined the fabric of my being and introduced demonic possession into my life experiences, but I mean, you can kind of understand why my parents think Dex Foray is public enemy number one.

Obviously, they don't approve of my new life. I can tell that from the things they aren't saying and the questions they aren't asking. They don't even wonder when or if I'm coming home; it's just such a non-issue that it's become an issue. At least for me. I *want* them to care. I want them to say something, even if it's just to scream at me.

The only person that I talk to truthfully on a daily basis (even if it's just mainly through texts) is my younger sister Ada. She's happy for me, happy that things are going well with Dex (even though she often starts the conversation with, "You guys still together? Yes? Okay cool,") but she doesn't pull back from telling me how badly she wants me to come back home, even just for a visit.

The thing is, I'm totally scared. One part of me wants to go back, to try and smooth things over and make things right. Maybe if they see Dex again, months later and in a better context, they'll learn to like him. To see the things I see. To see how well he treats me. And I want to see Ada and hug her and make her feel like she doesn't have to face my parents alone. But the other half of me thinks it could be a mistake—that they'd never open up to him, and I'd regret even trying to make amends. I could make things worse.

I needed a sign.

"Ouch, Jesus," I swore at the stabbing pain at my wrist. I glared up at the burly, bearded tattoo artist who was glaring back at me.

"Try not to flinch," he said gruffly, his gloved hand hovering over my bared wrist.

"You're almost done, honey," Rebecca said in her soothing British accent, patting my other hand. "Few more minutes. Looks fab."

I sighed and tried to relax my body. Now that I wasn't daydreaming, everything was very real. I was with Rebecca, lying on my back in a Seattle tattoo parlor, getting some ink on my wrist. My first tattoo, and though it didn't hurt as much as I thought it would, it was still extremely uncomfortable. It probably didn't help that it was on one of the more sensitive areas. I was just lucky I decided to go with one color of ink—blue—instead of getting it filled in.

Oh yeah, I was getting a tattoo of an anchor. Cliché, I know, but I got it for Dex. After all, he had a tattoo inspired by me on his shoulder, and I figured it was only fair. And, you know, he was my anchor. When he'd given me the anchor silly band back on D'Arcy Island, that stupid little gesture meant so much to me. Then, when I'd ripped it off after, well, the "incident," I'd missed that symbol. Through all the ups and downs we'd gone through, in the end, he was still my rock. And an anchor was a hell of a lot sexier than getting a big ass boulder tatted on you.

"He's going to be so surprised," Rebecca said as the tattoo machine resumed its buzzing.

I ground my teeth together against the vibrating prickles. "Uh huh. I hope so."

I asked Rebecca to accompany me here so I wouldn't have to go through it alone. I wanted it to be a surprise for Dex, so I just told him we were going out and doing girly things. I know his dirty mind was probably imagining us heading to some International Pillow-Fighting Convention, and a tattoo parlor was the last place he'd think of. I wasn't really the tattoo type—my interests in life were so wavering and fleeting, but my love for Dex was as permanent as ink. I wanted him to know that.

"Okay, you're done," the man said, lifting away the needle, the room growing temporarily quiet without the constant buzz.

"For real?"

He grunted in response and motioned for me to sit up. I slowly did so and stared at my left wrist. It wasn't bleeding like I thought it would be since I'd felt him periodically dabbing it with cloth as he worked. The tattoo was shiny and raised, the skin around it red, but it looked beautiful. Simple but beautiful. And I suddenly felt infinitely cooler.

I looked up at Rebecca for her approval as the artist started wrapping it in black plastic. Her matte red lips were stretched into a smile, her eyes sparkling with delight. In fact, she looked borderline ecstatic which I found almost odd.

"He's going to *love* it," she said. "Really, really. It's going to mean so much to him."

I smiled. "Good."

It's not that Dex didn't know how I felt about him. After what happened to us in New Orleans, and how he'd almost died right before my eyes and I almost lost him in so many ways, I'd had verbal diarrhea of the lovey-dovey kind. But for some reason, at times I could tell it was hard for Dex to believe me. When I told him I loved him, he had a knack for turning it into a joke, like, "You say that to all the boys," and while he played it off in his cheeky way, I could tell it came from somewhere. I hoped the tattoo would ease that for him.

Like I said, they'd been the best two months of my life, but things weren't perfect. It's hard to truly appreciate things when somewhere in the back of your mind you're waiting for the other shoe to drop.

I swung my legs off the table, admiring even the black plastic around my wrist. That, combined with my new twelve-hole forest green Doc Martens and my leather jacket that was too hot for the surprisingly warm May weather, I felt better than I had in weeks. See, along with the whole impeding feeling of doom that I couldn't shake (and I had no idea what it was about either), I'd gained some weight after moving in with Dex. I could blame his diet all I wanted, but the fact was he ate fairly well and still went to the gym every day, so there goes that excuse. I knew they were "happy pounds," like the in-love equivalent of the freshman fifteen, but it still had me a bit bummed out. Dex loved me the way I was, but I still felt like I had to be something he could show off, something like his ex-girlfriend Jenn. I'd lost the shape I worked hard for over Christmas, and I always had that fear one day he'd realize I wasn't good enough for him.

"Come on," Rebecca said, tugging on my arm toward the cash register. "Let's get you home to your man." She clicked her way over to the counter in her sky-high red heels, her small ass sashaying in her pencil skirt. Rebecca was the opposite of me. Since she and Emily broke up, she'd been doing nothing but losing weight, something she didn't need to begin with.

It didn't help that when we had our last meeting with Jimmy Kwan at Shownet over Experiment in Terror, he brought up the fact that Rebecca should be in front of the camera. He wasn't trying to boot me off, so he said, but that two hot girls were better than one. Luckily Rebecca refused, saying she was only good as a production manager and that her days of hosting ended when Wine Babes did. And even though Rebecca was his good friend, Dex agreed. I probably would have hit him if he didn't.

Ever since we'd come back from New Orleans, we'd done about five shows together as a "threesome."

It wasn't until the fourth show—investigating the haunted town of St. Augustine in Florida—that we really found our rhythm and clicked. Though filming hadn't changed much, Dex and I had to adjust to a more regimented schedule, running on Rebecca's time now and not our own. I had to admit it helped—we never wasted too much time in one space, and we were always in the most opportune areas, but there was a learning curve all the same. We had to stop being "Perry and Dex" and remember that Rebecca was counting on us as well. Then there was the fact that Rebecca wasn't, well, she wasn't like *us*. She rarely saw anything supernatural, and I know it started to bug her too when Dex and I would be freaking out or talking to ghosts, and she'd be staring at nothing. By the fifth episode, a haunted library in Eureka, Rebecca decided she'd only be around the actual filming when we needed a hand—otherwise she'd be somewhere else and leave the ghosts to us.

"I wonder where we're filming next," Rebecca commented as we walked down the street to her car.

I shot her an odd look, wondering if she'd heard my thoughts. I still had this tendency to project my thoughts and lately I'd been picking up on other people's. It usually happened with Dex, though on occasion I'd find it in some random person. But Rebecca had never been on the receiving end of Perry telepathy. At least not yet.

"Did you hear what I was thinking?" I asked.

She smiled. "No, and believe me, the day I hear you, you'll know. It's just we both know that Dex is having that meeting with Jimmy today. I'm assuming it won't be about me being a host since I nearly ripped him a bloody new one. Hopefully it will be another assignment." She unlocked the door to her hatchback and I got in in the passenger seat. "I mean, it's been three weeks since we returned from California and I know the library episode wasn't a complete disaster."

I nodded as she took us out of the Queen Anne district and headed back to downtown Seattle. I rubbed the plastic over my tattoo, wanting to peek at it again but having to restrain myself. "I know. It's like I know there are tons of paranormal hot spots all over the country—more now than ever, according to websites."

She brought out a cigarette and rolled down the window before lighting it. "I sent a bunch of suggestions to Jimmy too, but I think after Florida, he wants to keep us closer to home."

"Because he's cheap."

She exhaled a cloud of blue smoke. "I guess having a sponsor didn't really help."

"At least it's paying for your salary. We didn't have that before."

She gave me a shy glance. "So you're saying you don't totally resent me for being on the show with you?"

I looked at her incredulously. "What? No! What makes you say that?"

She shrugged. "I don't know. I feel like the third wheel sometimes."

"You *are* the third wheel," I said. She gave me a half smile and I quickly continued. "Meaning, you're the wheel. You steer us, you keep us going in the right direction. Yeah, it's different for me and Dex, but sometimes I think it's because our relationship has changed too. Everything is different from the way it used to be and that's not a bad thing. Thanks to you, the shows are tighter and we're not wasting as much money, and Jimmy doesn't yell at us as much. The shows look better too—just having you around to put up a second light or whatever. Seriously, Becs, you're awesome. You're the reason Dex and I can still do this. You're a lifesaver."

"Well, you're way more fun to work with than Jenn," she said. "Though that's a given."

Sometimes I'd forgotten that Dex started out at Shownet by being the cameraman for *Wine Babes*, filming Jenn and Rebecca as they talked about pairing certain wines with McShit from McDonalds. That's how he hooked up with that bitch to start with. I tried to shrug off the questions, wanting to ask Rebecca what they were like when filming together versus the way Dex and I are. I was under the impression that they were off humping like bunnies every time they worked together, and though Dex and I weren't that different, I think he was slightly more professional around me. Which was good...right?

I rubbed my lips together, keeping my mouth shut, and sat back as Rebecca put Lana Del Ray on her stereo. I let the music rush over me and fidgeted in anticipation of Dex's reaction to my tattoo. I really hoped he wasn't going to think it was too much. Sure, we'd been together for two months as an actual couple, but things were still so fresh and new for us in so many ways.

CHAPTER TWO

We found parking on the street just as the monorail trundled past our apartment, heading down 5th Avenue, and made our way up to the apartment. As soon I as stuck my key in the lock, I heard tiny little paws and claws scampering on the ground and knew Fat Rabbit was launching himself across the floor at rocket speed.

I turned around and eyed Rebecca's bare legs. "Be prepared." Fat Rabbit had already ruined countless pairs of tights from jumping on her, much like Dex had ruined countless pairs of underwear by ripping them off of me.

I eased open the door to see the drooling, elfin little face of Dex's French bulldog jumping up at me, emitting frantic barks of joy. I'd gotten used to the little bugger, but Dex was still his master, his alpha. Fatty Rab treated me like another dog, which was fine since I didn't have to be the one to discipline him. Actually, it was kind of charming when Dex did have to lay the smackdown on him (not literally of course). There was a warm feeling in the back of my head, the surprising idea that he'd be a very good father.

But that was my silly brain always getting ahead of everything. I constantly needed to remind myself to concentrate on the present before my mind started fantasizing about all these ridiculous plans for my future. One step at a time....

I shooed the dog away with my boot, knowing Dex wasn't home yet, and we walked into the apartment. Not a lot had changed since I moved in. It was my place too now, and it felt like it, but it wasn't like I'd always harbored dreams of redoing Dex's place. I had some vintage travel posters framed and put on the walls alongside signed concert posters, a few skull-embossed pillows added to the couch, a potted plant in the corner near the balcony, and a small herb garden I started on the windowsill, but that was about it. It was very us—whatever that meant.

I made Rebecca and I a cup of coffee with our new espresso machine, somehow managing to spray coffee all over my shirt. While I was in the bedroom changing, I heard Dex come in. Well, I heard Fat Rabbit erupt into a chorus of happy barks.

I slipped on a long-sleeved Henley, unbuttoning the top few buttons (Dex always said you gotta work with what god gave you), and made sure the sleeve covered the plastic over the tattoo. I poked my head out the door to see him throwing his car keys into the bowl on the kitchen counter before scooping Fat Rabbit into his arms.

Dear Lord, there was never anything hotter than watching Dex cuddle his dog. And as usual, he was looking good. The "pinch me, is he really *my* boyfriend?" kind of good. I literally asked myself that every single day.

He was wearing his only pair of blue jeans (most of his pants were either camo, grey, or black) that were so worn it looked like he'd had them since he was a teenager. They made his ass look amazing, regardless. On his feet were his black army boots. His t-shirt was white, not too tight, but you could still see his amazing shoulders and pecs, and his biceps popped with that early summer color. He'd picked it up at some thrift store, probably because it said *Ride the Mustache* across it.

He gave Fat Rabbit a kiss on the head and said hello to Rebecca.

"Where's Perry?" he asked. Before she could answer, his dark eyes quickly flew over to me and he smiled as bright as day, his dimples showing on his scruffy face. "There's my woman."

It felt like warm honey poured down my spine and feather-winged butterflies flew up my limbs. All it took was to see him, to hear those words that I was *his*, and I was falling in love, so hard and so fast all over again. It made me forget all my problems, lifted that ominous weight off my back. He worked better than any anti-depressant.

I grinned back at him as he put Fat Rabbit on the ground and walked over to me. He put his arm around the small of my back and pulled me close to him before kissing me softly on the lips. He pulled away and brushed my hair behind my ear. From the way his dark eyes were glinting as they searched mine, I had to wonder what was on his mind, if somehow he already knew about the tattoo.

"Hey kiddo," he said, voice rough and soft at the same time.

Rebecca cleared her throat from across the room and Dex looked back at her.

"Sorry," he said, though I knew he wasn't. "I guess you don't want to get in on this action. Do you?"

She rolled her eyes and I quickly smacked him across his chest. He grinned cheekily back at me and ran his hand through his thick black hair before taking mine in his and leading me over to the couch.

"Now I can tell you two are hiding something from me because you both have these devilish little girly smirks on your faces," he said as he sat me down.

I looked over at Rebecca, eyes wide, and she quickly shrugged just before he turned to her.

"But," he continued, giving her the stare down, "before I get it out of you by nefarious means, we have to talk about the show."

I swallowed hard, a lump forming in my chest. I really hoped Jimmy wasn't ragging on him again about making Rebecca the host. Dex noticed the look on my face and said, "Don't worry. I think this is very good news."

Rebecca stepped closer, folding her arms. "Well, what is it?"

"We've got a show. And it seems like it's going to be a good one."

I exhaled noisily at that.

"It's about time," Rebecca said. "Where?"

He took in a deep breath before saying, "A haunted school. On the Oregon Coast." He looked at me expectantly. "It's just an hour away from your Uncle Al's."

I wasn't sure how I felt about that. "Oregon?"

"We're going back to the beginning, baby," he said, wagging his brows. "Only there's no lighthouse this time. As shit-your-pants scary as that Old Roddy fucker was, we've got a school of dead children. But we can handle it. And if we can't, well that's what Jack Daniels is for."

Rebecca pursed her lips. "Okay, I'm going to need a bit more information than school of dead children, Dex. What was wrong with all the suggestions I kept giving to Jimmy? There are heaps of haunted places around with actual documented phenomenon. In all my research, I've never come across any kind of haunted school before on the Oregon Coast."

"To be fair, Becs," Dex said with a leveling gaze, "you've only been doing research for, what, two months? Jimmy said this just came to his attention the other day. He's already discussed it with the sponsors and the school and they've all agreed to it." She frowned at that, probably feeling that her role as production manager was getting stepped on a bit by Jimmy himself. "And anyway, he showed me the location and gave me the lowdown on the whole place. It seems legit."

He walked over to the fridge and pulled out a beer. "Anyone want one?"

Rebecca and I shook our heads while he came back, swigging on a bottle of Heineken. He sat down on the couch beside me, his arm coming around my shoulder.

"Where on the coast?" I asked him, my mind still stewing over the fact that I'd be not only returning to Oregon, but near the place that started it all, the place where I first met Dex. It was a fucking trip to think how full circle this could be, to go from running into him in the lighthouse and staring at his face for the first time to sitting beside him in *our* apartment, his arm around me, in love. Did I even realize at the time what this strange man would become to me? Everything.

"There's a small town called Gary on the coast, just north of Tillamook. I know you and I have driven past it before."

I frowned, my memory jogging in place.

He continued, "There's a giant smokestack there leftover from a mill that no longer exists. I remember you telling me it looked creepy. I thought it looked like an ancient dildo."

"You would," I said. I had a faint image of it in my head. "Is there a large G carved into the mountainside?"

He nodded. "Yeah. The town itself is nothing to look at, but there used to be a sanitarium there. Sea

Crest. Until the 50s it was used for children with Tuberculosis. They believed the fresh ocean air would, I dunno, clear their lungs or something. But it never did. There was no cure until there was a cure. It was basically a house of death. The kids would die in the end, all of them dropping like flies. You came in to Sea Crest by the front door and you came out by the morgue."

I shivered despite it being warm in the room.

"Sounds like a bloody good time," Rebecca said under her breath.

Dex slapped his knee, making me and Fat Rabbit jump. He seemed to be a little too enthusiastic about this. "Speaking of blood, when the patients died, the doctors would put them on this special slab and drain their bodies of blood. Apparently in the upper floors of the school, you can see the rivers of blood in the floor that they couldn't seem to clean away."

"How is this still being used?" I asked. "I mean, a school?"

He shrugged. "I know. Apparently it's a grade school for artistically gifted children. Their old school was in Tillamook but it burned down a couple years ago. Parents didn't want to have to pay for a new building with an increase in tuition so they decided to take over the old sanitarium."

I snorted, trying to ignore the prickles of unease on my neck. "Great. All we need is a bunch of creative art kids in a school full of ghost kids."

"That's the thing," he said. He paused to take a swig of beer and settled back against the couch, his hand rubbing my shoulder. "Things have been fine until recently. That's probably why, Rebecca, you didn't hear about the place before. They have a new teacher for painting and drawing, Brenna McDonald or McSomething, and she's the one who reached out to Jimmy. It all seemed to start the minute she got there."

"And so she actually wants us to film it?" Rebecca asked.

"So she says."

"And the school doesn't have a problem with it?"

"He said they didn't. Maybe they want the school to have some notoriety. I don't know, but we're going. On Sunday we'll pack up the Highlander and go for it."

"That's like in two days," I pointed out.

"Then it's time to call your uncle and let him know you'll be in town. Maybe we can drop in on Sunday for dinner. I'm sure he'd like that."

I licked my lips. "I haven't talked to him in forever."

"So maybe this is the opportunity to start making amends."

"I don't have a problem with my uncle," I said rather defensively.

Dex tilted his head. "No, not with him...but...well, we'll have to drive through Portland to get there."

Ugh. He was right. There was no way I could go to Oregon and not see my family. Even if we took the coast, if Ada ever found out that I'd been in the state without seeing her, she'd kill me.

Rebecca pulled out her cell phone and eyed it before slipping it back in her purse. "I suppose that means I only have a few days to prepare. I better get started."

"Hey now,"Dex said, leaning forward. "You're not going anywhere. Now that you know the show, I want to know what you two were up to today."

She gave him a smirk and started for the door. "I think maybe Perry needs to tell you. In private."

Before I could say anything, she wiggled her fingers at me in a goodbye and left the apartment, closing the door behind her. My nerves suddenly started misfiring. I couldn't believe I was actually nervous around Dex. My tattoo started tingling underneath my sleeve.

"Well?" he said expectantly.

I slowly turned my head to look at him. He was holding the bottle of beer at his mouth, taking a beat to grin at me before having a sip. He wiped his mouth with the back of his hand and dipped his chin, his eyes boring into me, framed by those cocky brows. He certainly had a way of making me talk. Or a way of making me jump him.

"I, uh...I did something today," I started, picking at the lint on my leggings.

He leaned in closer, bumping his shoulder against mine playfully. "Oh yeah? Is this the part where you tell me that you and Rebecca are running away together?"

"Does your mind always go there?" I asked, even though I knew the answer was *yes*. Once a pervert, always a pervert.

"Not always," he said slowly. A grave look came across him. "But seriously. What is it? What did you do?"

I took in a deep breath and avoided his eyes. I stared at Fat Rabbit who had flopped down on the rug. "I did it for you."

I could feel him straighten up. "You didn't murder someone, did you?"

"Some blood was spilled...but no." I tried to find the words. This was actually kind of hard. You'd think I was proposing to him or something. There was so much that I felt inside for Dex, but for some reason it wasn't always easy to express the way I was feeling. Sometimes I totally felt like a dude.

"Okay, here," I said quickly, pulling back the sleeve and placing my wrist on his leg.

He eyed the black plastic with surprise. "You got a tattoo? *You* got a tattoo?"

"Uh huh," I said, and very carefully began to peel away the edges of the tape. "Ta-da."

The skin around the anchor was a darker red and the ink wasn't as vibrant as earlier but it was still there. Obviously. And suddenly it hit me how permanent this was. I mean, I knew before that it was—it was a tattoo—but holy shit, what the fuck had I just done?

"What is this?" Dex asked quietly, his fingers stroking alongside the ink as he stared intently at the anchor. My heart thudded loudly in my chest, my skin sensitive to his touch. Yup. I'd just gotten a tattoo for Dex and I was just realizing it would be embedded into my skin for the rest of my life. What if we broke up? What if this was too much too soon? What if he hated it?

I tried to pull my arm away but he swiftly wrapped his long fingers around my wrist, careful not to touch the tattoo, and held it closer to his eyes. "Perry?" His voice was even lower than before, barely above a whisper.

I tried to clear my throat. "It's...it's a tattoo. Of an anchor. It's for you. Because...Dex, you're my anchor."

His grip tightened and he looked up at me, his brows furrowed. I went on, licking my lips, trying to keep my voice steady. "You...make me feel sane in this crazy world. You give me hope. You give me life. When I'm with you...I can't even believe I'm with you. It's like that every morning. Like I'm dreaming, but I'm not."

I had to look down, his eyes were getting too intense for the words I was saying. "I just...I wanted you to know that. I know I can seem...distant sometimes. I know I'm always in my head and sometimes I'm just a little too quiet. But you're the most important thing to me. You keep me grounded, you hold me in place, you make me feel real. I love you, Dex. I hope this lets you know that."

He didn't say anything. My heart rate sped up, the apartment thrummed with the silence. Shit. Shit, shit, shit. I just fucked it all up, didn't I?

I exhaled shakily and turned my head to look at him, to see the damage.

His eyes seemed frozen in a state of shock yet awash with some unreadable emotion, his Adam's apple bobbing as he swallowed hard. His grip on my wrist never changed. I was afraid the silence would bury me. I was afraid I'd made a mistake.

Then something remarkable happened.

The fear vanished.

He burst into a smile with the energy of a million fires, gleaming white teeth against dimples. His eyes seemed borderline watery and he shook his head back and forth so his hair flopped on his forehead.

"I love the fuck out of you," he said, almost in awe. "Come here."

He grabbed the back of my head, bringing my face toward him and held me firmly in place while he kissed me hard. There was heat and tongue and hunger all in one. It made me feel impossibly giddy, impossibly light.

He stroked one hand down my cheek and pulled away, whispering, "Did you seriously do that for me?"

I nodded. "Of course I did."

Dex grabbed my face in both my hands and kissed me again. "You have no idea how that makes me feel. No idea."

"Good, right?" I whispered.

"Good? Oh, baby, better than good. You just made me feel like a fucking king." His lips trailed to my ear. "I owe you for this. Big time."

I gave him a sassy grin, suddenly exuberant at how much he liked the tattoo. I had no idea it would mean so much. My eyes darted over to the bedroom and back. “Well, I can think of a few ways you can repay me.”

His eyes blazed. “You don’t have to tell me twice,” he growled.

He got up, and in one easy motion, scooped me up in his arms. I cried out in surprise and put my arms around his neck as he carried me over to the bedroom and kicked the door shut before throwing me on the bed.

“Your clothes need to come off, now,” he commanded, immediately dropping to his knees and pulling me forward so my legs went over the edge of the bed. He parted my thighs and went between them, running his hands up my legs until they were under my skirt. “In fact, I don’t know why you bother wearing clothes at all,” he murmured as he slowly began to peel my leggings off.

“Boots first,” I pointed down at my feet without raising my head.

“You and your fucking Docs. Baby, they look great on you but twelve holes are a bitch to undo.”

“Then leave the boots on.”

He paused with my leggings around my knees and I could feel him giving me a steely stare. “Who’s the boss in the bedroom here?”

“Tony Danza?”

He lightly smacked the side of my thigh. “It’s going to be harder and it’s going to be on that fuckable ass of yours if you talk back again.”

I grinned to myself and bit my lip. His large hands went up and pulled down my boy shorts, pressing my legs slightly together to get them off. Then he ducked underneath my legs so he was trapped between me with nowhere to go but my lady bits. Not a bad predicament for me.

“This is going to be tighter than usual,” he said, his breath hot on my inner thighs. I could feel the rough scruff of his face brushing against my skin as he made his way to my slit. “I’m going to eat your pussy clean,” he murmured right before I felt his lips on mine, his warm, wet tongue dipping in between.

My breath hitched from the sensation before I relaxed, smiling again at his dirty talk. He made me blush so hard sometimes but it still turned me on anyway. And fuck, he was insatiable when he was between my legs. He acted like it felt as good for him as it did for me, and then it was double the turn on.

I know, I was fucking lucky.

I let out a little moan as his tongue flicked my clit and my hands gripped the sheets, holding them tighter and tighter as I felt myself swell and open wider for him. He responded with a moan of his own, the vibrations nearly sending me over the edge, as he slowly inserted two long fingers inside me. He made a come hither motion, knowing exactly the right moves to make, and I couldn't keep it together much longer.

"I want you inside me," I groaned.

He paused, his lips brushing against me as he spoke, sending shockwaves of honey through my veins. "What did I tell you about talking back?"

"Oh, I'll talk back to you," I said deliriously, rolling my head from side to side.

"No, you taste too fucking sweet," he said gruffly. "You're coming now."

His head went back down, his tongue sweeping over my clit, his fingers coaxing me until seconds later I was crying out his name, my body rocked by spasms. I barely had time to piece my reality back together when I heard him kicking off his boots and unzipping his jeans.

He grabbed me by the waist and rolled me over, giving my ass a hard smack with his hand. I could feel his balls pressing against my thigh, something else that turned me on.

"That's for talking back," he said. Suddenly he was flipping me over again until I was facing up. I took in the sight of his cock, his hardened muscles, as he leaned his taut body over me, feverish intensity in his eyes. "And this, this is for the tattoo." With one hand he grabbed my face while the other guided himself inside of me. He kissed me so passionately I felt like I couldn't breathe and it didn't even matter.

He pulled away, his eyelashes grazing against my cheeks and whispered, "Thank you. Thank you for letting me in." There was so much sincerity in his voice, this funny man of mine, that I couldn't help but put my hands on both sides of his face, feeling the strength in his fine jaw, and looked him deep in the eyes until I hoped he could see my soul.

"I'm not letting go of you," I said softly, feeling like my heart was beating just for him. "Not ever. This is permanent."

The words felt so heavy leaving my lips, but they were nothing but the truth.

Dex proceeded to make love to me right there—I mean really *make love*. That looking deep into your eyes, slowly devouring every inch of your body, coming so hard that it feels like your souls are fusing together as one, seeing stars, kind of love. Cheesy maybe, but god I loved him, and this, us, felt so incredibly real. So incredibly right.

When we were finished, I kept the bandage off the tattoo and a smile on my face for the rest of the day.

CHAPTER THREE

I woke up in a cold place. That's all I could feel, this terrible chill that enveloped my body from inside and out, an icy hand that gripped my organs and froze my heart.

Where was I? I tried to open my eyes but my lids seemed fused together. I was lying down, on my back somewhere, seemingly all in one piece.

Another dream? I hadn't had a nightmare or anything like this for what seemed like months.

Perry, a familiar voice came floating into my head. *Open your eyes, darling.*

I did as the voice asked and saw nothing above me but grey, heavy clouds. I slowly sat up and when I realized what I was looking at, I was struck with a mix of fear and relief.

Everything around me was grey—monotone—fields that stretched on forever with grass that did not move and air that felt thick like soup. Smelless. Soundless. Tasteless.

In front of me was my grandmother, Pippa. She wasn't close, just a few yards away, but even then I could tell there was a marked change in her. Despite the fact that she was dead, the times I had seen her in the past she'd looked a lot more vibrant. Now she was skinnier, and dressed in a shapeless dress and long coat that hung off her bones. Her hair was thinning more, the curls dull. There was no makeup on her face at all, making her look both more human and more vulnerable.

"Pippa,"I said, never feeling comfortable enough to call her Grandma. "Where am I? Am I in the Thin Veil?"

We are somewhere I think is safe, she said without speaking.

Am I dreaming? I asked, remembering I could just think it and she would hear it. I was wearing every day clothes, not Dex's t-shirt I fell asleep in every night. This *had* to be a dream.

She held my gaze steady, her eyes still full of life even though the rest of her seemed to be wasting away.

I'm sorry I haven't been around, she said.

I swallowed and nodded, noticing the tense tone of her voice.

Things are changing over here, she said. *Things are changing for me. I'm afraid I won't be able to see you very often.*

Why?

I don't know. But I feel it. I know you can see it in me. Though I am dead, I am also dying. And you...you are growing stronger.

I bit my lip. *I don't understand. Stronger how?*

You are able to put your thoughts in other people's heads and you're starting to pick up on their thoughts. Not with everyone, but with others like you. Like me.

So? I mean, what's the use in that? I don't want that, I don't want people to know what I'm thinking, and I don't want to know what they're thinking.

You will learn to block your thoughts and learn to block theirs. But that is beside the point. You are gaining these gifts at rapid speed, which means you have the capacity for immense power.

I'm not a fucking superhero.

Don't swear, Perry, she chastised me, her nostrils flaring.

Sorry, I replied.

I'm trying to warn you.

Then come out and say it. You know this passive aggressive dilly dallying has never worked in my favor.

I would tell you more if I knew for a fact, for certain. Alas, I do not. She looked up at the sky, frowning. I followed her gaze but saw nothing out of the ordinary for whatever world we were in. She went on. *But I do feel things, and I have...instincts...that I never had when I was alive. The demons on the other side are growing. The ones that make it through to the Veil are strong. The ones who make it through to your side are even stronger. It gets worse each year.*

My heart slowed a few beats, but still I raised a brow, forcing myself to be cynical rather than scared. *Is that so?*

She smiled lightly which only made her hollowed out cheekbones more pronounced. *You feel it. Everyone on your side feels it. The disasters, floods, hurricanes, tornadoes, earthquakes. The daily violence. The fall of humanity. Everything crumbles for a reason.*

So what do I have to do with the fall of humanity? I asked. What she said did make sense but you could probably say that about humanity at any time during our planet's history.

You don't have anything to do with it. But maybe you will. Or someone you know will. Someone who is as equally special as you.

Dex, I said, exhaling slowly.

Yes, she said. *I think he might be a target. Could be. Or maybe your sister. Or maybe other people that I do not know. I just know that when demons get to the other side, they look for a host and they go after the ones with power.*

Been there, done that, I said, narrowing my eyes at the memory. *Have the t-shirt.*

This isn't the time for jokes, Perry.

Well what the hell am I supposed to do about it? I asked, raising my hands in frustration. *I don't even know where I am and you're telling me that more demons are looking for people like me.*

Her eyes turned soft, her mouth grave. *I just wanted to warn you. Nothing I said is necessarily true. It is just what I feel and what I fear. If something did happen to you, to Declan, to Ada, to...*she trailed off and swallowed hard. *Just know I had to tell you, even if it turns out to be nothing.*

Well, let's just hope it's nothing then, I said, *because honestly, dealing with this seeing ghost business is hard enough. Thank God for Dex, because if it wasn't for him, I wouldn't know how I'd cope in this life, always seeing things that others can't.*

It is lonely. And I wouldn't wish it upon my greatest enemy. I felt a life of isolation and sorrow roll off of her and onto me.

Suddenly her head jerked up, and this time there was something to see in the sky. I couldn't quite make it out; it seemed to be both very close and very far away. It looked like a bat, a giant black one, with a wingspan that grew larger as it grew closer.

"Time for you to go," Pippa said.

Everything shimmered, rippled, a dance of air on a palette of grey.

Then I was back in the apartment, standing in the living room in Dex's t-shirt, my legs and feet bare and cold. I heard a little snuffle from beside me and saw Fat Rabbit roll over on the couch, seemingly asleep and uninterested.

The fuck just happened? Was I sleepwalking, dreaming I was in the Veil with Pippa? Or had she actually, physically brought me there? Wasn't that supposed to be dangerous in a way?

I just know that when demons get to the other side, they look for a host and they go after the ones with power.

I shuddered at her words as they played over in my head. I'd already faced my demons, I'd already gone to hell and back. There was no way that could happen to me again. No way.

But what about Dex? asked the voice in my head. Ada?

I knew I'd do whatever I could to protect both of them. But I also knew I couldn't freak out over an unsure warning in what might have been just a dream.

It *had* to be a dream.

I sighed. I headed to the washroom to pee when suddenly there was a burst of vibration and a buzzing sound. With my hand at my chest, I spotted Dex's cell on the kitchen counter, dancing and skipping from a muted phone call.

I frowned and quickly went over to it. Not only was it four in the morning, but the number was 1-234-56789123456789, something I had never seen before.

I picked it up and pressed answer. "Hello?" I said quietly, not wanting to wake Dex if I didn't have to.

There was silence though I thought I heard breathing.

"Hello?" I asked again.

Someone cleared their throat. "Sorry. I may have the wrong number. Is...is Declan Foray there?"

"Declan?" I asked, always finding it funny when people addressed him by his full name. "He's sleeping."

"That's a shame," the man said. I couldn't really figure out if he was young or old. He had a clipped way of speaking.

"Can I take a message?"

"Who is it that I am speaking to?"

I paused, feeling funny about the whole thing. "Perry," I said reluctantly.

"Are you his girlfriend? His wife?"

I would have snorted at that if I wasn't so creeped out.

"Who is it that *I* am speaking to?" I asked.

"I must have the wrong number," he mused slowly. Then the call went dead.

I stared at the phone, trying to wrap my head around it. Then I shrugged and headed back to the bedroom. It was time to go back to sleep.

***

I didn't really remember the phone call, nor my dream about Pippa, until a couple of days later when we were getting ready to leave for Oregon. I left out the dream since it was probably nonsense anyway—I *was* under a lot of stress when it came to seeing my parents, so my mind was probably concocting a bunch of nonsense—but I told Dex about the call. It didn't seem to interest him a bit so I left it at what he thought it was—a pushy telemarketer in the night.

"The dog sitter will be here in ten minutes," I yelled at Dex from the bedroom. He was in the bathroom and taking forever. "And then we have to be out of here."

I heard him mumble something that sounded like, "Relax, kiddo," followed by the buzz of his electric razor.

I sighed. Rebecca had been Fat Rabbit's regular dog sitter until she joined our team. Now we'd been trying to find the right one for a while. The last one we had was Dex and Rebecca's friend Seb, and when we returned home, we were paranoid that Seb had turned the place into a marijuana grow-op. Even the dog seemed to be extra lazy upon our return. As soon as the new sitter, Ana Rita, showed up, we'd take off for Oregon.

I still hadn't told my parents about it. In fact, I hadn't told Ada either. We'd decided to head straight to the coast and then stop by Portland on the way back, so at this point I'd only called Uncle Al. He sounded overjoyed to hear from me—it's wasn't like I regularly talked to him anyway—and it calmed my nerves a bit.

But only a bit.

Because I was pretty fucking nervous about this whole thing. The child ghosts at this school weren't even entering my head—I was worried about my parents and their reaction to me showing up. I was worried about how they would or wouldn't accept Dex. Even though I'd cut the ties and I was more than old enough, they were still my parents and they still had a strange hold on me.

I looked over my shoulder at my small suitcase I'd packed on the bed. Then I looked at Dex's duffel bag on the floor. I peered inside. It was completely empty.

I rolled me eyes and ran over to the bathroom door and pounded on it. "Hey, you haven't packed yet!"

The buzzing stopped momentarily. "It'll take me two seconds."

Right.

I went back to the room and started flipping through his closet, pulling out a leather jacket, a cargo coat, a hoodie, and a long-sleeved dress shirt for when he'd meet my parents again, then headed to his dresser. I rummaged through his drawers, picking out a few t-shirts and folding them before I tackled his boxer briefs. I only pulled out one pair before I heard the bathroom door open and Dex cry out, "What the hell are you doing?"

I whipped around to see Dex charging toward me and slamming the drawer shut. Thank god I removed my fingers just in time.

"What's your problem?" I asked him, noting how his body was now blocking the entire dresser, his eyes wide with panic. He'd trimmed down a lot of his beard and 'stache so it was just sexy scruff, and put in his eyebrow ring. He was looking good. But obviously nuts.

"What are you doing?" he asked again.

I gave him an odd look. "I'm trying to pack for you."

"I told you I'd do that," he said, though he was starting to relax.

"Well I'm not counting on that. Why are you acting so sketchy? I'm allowed to touch your underwear."

"Not when there might be skid marks on them."

"Ew!" I wrinkled my nose. "Holy TMI, and also, don't you know where the damn laundry basket is?"

He shrugged. "Now that you know what you're up against, you can continue packing if you'd like."

I shook my head and gave him a wave of disgust. "No thank you, it's all yours."

He grinned at me like he'd won some kind of war, and I could do nothing but take my suitcase out to the front door just in time to hear the buzzer from downstairs.

Fat Rabbit immediately started barking, staring up at me with a forlorn expression on his wrinkly face.

He always acted a bit weird whenever we went away and the suitcase was a clear sign. I hoped he wouldn't give the new sitter too much trouble.

I buzzed the woman up and turned to see Dex strolling proudly out of the bedroom with his duffel bag in tow.

"See," he said, "packed in seconds flat."

I narrowed my eyes suspiciously, figuring he'd probably forgotten a bunch of stuff like deodorant and socks.

When he got next to me, his face grew serious and he reached out to touch my hand, holding onto my pinky. "Are you okay? You're the one who is acting a bit sketchy lately."

I nodded but still said, "I don't know. Just feeling antsy for some reason."

He raised his brow. "Some reason? Kiddo, going home to see your parents isn't some reason. It's a big deal and it's okay, I get it. But I'm here for you, you know that. Right?"

There was a quick knock at the door which set off Fat Rabbit again so I quickly shot him a smile. Having his support would help, but it wasn't enough to make my nerves stop rattling.

I opened the door to see a pretty woman with a warm smile and honey-tinted skin, dressed in form-fitting yoga pants and a tank top that conformed to her lithe body. Immediately I felt a prickle of insecurity and self-loathing, mentally comparing my body to hers.

"You must be Ana Rita," I said, trying to ignore my shortcomings. "I'm Perry, come on in."

"Thank you," she said warmly. I saw her eyes flit over my shoulder to Dex and her smile broadened. "Hi. Dex, right? We spoke on the phone."

Dex nodded and shook her hand. "Thanks for agreeing to watch the little bugger. Hope you're prepared for lots of farts in your future. From the dog, of course."

She went down into a crouch to pet Fat Rabbit who was wriggling all over the place like a spazz, drool flying everywhere. I watched Dex carefully to see if he was checking her out. If he was, he was being real subtle about it.

"You sure you're comfortable staying here?" he went on while Fat Rabbit finally calmed down enough to be sitting in front of her. "Fat Rabbit doesn't do well in other people's houses, he tends to take dumps in your shoe, so we just find it easier to have people come here and sit for him."

She glanced up at him, brushing her light brown hair out of her face. "It's no problem. It's nice to have a change of scenery from time to time. You sure you're comfortable with me being here?"

"Any friend of Rebecca's is a friend of mine," he said, and then gestured over to the kitchen counter. "Instructions are there. Call us if you have any problems."

I waved goodbye to Fat Rabbit while he bounded past Ana Rita and over to Dex where he delivered a bunch of last minute sloppy kisses. Once we were in the elevator, I looked over at him. "She seemed nice."

He shrugged. "As long as the dog is alive when we come back, I don't care." I guess I was staring at him for too long, studying the set of his firm jaw, because he looked over at me with interest. "What?"

"Nothing," I said. Like hell I was going to tell him I was feeling unworthy because the dog sitter happened to be a hot chick. I needed to get the fuck over myself before I royally screwed things up one day. A guy can only tell you you're beautiful so many times before it seems like a lost cause, and I didn't want to seem like one with Dex.

He studied me for a moment and I could tell he wanted to say something, but thankfully he let it go, probably chalking it up to my nerves again. Once in the parking garage, we loaded our bags in the Highlander, Dex having brought the camera equipment down earlier, and headed off to pick up Rebecca.

We drove down the interstate until we got to the turnoff at Longview and started heading out to the

Pacific. The minute the Highlander was heading west, away from the direction of Portland, I let out the longest breath of air.

Rebecca, who had been talking nonstop about a chick she met at a party the night before, leaned forward and tapped me on the shoulder. "Relax, Perry."

I shot her a smile over my shoulder. Even though we were heading to the coast to look for ghost children, she still looked fabulous in a retro cherry-printed white sundress, a lace cardigan, and cat-eye shades. "I'm good."

"Anyone feel like having a late lunch in Seaside?" Dex asked.

"As long as we're at Uncle Al's by seven, sure," I said. I used to go to Seaside all the time as a child so it would be nice to visit the quaint town with its promenade, crashing waves, and old timey shops. I hoped I could avoid the enormous candy stores where I used to spend hours picking out saltwater taffy.

An hour later we rolled into town, wrestling with early-season tourists for a parking spot. We grabbed a quick bite to eat at a chowder place that Dex swore on the bible was the best he ever had, and he wasn't far off. We still had a bit of time before we headed down the coast again, so I suggested we go for a walk on the beach. It was sunny and warm, with just a light breeze, and on the Oregon Coast you had to take advantage of that when you could. I guess Rebecca thought we wanted some privacy because she told us to go ahead; she wanted to do some shopping in town. I didn't know what she could possibly buy aside from chocolate-covered bacon and clothing with tacky seagulls printed all over them, but we left her to her own devices and headed out to the sand.

"Fuck me, this feels good," Dex said as we stood at the top of the steps before heading down onto the beach. The ocean was blue and glittering from the sun, the sand glowing golden white. Kids ran up and down with their kites, making sandcastles and running back from the cold surf.

Dex took in a deep breath. "Feel that sea air. That's got to be good for you."

I gave him a funny look, shielding my eyes with my hand. "We live by the ocean, Dex."

"Bah. Puget Sound doesn't count," he said. "I mean the real ocean. This. There's nothing between us right now and Japan. Just water and waves. Makes you feel free."

"You don't feel free otherwise?"

He gave me a lopsided grin and took my hand in his. "Come on."

He led me down through the dunes, my boots slipping awkwardly as I walked, until we came to the hard-packed sand near the pounding surf. We walked side by side, not saying anything to each other, just watching the people around us, the miles of flawless beach, the sand dollars that crunched under our feet.

We stopped where the pine-dotted bluffs of Ecola State Park jutted out into the water and the beach curved inward, and sat down on a washed up log. Out on the waves, surfers vied for the perfect set, looking like vertical seals in their shiny black wetsuits.

The light wind tossed my hair into my mouth, already tasting like salt, my vision blurred by the strands. I felt Dex's fingers on my face, tucking my hair behind my ears.

"Feels familiar," he said in a low voice. "Doesn't it?"

I thought about it for a second and realized it did. Even though the cameras were back in the car and we were just sitting here looking at the coast, the smell of sea spray, the sound of surf and the feel of sand under my feet brought me back to when we first met each other, just an hour south of where we were.

I looked him over, remembering how he was when I first met him. He still had on the same newsboy cap, though now his eyes were dark and shiny instead of dark and manic. There was no cigarette dangling from his crooked smile and his mustache was trimmed beyond rapist standards. It was still Dex but now he was my Dex. It was kinda hard to wrap my head around it now that we were back at the beginning.

"It feels good," I told him. "Weird. But good."

"Just like me," he said before sucking in his lower lip and turning his gaze to the shore.

"You're better than good," I said.

He nodded with a smile. "And weirder than weird?"

"I think we both are, when you think about it. You're the only person I know that knows what I'm talking about when I say I saw the creepy lady in black at the convenience store."

He pulled the brim of his cap down, shielding his eyes from the glaring sun, and stared at the grains of sand that danced at his boots, whipped around by the wind. "I'm starting to think the douche magoose who works there thinks we're both a bit nuts."

"His name is Paul," I said sternly, sticking up for the harmless hipster who works at the store across the street from us. "And yeah, he probably does. I just pretend I don't see her. I do that with everyone."

He gave me a sideways glance. "How often do you see them?"

It suddenly struck me as odd that even though Dex and I suffered from the same affliction and were intimate with each other on a daily basis, we never ever talked about the things we saw. I chose to suffer in silence, even though I knew he'd understand if I told him.

I brushed a wayward strand out of my eyes, mulling it over. "At least once a day. I think. It's hard to tell, in Seattle anyway. Sometimes I think I'm looking at a ghost but it turns out to be a meth head."

He put his elbows on his knees and his fingers together like a steeple. "Do you ever get scared?"

I snorted. "Yeah. Of course."

I mean, they were ghosts. We weren't seeing puppies. We were seeing the dead, and both of us knew very well that the dead had the power to kill us. Of course, they had the power to kill anyone, but when they found someone who was actually able to see them, able to communicate with them, it made things a bit riskier. They wanted to be around us, they wanted the attention they so rarely got. That's why when we went ghost hunting with Rebecca, she was never in any real danger. It's not that she wasn't scared herself, there were a few times where she was freaking out on behalf of what we said we were seeing, but we both knew the ghosts wouldn't usually bother with her. She didn't see them, so she didn't really exist herself. Sometimes I felt like Dex and I were the ghosts—that the dead could only see us—and every other normal person was just a passing shadow to them.

"Me too," he said, his eyes focusing now on the surfers. "I keep thinking I'll get used to it, but I never really do. Some days I can just kind of, you know, gloss over them. The old man bleeding on the sidewalk that people are walking past...I can almost pretend he's real. As if that fucking makes it better. But I can ignore it. Then sometimes I have a strung out woman with a broken neck in my face, flies coming out of her nose and..." He trailed off and I saw a shudder roll through him.

I reached for him, putting my hand gently on his leg. "I know what you mean."

"And then it just slaps me in the face. Hey, I'm a fucking freak. Hey, this is the reason I was put away in a mental institute. Hey, this is never ever going to go away."

"Unless we go on medication," I said quietly.

He shook his head. "No way, baby. I've seen the light. I can't go back to hiding from it. This is me. This is us. No other way around it, we just have to deal." He tilted his head down and eyed me. "You know that. It's us against the world."

We both fell into silence that was occasionally punctuated by the cry from a soaring gull. How right he was.

Eventually he cleared his throat and gestured to the houses that lined the beach to the right of us.

"Could you imagine yourself living here in five, ten years?"

I eyed the houses, all of them grand with large landscaped lots and views to die for. "Sure. I guess. It's nice here. But I think I'd have to be independently wealthy."

"So say you were. Say you could live anywhere. Where would you live?"

I pursed my lips as I looked at him curiously. "Why are you asking?"

"Why not? We've never really discussed our future with each other...have we?"

I swallowed hard, those damn butterflies making an appearance in my insides.

"Of course," he went on, "I'm being a twat in assuming that I'm actually in your future..."

I gazed at him steadily, my eyes focusing on his ear, where just the tip had been left scarred from his counter with the voodoo priestess in New Orleans. "Dex. I just got a tattoo for you. I let some humorless dude brand me with a needle and ink in a place I look every single day." I waved my wrist at him. "Of course you're in my future. You're the only thing I know about the future."

His eyes blazed passionately before he broke his stare. "Then if that's true...where do you see us?"

Now what was he getting at? What did he want me to say? That in five years I wanted to be married to him, to have his babies, to be putting up a white picket fence? These were dreams that I rarely allowed myself to entertain...none of that ever seemed possible for us, no matter how in love we were.

"I see us...happy," I answered feebly.

"Doing the show?"

"I don't know. I don't think so. It doesn't feel like enough, if you know what I mean." His blank stare told me he didn't. So much for mind reading. "I mean, I think, I *feel*, like the show is a means to an end for now...but it's also the beginning of something, not the end. I think one day we'll be doing something that's more...respectable. Something that matters."

"And me?"

"And you're there with me. I don't know what it is, but we're doing it together."

"I don't think you can count wild monkey sex as a career, Perry."

"I'm counting it as a perk," I said with a smile. "But I think we're both destined for something more. I've always felt that, right from the very start. I think in five, ten years, Experiment in Terror will be a memory. A scary, kind of fun and meaningful memory, but something in the past."

"And we could be living in Seattle...or Seaside..."

I took my hand off his knee and started pushing my fingers into the cool sand. "Anywhere. San Francisco. Boston. Anywhere. As long as I'm with you, I'm happy."

I could feel his eyes boring into me, and by the time I looked back up, he had taken out his phone and was glancing at it. "We oughta get back to Rebecca. She's probably getting sucked into a timeshare by now or getting cotton candy stuck in her hair."

Dex helped me up off the log and took his sweet time brushing the sand and bark off my backside. When we were back at the Lewis and Clark statue at the end of the promenade, he put his arm around me and pulled me in close. "Are you ready to say hi to Uncle Al and your dopey cousins?"

Are you ready to start making amends with your family, is what he was really asking, even though my uncle Al was barely part of the equation.

I let the strength and warmth of Dex's hold wash over me and nodded. As long as he was at my side, I'd manage.

At least I'd try.

CHAPTER FOUR

It was just before seven when Dex pulled the Highlander down a coastal lane past the beach town of Manzanita. Uncle Al's property took up a large chunk of land that I was sure the state was eager to own. There were pastures and an abandoned barn where an old dairy farm used to be, a couple of miles of beachfront, as well as a small forest that dipped into the shores of Nehalem Bay. And, of course, somewhere on the bluffs, the charred remains of a lighthouse that may or may not have blown up on our behalf.

"God, this is weird," Dex said under his breath as we parked at the end of Uncle Al's driveway. The house, a large rancher, looked the same, and my twin cousins, Matt and Tony, had their two cars parked outside. I remembered Matt's truck well—Dex and I had to share the backseat together rather awkwardly.

"Oh, it wasn't awkward for me," Dex said with a knowing smirk as he jammed the Highlander in park.

I flushed at the unexpected intrusion. "Could you hear me think that?"

He slid his hand across the steering wheel. "First time in a while, but it was so worth it."

"You heard her thoughts?" Rebecca asked, leaning forward. "Lucky duck. I never hear anything."

I gave her a look. "You know you're not missing out."

"Well now I want to know what wasn't awkward."

Dex turned to her. "Perry and I were squeezed in the back of that old truck there while we went down the road. Her boobs were banging around from the potholes and I was trying to keep my massive erection hidden."

She wrinkled her face. "Ugh. Nevermind, you guys keep your thoughts to yourself."

I frowned, both turned on and strangely flattered. "You had an erection from that?"

Rebecca's manicured nails fluttered in my face. "I said, keep your bloody thoughts to yourself. I don't want to hear about anyone's erections. Boobs, maybe."

Dex sighed. "Rebecca, you're missing out on so many beautiful wonders about the male body." He gave me a sly look. "And yes, I had a hard-on most of the time I was around you. Why do you think I was so fidgety? It wasn't always the meds, baby. It was your tits and ass and face and everything else I thought I could never have."

I couldn't help but smile at that, at finding out what he first thought of me. And now I wanted to prod him for more. God, I was such a doofus.

Fortunately Rebecca was spared from further tidbits because the front door to the house swung open and Uncle Al appeared in the doorway, eyeing us suspiciously like we were lost tourists or trespassers.

I took in a deep breath. "We better get out and say hello before he pulls a Clint Eastwood on us."

We climbed out of the car, the scent of the dunes and meats grilling on the BBQ bringing me back again.

I'd last seen my uncle and cousins in December, so there wasn't much difference to them over the last six months. But oh, wait. Behind the jovial grin of Uncle Al and his thinning slicked back hair was the look of a man in peace, a man in love. Before I had a chance to wonder if he was still with the woman he had been seeing, I saw her appear behind him: a tiny woman with vivid eyes and a long, delicate face. Marda, I think her name was.

I quickly tugged down the sleeve of my shirt, planning to keep my tattoo hidden from him until my parents had a chance to see it.

"Perry!" my uncle exclaimed, throwing his arms open. As if I were a little girl again, I ran over to him with a shy smile on my lips and threw myself into his embrace. He smelled like this strong cologne he always wore but I inhaled the scent anyway.

"Hey, Uncle Al," I said as I pulled away, looking up at him. "You're looking great." A little bit tubbier but I wasn't one to talk. Looks like we'd both put on the "love pounds."

"Perry, bella," he said, giving me another quick hug. "You're still blind, I see." He winked at me and then turned to his lady friend. "You remember Marda, of course?"

"Of course," I said, offering my hand to her but she pulled me into a hug instead. I felt like I was crushing her bones. "Nice to see you again."

I looked behind me at Dex and Rebecca who were hovering between us and the car. Dex was trying to smile but I could tell he was nervous; he'd taken off his hat and was holding it anxiously in his hands. You'd think he was about to meet the President or something. It was actually damn endearing.

"This is Dex and Rebecca," I said, though I knew he knew who Dex was. He knew very well. Not just because of the ruckus we caused in his lighthouse, but because he saw how in love with Dex I had been. He was the one who told me that my infatuation for him was creating a hole in my heart and that I'd get hurt and be stronger for it. Well, he was kind of right about all that.

"Hello, Dex,"my uncle said, walking toward him to shake his hand. Dex smiled sincerely and I could tell he was giving him one hell of a handshake. It was a lot different than the first time they met. Dex was really trying to make a better impression.

"Thanks for having us over," Dex said. "Really appreciate it."

Oh boy, was he ever trying.

Even Uncle Al seemed a bit taken aback, raising his brows before shrugging. "It's no problem at all. When Perry said she was coming for a visit, I was overjoyed. We all were. We never get to see her anymore." I detected a bit of strain in his voice when he said that, probably thinking about his brother. I wondered how often he talked to my parents and if they talked about me. I guess I'd have to pry him for info after he had a few glasses of wine.

The rest of the introductions to Rebecca and Marda were quickly made before we made our way into

Uncle Al's cozy living room to have a drink. The twins were nowhere to be seen; apparently they were at the beach trying to impress some neighborhood girls, much to Uncle Al's dismay. He said Tony and Matt were still a bunch of troublemakers, and when you added women to the mix, it usually ended in disaster.

"Ain't that the truth," Dex joked as he sat down on the loveseat. He looked up at me with an expectant expression, wanting me to sit with him. To tell you the truth, I hesitated. With Rebecca taking an armchair and my uncle and Marda on the couch, there wasn't anywhere else for me to go, but I didn't want to immediately announce to Uncle Al that Dex and I were a couple. I mean, I figured he knew since I was living in Seattle, but then again, I had no idea how much my uncle knew about the falling out.

Dex didn't let me hesitate for long. He reached up and pulled me down by the arm until I was sitting back in the loveseat and his arm was placed snuggly around me. I dared to meet Uncle Al's eyes. He was staring at us with judgement. Figures. But before I could feel uncomfortable about it, he wiped the expression off his face, as if he realized he was doing it, and got off the couch.

He pointed at me and Dex. "What do you two want? Beer? Wine?"

We both took a beer while Rebecca went for a small glass of wine. The wine would be better on my figure but beer was easier.

We lapsed into easy chit-chat, most of the attention on Rebecca since she was from England, and Uncle Al waxed poetic about his time living there when he was a "young lad." Rebecca wasn't always the most talkative person but she certainly was tonight, maybe because she felt awkward, maybe because the whole situation was still a teeny bit awkward in general. Yeah, the whole elephant in the room? It was languidly parked behind Uncle Al's couch and no one would dare to look at it.

Finally Matt and Tony came home to alleviate some of the tension. Like, straight up.

"So you two are shacking up now," Tony said as he nodded to Dex. "Cool."

I rolled my eyes. "I live with Dex, if that's what you mean." I quickly eyed Uncle Al who just clucked his tongue and excused himself to go check on the grill. Marda followed after him, the screen door swinging shut.

"I had a feeling this would happen," Matt said as he grabbed a beer from the fridge. Though they were under twenty-one, the rules were always lax for them.

"You did?" I asked.

He grabbed an extra can of beer for Dex and threw it at him. Dex caught it without looking, also eager to hear what Matt had to say.

"Totally," Matt went on, leaning against the counter and cracking the beer open with a loud *snap*. "Don't you guys ever see those movies where the girl and the guy are, like, under *duress*," he said duress like he just learned it from his Word of the Day toilet paper, "and they totally hit it off after? Like *Speed* with Keanu Reeves and Sandra Bullock. Meet on a bus. Bus gets a bomb on it. They make out. Awesome flick, even today."

Dex grinned and then took a large swig of beer. "Thanks, man. I think Keanu Reeves is a fine actor if you put him on mute. Otherwise, it's..."

And then Dex launched into his repertoire of Keanu impersonations. They weren't half bad, and I'd heard a lot of them before, but when the twins encouraged him to try talking like Jeff Goldblum, I had to draw the line.

Luckily Uncle Al came back in with the grilled chicken and everyone gathered around the table before Dex could continue talking about Chaos Theory.

"So, Perry," Tony said as we all dug into the food. The chicken was grilled perfectly—no surprise there. Uncle Al took the barbeque to a new art. Summer was almost here, but I knew he'd been using the grill all winter long.

"So, Tony," I said to him, pointing my fork at him with a smile.

He looked to me, Dex, and Rebecca. "Tell me again why you're here. I mean, in Oregon. On the coast. It's another episode, right?"

I felt defensive for one second before I remembered that both Matt and Tony watched the show and totally believed in what we were seeing—and doing.

My shoulders relaxed. "Yeah, it's a haunted school."

"No way," said Matt. "Not the one in Gary that used to house the sick kids."

"The very one," Rebecca said. It was the first thing she'd really said to them other than, "Hi, I'm Rebecca," and the twins eyes flew to her and her cherry-print dress.

"And you're the new partner," Tony said, trying not to drool. "You know, I used to watch you on Wine Babes all the time."

I groaned internally. I felt like I was about to have fucking déjà vu.

"Were you ever in Maxim like Jennifer was?" Tony asked.

Yup. Déjà vu. My upper lip involuntarily curled. Dex put his hand on my knee. Uncle Al looked at me with a dry expression.

Rebecca let out a laugh. "Me, in Maxim? Oh mercy, I'm not a bloody whore, you know. My tits and arse aren't for the world to see."

And Rebecca saved the day.

"That's a shame," Tony supplied.

"Anthony!" Uncle Al warned. "Eat your damn food and shut up."

"Back to the ghosts," Matt said, always the smarter one. He eyed me closely. "Have you been there before? It's really fucking creepy."

"Language, Matthew," Uncle Al said.

Matt took a long gulp of his beer, staring at his dad over it before saying, "Whatever, Dad."

"No, I haven't," I said. I haven't been to Oregon for months, I wanted to say. "But apparently all the hauntings started recently."

"Don't you think that's odd?" he asked, leaning forward like it was a conspiracy theory.

"Why?"

He took a lazy bite of chicken. "I don't know. We always knew about that place…our friends live in Gary and they'd go there at night, way before it was a school. They said they'd see soccer balls going down the dark hallways by themselves and shit. They'd hear, like, the wheels of a gurney being pushed. Children crying. It's just funny that the school has been operating for a while and only now they think there are ghosts."

I thought back to the teacher, Brenna McSomething, who reported the hauntings. I had to wonder if she was anything like Dex and I, if her very presence caused things to happen. And if her being there caused the hauntings to increase...what would it be like for Dex and I?

"Perry?" Dex asked gently, his hand pressing down on my leg.

I looked up at him and his deep, dark eyes, and realized that everyone else was staring at me. "Sorry," I said. "Must have zoned out."

"Matthew, please stop with this ghost talk," Uncle Al chided him. "It's not appropriate for dinner."

Matt mumbled an insincere sorry and Marda quickly took over the conversation by asking us if we were hooked on any TV shows. Rebecca, her, and Tony got in an argument over Breaking Bad for a bit until it was time for dessert.

Dex leaned into me, his breath hot on my neck. "I really hope they're serving pie," he murmured.

I flushed from my head to my toes and bit my lip. I shot him a sly glance, glad my hair was shielding my red cheeks from everyone else. "You remember that, do you?"

His gaze intensified, mouth parting open. "You have no idea. Of course, you were the one who was baking it."

"You know you can have pie any time you want," I teased him.

"Are we talking pussy or pie right now?"

I giggled, hoping no one could hear him. "Take your pick."

Alas, it wasn't pie but plain old ice cream with chocolate syrup. I opted out of it, relishing another beer instead. As soon as we were all finished, Rebecca and her impeccable manners started taking all the plates over to the sink to do the dishes, and naturally I had to help her.

Meanwhile, Dex took that moment to pour Uncle Al another glass of wine and ask him if he could speak with him, in private.

Rebecca and I exchanged a look as my uncle agreed, looking as surprised as we were, and the two of them walked out of the kitchen and into the backyard that overlooked the beach. I could barely make them out through the window above the sink.

"What's going on?" I asked Rebecca. "I know he hates doing the dishes but..."

She glanced out the window, watching as their shapes disappeared into the darkening sky, then busied herself with the scrubber brush. "Oh, I don't know. I guess Dex just wants to make a good impression, that's all."

"Did he tell you that?"

She paused for a moment before scrubbing at a tough stain. "Not in so many words. But he's here for you, Perry. He just wants everything to be okay. And he wants your family to accept him. He knows it's an uphill battle but you know Dex. He's determined once he puts his mind to something."

I know I doubted Dex every now and then but hearing that really made me feel good inside. Solid. I could only hope that whatever he was saying to Uncle Al, that my uncle was being nice about it all.

They were only out there for five minutes before they came back inside. Uncle Al came in first, his face red, but whether it was from wine or anger, I didn't know. Dex followed shortly after, his beer almost empty and dangling loosely from his fingers. While my uncle disappeared into the living room where the twins were watching a movie with Marda, Dex loitered in the kitchen for a moment. He didn't meet my eyes, and instead pulled out a chair and sat down.

I glanced at Rebecca, who gave Dex a strangely sympathetic glance before she turned back to the dishes.

"Dex," I said quietly.

He looked up. His face was open, expression blasé, but there was something troubling about his eyes. They looked haunted.

"Are you okay?"

He smiled but it failed to make his eyes crinkle. "Yeah, I'm fine. Bit of heartburn though."

"Maybe it's the beer," Rebecca suggested.

He answered that by finishing it off and getting back up. He headed for the front door. I hastily put down the plate I was drying and ran after him, stopping him just as he put his hand on the knob.

"Where are you going?" I asked, feeling suddenly uneasy about his change in mood.

"Got a bit of a chill," he explained, looking over my shoulder toward the living room. "Summer's not here yet. I have my jacket in the car. I'll be back." He leaned forward and kissed me lightly on the cheek before stepping out into the night.

I went back to helping with the dishes but wasn't the least bit surprised to see that Dex didn't come back in until we were done and watching some lame ass Ben Stiller movie with everyone else. There was no room beside me on the couch, so he sat on the ground, his legs stretched out in front of him. He wasn't even watching the movie; instead, he was staring blankly at a spot on the carpet.

I felt a pair of eyes on me and looked over to see Uncle Al staring from across the room. It took everything I had to keep from glaring at him in return. I came here hoping to make amends with at least part of my family. I had no idea what the hell my uncle was thinking, but whatever he heard about me from my parents, it was obvious that it was affecting him in some way. If he said something upsetting to Dex, I could damn well count on him feeling the same way about me.

I waited until the movie was over before I decided to confront him.

"I really hope you don't mind sleeping on the couch," Marda said to Rebecca as she started to pull the bed from it.

"Perry and I would be happy to take the couch if Rebecca wants the guest bedroom instead," Dex said. To hell with that, I wanted privacy to talk with Dex about what was going on. But while the three of them were having a debate over it, I took the moment to ask Uncle Al if he had any Sleepytime tea.

He gave me a curious look but walked into the kitchen where I followed him. He pulled open a cupboard and started riffling through tea boxes. "Marda is the tea drinker in the house now. Are you sure you don't want a glass of wine? Always helps me."

"Nah," I told him, leaning against the counter. "Wine only makes my body sleepy but it doesn't quiet the mind."

"Having trouble sleeping?"

"Can you blame me?" I asked directly.

He paused, box of chamomile tea in hand before placing it in front of me. "I'm afraid this is the most relaxing tea we have. I can ask Marda if we have anything else."

I quickly reached out and grabbed his arm. "No, don't bug her about it, it's no bother. Chamomile is just fine." I glanced at the living room where I could still hear them arguing over the couch. Rebecca seemed to be whining, given the rising pitch of her voice. "Look, I was hoping I could talk to you. You know, niece to uncle."

He sighed quietly. "Right. I thought you might want to. Well, I want to talk to you too."

Interesting. I nodded. "Okay then. Shoot."

He lips twisted wryly, an expression that made him look a lot like my dad when he was getting into scholarly mode. "You asked me first. The table is all yours." He gestured to it, and while I sat down, he put the kettle on and pushed a box of ladyfingers in front of me. "Eat. You could use it."

I tried not to laugh. What was it with Italians thinking everyone but the most obese person was severely underfed? Still, I picked one up and nibbled at the chocolate coating while I tried to think of the best way to ask.

"I was just wondering," I began slowly, keeping my voice low so that the rest of the house wouldn't hear me, "what my parents have said to you. You know, if anything. If you know what happened."

He sat down across from me and rubbed at the lines in his forehead. "I know what happened."

"And? What was that? What did they say?"

"I talked to your father, mainly. Your mom didn't have much to say to me. She never really does, to be honest with you, Perry."

"Well, you and me both."

"They love you very much. You do know that, don't you?"

I felt a sting of tears behind my eyes. "I don't know," I said truthfully. "I guess they do, like every parent has to."

"No parent has to love their kids, Perry. It's a conscious decision. They love you because they do, not just because you're their daughter. They just don't understand you. They worry. They're afraid for you, that you're making all the wrong choices."

I felt myself stiffen. “I’m not making wrong choices. I’m making the only choice.”

He let out a breath. “The way they see it, the way your father told me, was that you were very ill...mentally ill. It was enough for them to really worry.”

That was putting it mildly. I was fucking possessed!

“And then when you were doing better, just as you got back and were recovering, you decided to leave and go live with the very man who put you in that terrible position.”

“They don’t know Dex,” I said, the anger rising in me. I struggled to keep my voice down. “They don’t know him, but if they did, they’d see he’s the only one who loves me unconditionally. He’s always been there for me.”

“Except when he wasn’t.”

I opened my mouth, ready to spew venom, but he raised his hand in a manner that made me shut up, like he was some mob boss.

“Perry, you can’t pretend what happened to you didn’t happen. You can’t pretend he didn’t break your heart like I told you he would.”

I shook my head. “He did. I know, but people make mistakes. They deserve second chances.”

"You're right. And I agree with you," he said, giving me a hard, steady look like he was trying to freeze me in place. "But not when you're not well."

"I am well. I've never been happier."

"I can see that," he said simply.

"Perry?" I heard Dex's voice from the other room and spun around in the chair. He came out of the living room and poked his head in the kitchen while Uncle Al got up and poured me my tea. "I'm going to bed now. Becs won the great couch debate. You going to be long?" His eyes went to Uncle Al and back to me, that strange haunted look coming back into them.

I shook my head. "I'm just getting tea. I'll come to bed soon."

He stared at me for a few moments.

Don't worry about me, I thought hard, trying to project it on him. I don't know if it worked or not. He just nodded sharply and said goodnight to both of us.

Once I heard the door to the spare room close, Uncle Al put the tea down across from me. "Careful, it's hot."

I blew on it for a long time before taking a scalding sip.

My uncle leaned back in his chair. "So what else do you want to know?"

I felt frustrated at the conversation and fidgeted in my seat. "I don't know. That, I guess. I wanted to know what they said. I guess they think I went off with Dex because I'm crazy."

"Perry, they just want you to come home, that's all."

"I'm twenty-three. My mom wanted me out of the house for the longest time, how could they want me back?"

"They don't think you know what's best for yourself at the moment."

I nearly smacked my hand down on the table but refrained myself. "I know what's best for me more than anyone else. I'm not crazy. I had a moment or two there but that's over."

"Is it?"

I narrowed my eyes at him. "What do you mean? Of course it is."

"And yet you keep putting yourself in these positions."

"*What* positions?"

He folded his hands on the table. "My brother told me what you and your sister were saying, that it was possession. Demonic possession. You know Daniel discounted that off the bat, because of his beliefs. But you know my beliefs. You knew what I felt about that lighthouse. I have no doubt that if you keep opening yourself up to this...this job of yours, that you're just putting yourself more at risk."

I couldn't believe my ears. "You believe that I was possessed?" I asked quietly. I wasn't sure that I could trust Uncle Al with the truth. We all played it off like I was delirious with a fever, all so my parents wouldn't fear I was following in Pippa's footsteps and have me committed. What if Uncle Al was baiting me? What if he'd tell my parents what I really thought, what I *knew*, happened?

I cleared my throat and continued before he could answer. "Well I wasn't possessed. I was just delirious. My parents made a bigger deal about all of it than they should have. And I didn't want to live in that. Living with Dex made perfect sense and I don't regret a minute of it. I just wish they could see that I know what I'm doing."

He stared at me for a few moments before shrugging, as if all the world had been on his shoulders. I knew he didn't believe the act but I was giving him no choice. "When you see them, you can tell them that yourself."

I took another sip of my tea, the liquid burning my tongue and doing the opposite of making me sleepy. When my mouth recovered, I asked him, "What did you want to talk to me about?"

"I think we've already covered part of it," he said. His eyes drifted over my shoulder to the empty hallway. "Perry, I'm your uncle. I'm not your father. I know that doesn't stop me from giving you advice though so I'm just going to talk. You can listen or you won't listen, it's all the same. I want you to be happy. But I also want you to stay happy. To think about your future."

"Okay," I drew out, thinking he sounded like he was going into a pitch for a high-interest savings account.

He sighed and reached for a cookie, weighing it in his hands. "I just don't want you to do anything foolish."

I raised my brows. "That's kind of vague."

"Dex is foolish," he said quickly, his words sharp like needles. "You may think you're in love with him, and I believe you are, and I also believe the man is in love with you, but...come on, bella, you have to step back from the situation for just one second and try and see it all from someone else's perspective."

I swallowed hard, a ball of fire expanding painfully in my chest. "Someone else like my parents?"

"They're older, they've been there, we've all been there. You're living with this man that you barely even know, a man who just broke your heart and ruined you."

"Barely even know?" I managed to say. "I know Dex, okay? I know him more than anyone in this world."

"Perry," he said, his voice tinged with impatience. "When was the last time you were here? Think about it."

I blinked stupidly. "Uh, September?"

"Right. September. You came here with Dex in September. What month is it now?"

"May," I said, my throat tightening.

"And how many months is that?"

I stared at him, unwilling to count. "I don't know."

"It's eight months. You've known this guy for eight months."

Holy fucking shit. Was that true? I'd only met Dex eight months ago? It felt like I'd known him for years, ages, eternity. After everything we'd been through...every episode, every experience, it fused our souls together, time be damned.

"It feels longer than that," I said feebly. But I wouldn't let him, my parents, win this argument. I straightened up in my seat and looked my uncle in the eye. "But so what? Lots of couples move in together when the moment is right. It's different for every relationship. It doesn't have to be a big deal."

"It will turn into a big deal when you commit to someone you realize you don't know at all. I'm divorced for a reason. Don't think I didn't think like you at one point."

I gave him a funny look. "I live with Dex, Uncle Al. That's it. We're not getting married. We've barely discussed the future at all. Calm down."

His eyes widened for a split second. "He's thirty-two. You're twenty-three."

"Age doesn't matter."

"It does sometimes. It does when you assume that just because you're not thinking of the future doesn't mean he isn't."

I nearly laughed. Uncle Al clearly didn't know Dex at all. "He just got out of a long-term relationship. He's not thinking about that shit."

"And are you?"

I stared at the wisps of steam coming off the mug of tea. Christ, I didn't know what I was thinking half the time. I wasn't about to tell him about my white picket fence idea, the conversation we had about doing something after EIT, about houses in Seaside, Boston, or wherever I said. I wasn't going to tell him about the maternal instinct that started kicking about when I saw him being a fur baby daddy to Fat Rabbit.

"I..."I started. "I'm just playing it by ear."

He shook his head slightly. “You’re in love, Perry. You’re head over heels. You’re playing it by heart, not ear. Like you always do.”

“Well what the hell do you want me to say? If I say I think about a future with him, you’ll get mad, and if I say I don’t, you’ll call me a liar.”

His eyes softened and reached out for my hand across the table. “Bella, please. I’m not mad. I just want to pull you out of it for just a moment, just so you can look at it from a different angle. There are so many things in life that make us happy in the short term. These cookies, for example,” he said, picking up the tray. “But in the long term, they can hurt you.”

“Maybe I’m tired of everyone always worrying about me getting hurt,” I said snidely, crossing my arms.

“Maybe we’re worried because you are always getting hurt,” he said, “and a person can only get hurt so many times before it really starts to ruin them.”

“Alberto, are you coming to bed?” Marda asked, appearing at the doorway in a silk night robe, a sleep mask smeared on her face.

“Just a minute, darling,” he said, flashing her his smile.

“No more cookies,” she said, wagging her finger at him. “You have to watch your heart.”

When she left, he looked at me and sighed. "I didn't mean to upset you. I'm just looking out for you as I always do. Wasn't I right about Seattle? About you going to stay with him and his girlfriend?"

I mumbled that he was. "But it doesn't mean you're right about this. I love Dex. I know him inside and out."

"You know him as much as you can know someone for eight months," he said. "Just don't forget that. And don't forget that most of that time, he was with someone *else*." He eased himself out of the chair, leaving me with that extremely sobering thought.

He kissed me on the head goodnight and then shuffled off toward his room. I sat there at the table, drinking my hot tea until it was gone, apprehensive now about going to see Dex. I hated that my uncle—and by extension, my parents—were able to instill this doubt in me.

Had I really only known Dex, my Dex, my Declan Foray, for less than a year? The last two months of us living together, that was the only time we were actually together as a couple. Plus we started up hot on the heels of his last relationship, one that lasted three fucking years. No wonder my parents were so against the whole thing. No wonder my uncle was. Aside from the people who knew us best like Rebecca,

Dean, and Ada, our relationship must look batshit crazy to the rest of the world.

Then again, what else was new?

I took in a deep breath, trying to calm my nerves, then placed the cup of tea in the sink. I wondered if Rebecca was up and ready for a chat, but the lights in the living room were out. I reluctantly made my way to the bathroom and then finally the guest bedroom.

I carefully slipped into bed, not knowing if Dex was asleep. I wanted to talk to him—I wanted to know what he talked to Uncle Al about and if it was anywhere near as brutal as it was for me. But I heard him snoring lightly, brought on by all the beers, and decided to leave it for another day. I turned my back to him, our asses touching each other but our upper bodies far apart.

CHAPTER FIVE

I was on a bluff, overlooking the sea. I didn't know how I was there, but I was. The grass was cool beneath my feet, the wind sweeping off the blackened ocean was rich with salt and chilled.

I'd been here before. Was I dreaming?

I looked down at my body and saw I was barefoot and in a simple, plain nightgown. The déjà vu was back in full force all over again, transporting me back to September. But instead of being beside a lighthouse, there was nothing there except the burnt remains and a few pieces of foundation.

I had to be dreaming. I never owned a nightgown like that, and the only time I ever did was when I was caught in a nightmare. I half expected the shriveled face of Old Roddy to appear, to remind me that what happened here, what started it all, was only eight months ago.

But he never came. He never popped up. As far as I could tell, I was alone. It was just me and that dark, wide expanse of the Pacific, beckoning me like a gaping mouth.

I stared at the ocean, those obsidian waves that crashed at the shore below, wondering if this was all there was to it. Then, after some time, I knew it was all beginning.

A child's giggle came from behind me and the punchy sound of a rubber ball being kicked. I turned around to see nothing but the lighthouse remains and the dewy grass that stretched back into the forest of thick trees. There was no child, there was no ball. But that didn't mean anything.

Suddenly I heard quick footsteps behind me and the feeling of someone running past, brushing against my legs. Right before my eyes I saw a child form from thin air—a young girl—who ran after a ball. She squealed as she went, her attention devoted to getting the ball and nothing else.

At least it seemed that way until she reached it and kicked it off into the forest. The girl stopped, and in her brief stillness I could make out her fine features, her long dark hair and neatly tied bow at the back, her plain dress and shiny shoes. She was no doubt a ghost—her complexion was more than pale and there was a slight transparency about her, but I still couldn't tell if I was really seeing her or if it was all in my head. My dreams had always been prophetic, but since the one that Pippa appeared in the other day, it was hard to tell if they were real or not.

No wonder my parents were so concerned about me losing my mind. It never really ended, did it?

The ghost dream girl cocked her head at me and I could see her eyes were nothing but black marbles, the soulless ones that ripped into you. "Can you go after my ball?" she asked, her accent untraceable but her words properly enunciated.

I swallowed thickly and shook my head. I'd been in that forest before, in real life, and it was terrifying as hell. Fuck that noise.

"But I need my ball," the girl said, her tone becoming harder. I noticed her little hands tightening into fists as the rest of her became more solid and less see-through.

"I'm sorry," I said meekly, my voice echoing. "I don't want to go in there."

The girl glared at me and flipped her hair over her shoulder before she started marching over. "You will go in there and get my ball."

She stopped a few yards away, and it was only then that I noticed a large spot of blood forming on one side of her chest, spreading slowly like a blooming rose. "You're not really here, are you? Not yet?"

I frowned, not sure what to say to that.

The girl took a neat step forward, her hands clasped at her middle. "Or are you? Are you here to play with us?"

Without warning, a large gust of wind blasted at my back, whipping my hair into my face. When I finally brushed it out of my eyes, I saw Pippa standing between me and the young girl. Just like in my dream before she was looking tired and pale, her thin body hidden by a coat. Her attention was entirely on the girl.

"You get away from here," Pippa said to her. "You leave her alone. She is not yours."

"But she can see me," the girl said matter-of-factly, a devious twinkle in those cold black eyes.

"Go," Pippa said, her voice louder and almost animalistic. The young girl stuck out her tongue but trotted after the ball, disappearing into thin air right before the trees. Pippa faced me with a weary expression.

"They keep finding you, don't they?"

"I don't get it," I said. "Am I dreaming again? Is this real?"

"You are dreaming but it is real," she said. "This is the safest way I can get to you. The Thin Veil is too risky."

I gestured wildly to the forest. "Then who the hell was that little girl?"

She gave me a slight smile. "I am not the only one who can get to you this way. You know this. Your dreams have always been very powerful, Perry, always. You've seen and experienced things that eventually happened to you. Every day you're alive and embracing who you are, you're opening yourself more and more."

"So what about what you said before...about having to watch out?"

"I don't think you should be here, Perry."

"Dreaming?"

"Doing the show. Not right now. It's just a feeling I have..."

"I can't keep going on your feelings. I have a life to live too, a living to make."

She reached out and grabbed my hand. Hers felt so delicate, thin and cold. "I know. But you're not in a good place right now. You're the strongest when you are strong and right now you are weak. You're succumbing to worry and insecurity."

"That's me, like ninety-nine percent of the time."

"Darling, please. I wish I could offer you more than just a feeling but you have to take it to heart. Go home. Go back to Seattle. Go be with Dex and concentrate on your life there."

"But the show is my life, at least for now. It's just a few days of filming, we've done this a million times before. When this is done, we will go back to Seattle. After we stop by my parents first. I've apparently got a lot of explaining to do."

Her eyes widened with intensity, her mouth becoming tight. "No. No, don't do that."

My heart started thudding around in my chest at her sudden change in tone. She was starting to freak me the fuck out. "No? What do you mean, no? It's my mom. Your daughter. I haven't seen her or my dad or Ada for months."

She shook her head. "No. I don't know why but I don't think that's a good idea. It's...too much. It's too easy. Everyone in the same place, all the eggs in one basket."

Now she was starting to sound like Creepy Clown Lady. "You're not making any sense."

"I know I'm not making sense. But it's wrong. It's wrong. It's bad."

"And the show, filming here, that's not the problem anymore?"

She shook her head still, her thin curls flinging around. She started wringing her hands together. "No. It's all wrong. You need to go back home."

"Just tell me why!" I exclaimed, almost stamping my feet.

"I don't know!" she yelled back. Her eyes dropped to the ground.

A light ticked on in my head. "Are you afraid of my mom and I making up?"

She didn't say anything for a long time, just staring at the grass beneath us. Another breeze blew past, my nightgown billowing around me.

"Are you afraid that if my mom and I make amends, that you'll lose an ally in me? That I'll turn against you?" I asked, studying her face. I took a step forward. "You know I'll never forget what my mother did to you."

I tried to reach out and touch her but she yanked herself out of my reach and stared up at me with frightened eyes. "Don't go. It's too much in one place."

She still didn't make sense but it didn't matter. She *was* worried that my mom and I might make up.

She probably feared that I would shun her or that my mom would do the same to me as she did to her. It explained why she looked so frightened.

"Pippa," I said slowly, hoping to convince her not to worry. I knew what was best for myself. But my grandmother was already fading before my eyes.

"Too much, too easy," she said, her voice croaking and then lowering itself until it was just a shadow of what it was. "Too much. Too easy."

And then she was gone.

***

I woke up to Dex's warm hand sliding up underneath my shirt, teasing at the soft area underneath my breast. I smiled and relaxed into it, momentarily forgetting about everything that happened. I pushed the thoughts of Uncle Al, of his warnings, of my dream, all the way to the back of my head. They wanted me to think about them, to weigh down my heart with worry, but I wouldn't give in.

I'd only give in to the naked man beside me.

"Good morning, sunshine," he whispered into my neck, his lips gently trailing down to my collarbone.

I lazily reached up and ran my hand through his thick hair. "Morning, baby." I glanced around us for a clock, seeing only framed horror movie posters. The twins must have decorated the room. “What time is it?”

“No idea,” he said, and from the way his teeth grazed the outside of my ear, I could tell it didn’t matter. “I think everyone else is up. But then again, so am I.” He took my hand in his and placed it under the sheets, right on his cock. No surprise, it was hard as stone and felt hot beneath my touch. He groaned in response, the sweetest sound to my ears.

I gave him a sly look, putting pressure on my hand, my fingers gripping him. Still, I told him quietly, “I don’t think this is a good idea. That door over there doesn’t lock and anyone could come in at any moment.”

He sat up slightly and put his hand behind my head, holding me there hard. His eyes looked like a fire had been lit in them. “I don’t give a fuck if anyone sees us or hears us. Do you?”

I swallowed hard, surprised at his intensity. The way his eyes were burning into mine, I knew that this had to do with what Uncle Al had talked to him about last. Hell, I don’t know why I wasn’t feeling like giving him a big fuck you either.

I shook my head. “No, I don’t.”

“Good,” he growled and then kissed me, tangling me in a wet, passionate kiss that made our tongues dance. I felt my body relax under his touch as his hands began to slip my underwear and shirt off. He tossed them across the room then put me on my back, his firm body pressing down on me. "This is real," he said, voice oh so low, so gruff it made me throb. "This is nothing but real. You and me. Us. You know that, don't you?"

I nodded. "I know."

"Perry, I love you," he said, his gaze drifting to my lips. "I'm not..." He paused. "I'm here. I'm staying here, by your side. This is more than just two people shacking up together. This is so much more."

"Dex," I said, my fingers trailing down his face. "Are you okay?"

He watched me for a few loaded beats before he closed his eyes. "Yes. Sorry. I'm okay, I'm just...I'm your fucking man, baby. That's all there is to it, I'm your fucking man. That is never going to change." He looked at me and grinned, his hair falling in his face. "And now I'm going to fuck you till we embarrass ourselves."

Before I could say anything to that, his mouth was on mine again and his fingers were sliding between my legs. He let out a moan when he felt how wet I was. It only took a minute of his deft exploration before I was close to coming so I shimmied out of his grasp and turned my self around so my mouth was at his cock. Naturally, my ass was at his face.

"Holy fuck," he said under his breath, and while I placed my hands firmly around his shaft, he gripped my hips and pulled me back a bit toward his face. Dex and I had been pretty adventurous in our relationship—I mean, nothing really compared to that night we had in the hotel New Orleans. But a sixty-nine was something new to me.

So while I concentrated on licking him from balls to satiny shaft, working him with my mouth, hands, and tongue as best I could, he was trying to get me off at the same time. And though I was one of those rare females who actually got turned on while giving a blow job (it helped that Dex was so perfectly endowed), it was hard to continue when his own tongue was sliding along my pleasure spots and making me forget where I was. Long story short—the sixty-nine position doesn't work. You both get too turned on to keep going. It's a beautiful failure.

"Fuck this," I said, letting go of him and turning around. I placed my legs on either side of his hips, straddling him, and guided him into me.

"You're taking charge today," he said, staring up at me with feverish eyes. He bit his lip as I started rocking into him and moaned again.

"You might want to keep it down," I whispered, vaguely conscious that Uncle Al, Marda, my cousins, and Rebecca were just a few rooms away.

"You might want to shut up and keep fucking me," he answered with a lazy smile.

That I did. I gently rocked back and forth on his cock, sitting up straight, my long black hair flowing over my shoulders as Dex enjoyed the view. I knew I wasn't the prettiest, skinniest chick around, and now especially, but from the way he always looked at me with my body on display like I was a platter of ripe fruit, I knew I had to at least try and work it. I played with myself, building up to an orgasm before he swatted my hand away and replaced it with his thumb.

"Don't take away my job," he murmured, and then pulled me down toward him, my palms pressing into the strength of his shoulders, my breasts swinging near his face. With his free hand he took my nipple into his mouth and sucked hard enough to make me cry out from the sweet pain.

When he finally pulled his mouth away, he gazed up at me. "This is real, baby. This is us. Now, always, us."

I could only pant from the increased pace from his thumb.

"That's it, ride me raw." He took a hard hold of my hip and made me ride him harder, faster, until I was coming at the same pace, my head thrown back in ecstasy. "Let me know how much you love to fuck me."

A cry or two escaped my lips, the throws of my orgasm flowing through every part of me and he didn't hold back either, muttering a stream of delirious obscenities as he grunted to completion, the headboard banging hard against the wall.

I collapsed on his chest, our breath heavy, our bodies sweaty and spent, while my mind slowly rolled around from being on cloud nine to being in...Uncle Al's house. My face burned red hot with the reality.

I looked up at Dex. "I was loud, wasn't I?"

He stroked the top of my head with his hand. "You're always loud, kiddo."

"Shit."

"Told you I'd embarrass us. Well, embarrass you. I don't get embarrassed."

"No, you really don't," I mused, brushing his hair out of his face. My god, I loved staring at him after sex. Every feeling I had for him was heightened and he could not have looked more handsome and comfortable.

A few moments passed, the both of us relishing each other's post-coital company before we heard a very faint knock at the door.

"Uh, guys?" It was Rebecca.

"We'll be right there," I said loudly before rolling out of bed.

"Sorry to interrupt, I thought I'd wait till you were done," she whispered before her heels clicked down the hallway.

I turned around to see Dex beaming at me. Great.

So yeah, I'm pretty sure the entire house heard our morning antics. Thank god we had to get moving and were late enough that our departure was hasty, even though both Matt and Tony were smirking like crazy when they said goodbye to Dex.

My uncle, on the other hand, looked like he was ready to kill me. I gave him a light hug as we left and told him I'd stay in touch. He didn't look too enthused, though just as I was leaving the house he grabbed my hand and squeezed it hard. "Take care, Perry," he said. "I mean it."

I could only nod. Whether he was concerned for the safety of my heart or the safety of my life, I knew I'd do what I could to be vigilant.

"Well that wasn't so bad," Rebecca said from the backseat, looking behind her at the house as we pulled out of the driveway and headed south on Highway 101.

"Says you," I said. "You were the charming British friend. You didn't have to answer to Uncle Al and his disapproval on repeat." I looked over at Dex at the wheel, his shades covering his eyes. "By the way, what did Uncle Al say to you? What did you guys talk about out there?"

I knew it was a bit risky asking this when we weren't alone but sometimes it felt like Rebecca was basically an extension of us, and it was obvious that something happened—I'd just been too carried away by my hormones that morning to figure it out.

He tilted his head, shrugging one shoulder like it was no big deal. "Nothing really. I just wanted to tell him that you were doing okay now. I didn't want him or your parents to worry about you."

"Didn't go well, did it?" Rebecca asked with sympathy.

He glanced at her briefly. "No, it didn't. He doesn't hate me but he's not a fan of the Dex charm. I guess first impressions really do stick around."

"To be fair, Dex," I pointed out, "most of your charm is in your dick. There's a reason why you piss off half the population."

"Ha," he scoffed. "Anyway, I tried. But you know what, fuck Uncle Al. Sorry. Really, Perry. I know he's your uncle, but his approval means nothing if he can't see the big picture. All it does is make me want to prove him wrong."

"Prove him wrong about what?" I asked.

He sucked in his lip before saying, "That we aren't right for each other. That you plus me equals disaster." He put his chin down and eyed me over his sunglasses. "Don't tell me he didn't make you feel the same way?"

He pointed out that we've only known each other for eight months, I thought to myself. But there was no point in voicing it. Dex knew it. I knew it. We all knew it. But we couldn't listen to what other people thought, family members or not. I know my mind wanted to go there. I know it wanted to think about it, I know I craved the approval like nothing else. But it couldn't matter. If Dex and I were to have a chance as a couple, it couldn't matter at all. We just had to do what felt right to us.

And it really felt damn good.

"It doesn't matter what he thinks," I said. I lowered my voice, even though I knew Rebecca was just as involved with our conversation as we were. "Your opinion is all that matters. And Becs, of course."

"Thanks," she said. "Who knew Uncle Al was such a stickler? Guess you're having second thoughts about seeing your parents now."

I let out a laugh. "You could say that. I'll still see them though and deal with that shit when we come to it. Until then...I guess we have ghost kids to film."

"Not that I want to put a damper on your attitude," Dex cut in. "But you do remember the last time we had, well, hell sent rugrats around us, don't you?"

D'Arcy Island. Between the ghost of the murdered Madeline and the leper baby, we had enough nightmare fodder from just that episode alone.

I suppressed a shudder. "I remember. What's your point?"

"My point is, for the last few days you've been so preoccupied with your family and whatever else in that sexy head of yours that you're coming across as, oh, I don't know, insanely blasé about the whole situation."

He was right about that. "I guess I haven't really thought about it."

Except in your dreams, a voice deep inside said. I pushed it away, not ready to think about it.

Dex turned around briefly to look at Rebecca. "Are you prepared for this?"

"That's a ridiculous question," she answered with a smart wave of her hand. "You're acting like I'm not your production manager or anything."

"But are you prepared for, you know...the children of the damned? Toddlers from hell? Art kids without Ritalin?"

She folded her arms and sat back in her seat. "I'm prepared for the usual—both of you freaking out over things that I can't really see. Then I retreat and let you handle the rest. I'm prepared for that. Whether ghosts come into the equation or not, I don't really care as long as you guys see them. And if you don't see them, as long as you guys film something that can pass for it."

I twisted around and gave her a steady look. "You do know that whatever we film, we see. We aren't bullshitting."

"Perry, I know that," she told me. "But from a business point of view, it doesn't matter. Make a masterpiece out of a floating paper bag if you can. Put a sheet on me. I don't care. Just so we get the shots."

I looked at Dex. "Boy, she's starting to sound a lot like you."

He smiled and rubbed at his scruffy chin. "What can I say, we both know what makes a good show and we both love to eat pie."

I rolled my eyes.

"Oh, Dex," Rebecca said wryly. "Please don't ever change."

"Wasn't planning on it."

As we drove down the coast, I put the window down and let the ocean breeze mess up my hair. The water was a moving metallic sheet and the sun was shining, flooding me with shallow happiness, though by the time we reached the one-street town of Rockaway Beach, wisps of fog began to float in. When we rounded a corner and passed the nondescript sign that said "Gary," population 779, we were totally enclosed in a massive grey cloud.

"Not the nicest welcome," I noted as I stared out the window. I could barely see beyond the road's guardrail—I knew the ocean was still out there, right at our side, but the thick fog obscured everything.

"No, it's not," Rebecca said. She tapped me on the shoulder and then placed the small handheld camcorder in my hand. "But it makes for a perfect intro on film. Perry, film this. Dex, find a place to do a U-turn and drive through again."

Dex and I exchanged a look at Rebecca's leap into production manager mode.

"It has begun," he joked in a low, ominous voice.

He yanked the Highlander into a U-turn, cutting off a Griswald-ish family in a minivan, and when I was finished holding on for dear life, I switched on the digital camcorder and filmed out the open window as we drove through again.

"Behold, the town of Gary," I said in lieu of narration. Rebecca had me doing voiceovers after the fact. "It looks like it kind of sucks."

I could feel her glaring at me but she couldn't argue. Gary did look like it sucked. Even though it was almost summer, the pines that covered the sloping mountainside were a faded green, bordering on brown. The houses looked weathered and were simple, most of them one story and either shuttered into darkness by the trees or fronting a small yard with a chain-link fence and cement walkway. All the curtains were sealed shut and I didn't see many gardens or the usual signs of habitation, such as kid's toys in the driveways or hummingbird feeders.

The town itself wasn't much better. I couldn't make out where the marina was or if there even was a waterfront area (though I assumed there was since we were in Tillamook Bay), so there wasn't really a focal point to it except for the main drag. There was a motel with a lighthouse motif, a few woodcarving and fish shops, a smattering of diners, and a corner store. Those were the only places that didn't have a For Lease sign across them or boarded up windows.

We'd just got there and already the place was making me kind of sad.

"So are we staying at the lighthouse motel back there?" Dex asked Rebecca.

She hummed. "I haven't made a reservation. The principal said we were welcome to stay on site if we wanted to. Apparently the school nurse now is set up where the old nurses' quarters used to be, so there's a few beds."

I nearly stopped filming. “You think we should sleep where the nurses slept decades ago?”

“Don’t tell me you’re scared,” she said teasingly. “I think it would be good for the show. Don’t you think, Dex?”

I could tell he was looking at me but I kept my focus on the camera. In the past, Dex would have been the first one to jump into something risky and stupid, but nowadays he was very careful and protective of me. He used to want me to be scared—now he just wanted to keep me safe.

“We’ll see,” he said, and from the tone of his voice I knew that if I didn’t want to stay there, I wouldn’t have to. It wasn’t so much that I was scared, but the idea of really old beds and mattresses gave me the heebie jeebies. I’d take a tacky hotel over that any day.

“Oh, that must be the smoke stack from the old mill,” Rebecca said excitedly as we neared the thing Dex once described as an “ancient dildo.” “You’ll want to take your next left after we pass it and follow the road up into the hills for four miles.”

Dex wheeled the SUV away from the coast and we headed up along a long, winding road that disappeared into the cover of trees. “Not exactly in the neighborhood, is it?”

"Apparently the TB patients had to be higher up to get the best benefits. Anyway, from what I gather it seems like all the children are from Tillamook anyway. I'd be surprised if this town had many families left in it after the mills all closed down." She nudged me gently. "Keep filming as we pull up."

Dex made a clicking noise with his tongue. "Hey, Becs, let's not try and take over my role completely. I know I was joking about the pie comment but Perry is off limits. Only I get to boss her around. Well, attempt to, anyway."

"Sorry," she apologized. "I guess I'm a bit nervous."

"Oh yeah?" I asked, keeping the camera aimed at the road and the rows and rows of trees that passed by. Dex was going to have a lot of editing to do after this.

"Yes, it's peculiar," she said, her voice less chipper. "I don't know why. It kind of started as soon as I saw the fog. Perhaps it makes me feel claustrophobic."

I had to admit, I was feeling a bit like she was. Though I knew it had nothing to do with the blanket of fog and more to do with the slightly sinister, totally apprehensive vibe that the area was giving me.

"You think you'd be used to fog, coming from jolly fucking England and all," Dex said.

She ignored that, and a few minutes later we were pulling through a pair of massive wrought-iron gates that were battle scarred with rust from the relentless ocean air. On either side of the gates was a crumbling stone wall about seven-feet high that stretched off into the dark trees.

Before us was the long, wide gravel driveway that led to an enormous white building. It was slightly reminiscent of the mental institution that Dex and I filmed at in Seattle but much longer and two wings and five floors. With its pointed apex, it looked a bit like a European castle or chalet hidden in the mountains.

The only thing about it that reminded you it was a school was a colorful rainbow mural that stretched along the outside wall of the first floor. Every floor above that, however, showed peeling paint and decay.

"We're here," Dex said slowly. "And I'm suddenly grateful for the ghetto school I ended up going to."

"No kidding," I said. We parked the car in the lot beside a private school bus that said Oceanside Arts Academy and got out.

The first thing I noticed was a change in the temperature and air quality. It was about five degrees colder up here and pierced your lungs. The fog was lighter too and you could see faint patches of blue sky if you looked above your head. I reached back into the car and quickly grabbed my Kyuss hoodie. Not very professional, but it was warm.

I looked at Dex and Rebecca as they stood beside me, staring up at the towering building. "Are we filming first or bothering with that later?" I looked at both of them to ensure I wasn't leaving one of them out. I knew Dex was feeling a bit slighted when it came to filming now.

"Well, if it were up to me," he said pointedly, "we would go in and look around first before we start with the cameras. But Miss Sims here made all the plans..."

She gave him a tight smile. "And Miss Sims agrees with you."

She turned and headed up the driveway to the front doors. Dex and I walked a few paces behind her, watching as she sashayed in her capri pants and striped boat neck top, like she was about to board a friggin' yacht in 1955.

I pulled at Dex's elbow and leaned into him. "Do you believe her spiel about claustrophobia, or are you getting the weirds too?"

"The weirds? Kiddo, I have the weirds in spades." He looked up again at the building, at the broken windows and moldy curtains of the upper floors. "This place is something else."

"You think it's going to be a good show?" I asked quietly.

His mouth twisted. "I'm not sure what good is anymore. I think—I know—that this place is definitely haunted as fuck. I'm just hoping we can get in and get out with our lives and sanity intact."

"If I knew better, I'd say you were being paranoid."

He frowned. "You know there is no such thing as paranoid when it comes to us."

"You two coming?" Rebecca called out. When we both turned to face her, we noticed a pale, heavyset woman standing at the top of the stairs leading to the giant oak doors. Rebecca looked back, jumping slightly as if she had a fright.

"Are you the TV people?" the woman asked in a nasally voice, the alabaster jowls of her neck swaying. She reminded me of a Disney villain, which probably wasn't the impression she was going for. But with her dark brown dress, severe eyebrows that looked like someone made em-dashes above her eyes, and mousy brown hair piled high into a topknot, it was hard not to make the comparison.

"The internet people, yes," Rebecca corrected her as she came forward up the stairs, dainty hand extended. "I'm Rebecca Sims, the production manager for Experiment in Terror. I was the one emailing you."

The woman raised her nose in the air, eyeing her carefully. I could tell her focus was fixed on Rebecca's polished red lips and nails. "I recall." She shook her hand and then turned her attention to Dex and I. Without realizing it, both he and I had stopped where we stood and were just staring at this terrifying woman. "And who might you be?"

I elbowed Dex to speak first.

He sprung right into it, marching forward and taking the woman's hand in his. He pumped it hard twice and then asked with that infectious smile of his, "I'm Dex Foray, the only penis involved in the show. And who might you be?"

I sighed. I should have spoken first.

I immediately went up to her, climbing the first two steps and shot her an apologetic grin. "What he's trying to say is he's the cameraman and editor. I'm the host, Perry Palomino. Thank you for letting us shoot here, Mrs…?"

She put her hands on her hips and with a frosty expression said, "I'm Ainsley Davenport, the principal of Oceanside. I'm afraid I wasn't expecting you until later this afternoon."

Ainsley Davenport. Though it wasn't Ursula, the name suited her to a tee.

"Sorry," Dex said, still smiling, which meant he was enjoying himself. "We had to leave our last lodging in a hurry. You know how it is."

She gave him a dry, steady look that stretched on for seconds. "I see. Well, I have a bit of paperwork and some calls to make so I'm afraid I won't be much help to you until school is dismissed at three. I can get the nurse to give you a tour and perhaps you can meet with Mrs. McIntosh then. She teaches painting. She's the one who...started this whole thing."

At that, she turned around and went back into the building. The three of us looked at each other. Should we follow? Stay here? But before we could debate it out loud, a beanpole of a woman in a loose blouse and white pants stood before us.

"Hi," she said in a voice so timid and quiet that I found myself leaning forward, trying to catch the words. "I'm Kelly. I'm the school nurse here. It's nice to meet you all."

We quickly made our introductions again, Dex being polite this time, then Kelly motioned for us to come inside.

Though the outside of the school looked like it was built hundreds of years ago, the inside, at least on the first floor, looked beautifully refurbished. The floor in the foyer was a shiny grey marble, the walls outfitted with wall sconces and intricate paneling. Ornate light fixtures gleamed from overhead. Though it didn't look like a hospital, it certainly didn't look like a school either.

"This is very lovely," Rebecca said admiringly.

Kelly nodded. She had this way about her that reminded me of a heron. Her movements were slow, lanky and calculated. "Down to our left are the administration offices. It's a small school, only about a hundred students, so we don't use all the space on the first floor. But Ms. Davenport made sure that every single corner of the first floor has been remodeled, some say even past its original glory."

"Is your room down there?" Dex asked. "Rumor has it that it might be our bedroom tonight."

She nodded again, not meeting his eyes. "If you'd like. It's a very nice room. Come this way, please." She started off down the hall, Rebecca's kitten heels clicking as she followed.

"Oceanside was a very nice school," Kelly called to us over her shoulder, "before it burnt down, of course. No one knows what caused the fire, but it destroyed absolutely everything. It was very strange and it displaced a lot of children whose parents...well, it's not for me to say. But we needed a quick substitute."

We passed by closed office doors with embossed names printed on frosted glass, complete with brass doorknobs. You'd think all this refurbishment and newness would do something to quell that creepy feeling I had, but instead I felt like the fog was following us into the building. I had to keep looking behind me to make sure no one was there.

Kelly came to a stop before an open door. She gave us a small smile, and now that I was closer to her, I could see she had kind green eyes that contrasted vividly with her strawberry blonde hair. “This school is for very gifted children who wish to specialize in the arts. Or whose parents think they should explore their talent. It costs a lot of money to attend here and yet you should have seen the fuss they made when it came to gathering funds to build the new school. Setting up Oceanside here was a no brainer for most people.”

“You don’t seem to agree,” Dex asked astutely.

She raised a brow. “I’d rather not work in an old sanatorium, if that’s what you mean.” She cleared her throat, looking around sheepishly as if she’d be reprimanded for speaking her mind, and then gestured to the room. “This is my office. If you go past the door in there, it opens up into the old nurses’ quarters.”

The first room was nothing more than your normal nurse’s office, though of high sanitary regard with its gleaming floors and sink, tidy shelves, and two single cots with tightly tucked in sheets. The walls were adorned with drawings from what I assumed were the kids, though they looked a million times better than any drawing I ever did. There were charcoal and pastel portraits of Kelly, watercolors of forests, and one portrait of a young boy holding onto a ragged teddy bear, dressed in 1930s garb.

"Every kid here has talent," Kelly said, catching my eye and then motioning us forward. We stepped through the doorway and looked at our potential dwellings as she flicked on the light. I guess I was expecting something rotten and decrepit but it didn't look bad at all. It was a little sparse—the children's drawings didn't extend this far and the walls were bare. There were four twin beds in a row, each separated by a gauzy curtain that attached to a rod on the ceiling. The beds looked like hotel beds—clean but not plush.

"So this used to be where the nurses slept back in the old days?" Dex asked.

"Half of this floor was like this," she said, patting the end of one of the beds. "There were five hundred patients here, sometimes more, and at least thirty nurses and administrators. Once people came to this place as staff, they never left."

"Never?" I asked.

She shook her head. "No. TB was considered the White Plague, you know. They all thought it was highly contagious, and until there was a cure, everyone was stuck. I'm not sure if you noticed, but halfway down the road between here and the town, there's a small building on the side of the road. It's hidden by trees so you have to look for it. That used to be the post office. The mail carriers would only come so close to the building for fear of catching the disease."

"Jesus," Dex swore. "So if you took a job here, there was a good chance you wouldn't see your family for a long time."

"Not until the 50s when the cure was found and the hospital was closed," she said sadly. "It explains why so many of the nurses killed themselves. Why so many of them...eventually went crazy."

The skin at the back of my neck puckered. Just great. Not only did we have the potential ghosts of kids who died from TB but also their nurses who went crazy and killed themselves. I started to have one of those "maybe this isn't a good idea, maybe we should pack up and go home, maybe I should listen to my crazy dead grandmother in my dreams" kind of moments, the ones that either mean nothing or make you regret not trusting your gut.

But then again, if it wasn't for doing the more *interesting* option, I would have never met Dex and would have never joined Experiment in Terror. There was something to be said about moving forward in the face of fear. I swallowed down my uneasiness and listened to Kelly.

"Nonetheless," she went on, "since the whole first floor was redone and the rest of the nurses' rooms were made into offices, Ms. Davenport kept this as it is to try and keep the flavor of the past. Her words, not mine. You're more than welcome to stay here though. There's a bathroom with showers just next door. Sometimes when I'm too tired after work to drive home, I sleep here."

"Anything strange happen to you?" I asked.

Her eyes grew momentarily large, focused on the door. "Just that."

We all turned to see what she was looking at. A small orange rubber ball came rolling into the office, bouncing to a stop when it hit the doorframe. It was followed by a few impish giggles that seemed to fade into the air.

I felt an absolute chill blanket me. I looked at Rebecca, my heart racing. "Did you see that?"

She nodded, though to my disappointment she didn't look the least bit scared. "It's a ball. Probably one of the kids from here, am I right?"

Kelly smiled at her. "You're right. He's from here. Except he's not one of Oceanside's students. He was from Sea Crest. And he died in 1932."

CHAPTER SIX

I looked over at Dex and almost smiled. I mean, as creepy as this was, it was almost fun to see the physical evidence of a ghost and especially in front of people who could be described as skeptics. Though when I looked back at Kelly, she was already smiling apologetically.

"I don't really see much," she said, as though she knew what I was thinking. Maybe she did. "Just here and there. Nothing terrifying, nothing that makes me want to quit my job. Sometimes I get creeped out, especially if I'm here alone. Sometimes things happen that I can't explain. But for the most part, I don't feel any...animosity here. Maybe Brenna will tell you differently, but aside from the never-ending ball game that Elliot plays with his friends, I don't ever feel uneasy."

"Elliot?" Dex asked as he walked over to the rubber ball. He picked it up in his hands, looking it over and then smelled it, as if that would tell him something.

"He's one of the ghosts that Brenna sees. Brenna McIntosh. Some other people report seeing him, too. That drawing in my office of the young boy with the teddy bear? One of the students, Jody Robinson, she drew that. She sees him. I just see glimpses, I get a feeling. But I don't actually *see* him."

"So you mainly stick to the first floor?" Rebecca asked. "Do you ever go upstairs?"

Kelly shook her head rather vehemently. "This is about all that I can handle. I can handle Elliot. I can handle the fact that he apparently has other friends, friends I never see evidence of and I'm happy to keep it that way. But when you go upstairs, things change. Only Brenna goes up there, and Carl, our custodian. I can't even get halfway up the staircase before I start feeling dizzy. *No one* goes upstairs."

"Well, it's fairly safe to say that *we'll* be going up there," Rebecca said. "Can you tell me—us – about—what we could expect?"

Kelly rubbed her hands up and down her arms as if she were cold. "I think I should keep showing you around." She walked out of the room as Dex came around to me and held out the ball.

"Touch it," he said.

I grimaced, pushing his arm away. "No. That's a dead kid's toy."

"But you're so good with balls."

"Shut up."

He put the ball on top of the first bed and we hurried after the two of them. Kelly led us back the way we came and down toward the classrooms. Almost all the doors were closed so we just read the signs on them as we walked past. Mrs. Collins. Mrs. Keats. Mr. Murphy. Ms. Ross. There were about fifteen rooms in total and the last ones we'd come across as we went further into the west wing were all the artistic electives.

"We're an arts school," Kelly explained, "but we still believe in having a proper, well-rounded education. Most of the teachers here just teach the basics for each grade—math, English, science, history. But two hours of every day the kids get to take art classes, and that's where the teaching becomes more specialized. Like Brenna, here."

We came to a stop outside an open door and peered inside. The room was covered in paintings with paint splattered stools and stacks of easels in the corner. At a large desk was a woman asleep, dark brown hair pooled all around her.

Kelly cleared her throat. "Like Brenna here," she said a bit louder, but even then her voice was quiet as a mouse.

"Brenna!" Dex yelled.

I smacked him on the chest as the woman jumped up from her sleep, her hair all in her face. "What? What?"

"You're a jerk," I told him.

He shrugged. "Got the job done, didn't I? Don't say I'm not a man of results."

Kelly waved at Brenna who was trying to clear her messy desk and appear like someone who hadn't just fallen asleep on the job. "Hey, Brenna, sorry to wake you. The ghost hunters are here."

Brenna got out of her chair and smiled at us. "Hi," she said exuberantly. For some reason I was expecting Brenna to look like a meek and put-upon person but that wasn't the case. She was young-looking, maybe just a few years older than me, with wavy brown hair and an apple-cheeked glow about her. "I'm Brenna McIntosh."

"I'll leave you guys with her now," Kelly said politely before walking off down the hall like a wisp of a person.

"Can I tell you how happy I am to meet you?" Brenna said as she came around the desk. Dressed in boot-cut jeans and a black tunic, she seemed even more personable. She stopped in front of me and pulled me into a hug. "Sorry, I'm a hugger," she said to my back while I was brought forward into a cloud of strawberry perfume.

"That's okay," I told her, getting my bearings as soon as she released me. "I guess you watch the show?"

"All the time," she said proudly. She looked over at Dex. "And you, I loved you in the Sasquatch episode, well at least the parts of it that you were allowed to air. But poor Twatwaffle."

He stuck out his lower lip in mock sympathy then sighed. "Yes. Thank god all good llamas go to heaven."

She didn't seem to catch on—or she didn't mind—his sarcasm because she went onto Rebecca next. "And you must be the new manager. You're doing a great job."

I could have sworn Rebecca blushed at that. "Thank you."

"Brenna," Dex began, "do you mind if we talk to you on camera? Is this a good time?"

"No problem," she said. "I've been preparing for this. It's too bad I fell asleep, I probably ruined my Hollywood face." She burst into a flurry of giggles.

"You look great," I reassured her as Dex touched my shoulder and let me know he was running out to the car.

"So are you sure you're okay with us filming right here today?" Rebecca prodded, ever mindful of a lawsuit. When Brenna nodded she went on, "Even with the kids and everything?"

"Oh," she said, "well I guess you shouldn't really film the kids. I mean, interview them and such. I think we would need permission for that. On camera, of course. Off camera I think it's fine."

"But doesn't the school care if the school—or their kids—are being featured in a ghost hunting show? That's bound to scare a lot of the parents, isn't it?" I asked. I know I'd be concerned.

She leaned forward, her hair swinging in her face. "Davenport doesn't care. She's been wanting to build a brand new school since the other one burnt down. As far as she's concerned, she doesn't care if parents get scared. It will only make them want a better school, the one she thinks we deserve."

"And what do you think?" Rebecca asked.

Brenna's eyes darted around the room. "I'd have to agree. I need this job though and I can't chance getting hired elsewhere. If we could move, I would be a lot happier."

At least it explained why they were so willing to go on camera. Still, with that amount of determination and attention, a part of me wondered if the whole thing wasn't exaggerated a little. Perhaps the little boy and his bouncing ball were a fake, perhaps we'd already been lied to. Perhaps there were no ghosts, just a faculty who really wanted a new school.

I looked quickly at Rebecca and I could see from the skeptical raise to her forehead that she was thinking the same thing. It was better to start treating this episode with a side of caution.

It wasn't long before Dex came trotting back into the room with his camera in hand. His eyes were dancing, his body buzzing with adrenaline. "Get this," he said, raising his camera up and flipping the viewfinder around for us to see. He pressed play, and as our four heads all converged around the screen, we watched as he filmed the ground, a paper plane lying at his feet. He picked it up and then aimed the camera up to the roof of the building. Within seconds, another paper plane came sailing down, barely visible against the foggy sky before it drifted lazily on an air current.

"There were only two planes," he said, placing the camera down and pulling one of the paper planes out of his pocket, rubbing it between his fingers. "But still, I think that's got to count for something." He looked at Brenna. "Does anyone have access to the roof?"

She didn't look shocked. "Just the custodian. I can get the keys. It's locked for safety reasons."

"So then it had to be a ghost," he said.

"Unless the custodian's taken up a new hobby," Rebecca said, though I knew what she was thinking. Davenport herself or even Kelly could be up on the roof, tossing paper planes over the side, knowing they'd provide a pretty good show. "Brenna was just telling us that Ms. Davenport doesn't mind if the school is featured on the show because they're hoping the parents will want to move their kids into a newer school." She stared hard at Dex, trying to pass on the message without saying anything more.

"Oh," he said. He looked at Brenna. "Tell me, sweetcheeks, you wouldn't happen to be pulling our leg about the whole ghost shit in order to get a new school, now would ya?" Leave it to Dex to be so direct. I knew for a fact that his bullshitting tolerance was pretty damn low.

Brenna's mouth turned down, her eyes becoming rounder. "No. No, not at all. This is all real. And it's only happening to me. No one else. They all feel it, they all believe me, but they don't see it like I do. In fact, it's gotten worse since I got here, at least that's what some of the assholes here say, like it's my fucking—sorry—my *damn*, fault. But I'm still the only one who gets haunted here. Me and a few students."

"Jody," Dex said slowly.

She nodded fervently. "Yes, Jody. They love her. Kyle too." She stopped and looked at me. "You have to believe me, this is happening. I want to leave. I want to go to the new school. And if you guys can't make the haunting stop, then at least the show will push the parents to make the move happen."

"You do realize that we aren't ghost whisperers," Dex said sternly. "Perry and I, we just see them. Our job isn't to fix anything, it's just to record it, report it."

"Like batshit journalists," I filled in. "Hacks. But we don't banish anyone or anything."

Except for that one time, I thought back to The Benson. I had to say that felt pretty good.

"I know that," she said, and for once her expression wasn't so jovial. "I'm just getting tired of this. And desperate. Please, you have to believe me."

Rebecca walked over to a chair and pulled it out. “Here, love. Why don’t you sit down and we’ll start getting to the bottom of this.”

Brenna smiled gratefully and took a seat. “Okay. We have about an hour until my next class, but I should be able to wrap it up by then. If I start wasting footage, just let me know.”

Dex quickly got the camera set up and I pulled up a chair next to Brenna, feeling like a chump in my hoodie. Rebecca put wireless mics on the two of us and we got started.

I asked Brenna to go back to the beginning, from when she first started at the school. She’d only been hired at the start of the semester. The last teacher quit and no one really knows why. One day she had a nervous breakdown and resigned. According to her student Jody, it was someone called Shawna that made the teacher leave. Brenna said she eventually found out who Shawna was, along with Elliot. Both of them Jody described as her imaginary friends. When teaching first graders, imaginary friends weren’t normal but they weren’t that uncommon, either.

“At first,” she said, “the only odd things that happened were just Jody talking about Elliot and Shawna as if they were real people. Often children with imaginary friends still know that they are imaginary. But Jody acted like they were as real as her other classmates. Only..." she trailed off, her brow furrowing. "Only Shawna wasn't someone that Jody liked...Jody feared her. That was another thing I found odd – I'd never heard of an imaginary enemy before."

"Not unless the kid is batshit crazy," Dex commented. I shot him a dirty look to which he shrugged.

She nodded. "I know. But Jody seemed well-rounded. And then when her classmate Kyle started talking about Elliot, I knew something was happening. They weren't messing with me, either. I'm pretty quick to see through children's games." She paused to look us each in the eye, playing with the timing of the story like a good teacher would do. "Then, I saw Elliot for myself."

I sucked in my breath as she continued.

"It was back in February, a month after I started. A huge snowstorm had set in on the coast, which was unusual. We get a lot of bad storms here throughout the year, but snow was rare. And so the power went out at the school and the kids were all sent home around noon before the snow really got going. We have a generator here but Davenport was worried about the roads becoming impassible."

I'd been given a ride in by my boyfriend because his car was the only one with four-wheel drive and so I was waiting for him to pick me up, just hanging out in the teacher's lounge with a few other staff and watching the storm blow in. When the last staff member left, my boyfriend called to tell me he was about fifteen minutes away. I went back to my classroom to make sure everything was okay and that the lights wouldn't come blazing on when the power returned. At that time, my classroom felt safe to me. The rest of the building, with the wind shutting open doors and howling through the halls, made my hair stand right up."

Finally, when I thought I should be waiting outside, I left the classroom and walked back down the hall. Suddenly the air turned as cold as ice, as if the storm itself had reached inside, and I heard a kick and the sound of a ball bouncing after me. I turned around to see an orange ball rolling down the hall. And, further down from that, was the silhouette of a young boy, backlit from the windows of the classrooms and the gauzy snowstorm outside. I asked who the boy was and he quickly turned around, as if spooked himself, and ran off down the hall until he disappeared."

"That was all fine," she said, catching her breath. "I was scared in a way but I wasn't creeped out. It was weird. It was interesting. I've always had weird things like this, unexplained things, happen to me before so it wasn't like it threw me for a loop. I just thought, oh, so that boy must have died here from TB. I was actually sad. Then the next day, before I even had a chance to ask Jody about it, she came up to me and said that Elliot was happy that I saw him. He hoped I would play next time."

A shiver went down my spine. I remembered my dream, the bouncing ball, the girl asking if I would play.

"Did you?" Dex asked.

She smiled sheepishly. "Not really. Next time it happened—it was also when everyone had left one night—I tried kicking the ball back but he wasn't too interested. He laughed that time, which I took as a good sign." She exhaled and looked down at the floor. "For a few weeks that was the extent of it. To me, the only thing haunting this place was Elliot, and he was harmless. That was until Jody started...getting sick. Well, acting sick."

"Which was it?" I asked. "Was she actually sick?"

She shook her head. "It's hard to say. She started exhibiting all the symptoms that TB patients used to but when it came time to examine her, nothing was wrong. She'd act like she couldn't breathe, yet Kelly would listen to her chest and say she was fine. She was kept home for a few days and when she finally came back...she wasn't the same."

I leaned forward in my seat, a chill on my limbs. "What do you mean, wasn't the same?"

Brenna frowned. "I don't know. She just...changed. When she came back, she was no longer the smiling, happy Jody. She was tired-looking, depressed. Scared. That's really what it was, she was scared. She started painting things, beautiful images that were so...disturbing." She got up, her chair pushed back with a loud groan, and went over to her desk drawer. She came back to us holding a stack of thick paper.

"It started with this one," she said, holding out the first picture. It was of the school, from the outside. There was no doubt that Jody excelled at watercolors. The painting was fairly accurate and there was even some realistic shading.

"Nice work," Dex said.

Brenna pointed at one of the upper windows. At first glance I thought Jody tried to paint in a window glare but I could see it was the face of a little girl, complete with a bow in her hair.

"Who's that?" I asked, trying to keep my voice steady. I didn't know how accurate the painting was, but it looked like the girl I saw in my dream.

"Jody said that was Shawna," Brenna explained. "Which was fine. But then she said Shawna was stuck on the fourth floor because of the *bad thing.* She smiled after she said that, too, like she was happy about it. I asked about the bad thing but she shrugged and ran off, like she didn't care anymore."

She handed me the next piece of paper. "This is what she drew the next time."

It was the school again, almost the exact same picture, only this time a few red lines were coming out of the fourth floor windows. The face of Shawna was now on the third floor. Though it was still just a kid's painting, Shawna's eyes were cold, hard dots.

"Plumbing problem?" Dex asked from behind the camera.

Brenna didn't smile. "No. Jody said that was the blood of all the dead children. She said it came from the room with the big lights. Now, Jody has never been upstairs to the fourth floor—none of the students here have—so I don't know how she knew that there's an autopsy room there, complete with big lights and a table where they put the bodies."

"Does the same table have a gutter around the edges to catch the blood from the, uh, deceased?"

She nodded. "You've done some reading."

He shrugged. "Dikipedia."

Finally she smiled. "What else? But you're right. They used to bleed out the bodies and the blood would collect around them. Super disgusting."

"I'm guessing she didn't know about that," I ventured.

"No. I thought maybe she heard it from someone so I asked her. She said she's been there, in her dreams, and that Shawna was making her go up there. Then she said that Shawna was on the third floor now because the bad thing wanted to be closer to her." She took in a shaky breath and looked at me. "And closer to me."

"What does the bad thing look like?" I asked. "I mean, what exactly is it?"

"You can see here," she said, holding out the third piece of paper. We all leaned in to get a closer look. It was nearly the same picture as before, only now Shawna was on the second floor and there was another face the next window down from her. This face was completely black and oblong, with long black hair and two white dots for eyes.

"That," she said, tapping beneath the face, "is the bad thing. And when I asked Jody if it was still on the second floor, she said it was already here. She said it was standing behind me."

I gulped loudly, nerves prickling down my back. "Did you look?" I whispered, totally terrified and totally enthralled.

She shook her head and gave us an embarrassed smile. "I couldn't. I was too afraid. I could almost feel it there. Even the rest of the students in the room grew quiet, like they could sense something else in the room, something…not of this world. I told Jody I'd look some other time and she said it would be back."

"And was it?" asked Dex.

Brenna looked down at the floor. She took in a deep breath and opened her mouth to talk.

Before she could say anything, there was a loud rap at the door. We all jumped in our seats at the noise, Dex swearing under his breath. I thought my heart was trying to make a run for it.

"Sorry to interrupt," Ms. Davenport said, standing stiffly in the doorway and eyeing us with mild interest. "Brenna, can I have a word with you?"

She shot us an apologetic look. "Yes, of course. My class will start soon. Mind if we pick up with this tomorrow?"

"Not at all," Rebecca said. We got out of our chairs and gathered in the hallway while Davenport stepped into the room, one fleshy hand on the door knob.

She paused there. "If you want, you can wait for me in my office. Or start making yourselves at home. You are staying here, aren't you?"

My partners both looked at me. It was my decision, my call—Perry was the precious one.

"Sure," I said, trying to sound breezy about it. "We can stay here. Will be a lot easier."

"You sure?" Dex asked, stepping forward and putting his hand on my shoulder. "We can stay in the motel, no big deal."

"I'm fine," I said, harder this time. "Really."

Dex didn't seem too satisfied with that answer, watching me closely to see if I was lying. I stared right back at him. Obviously staying in a haunted sanatorium with the bad thing was asking for trouble, but trouble was exactly what we needed for the show. I'd been down this road a hundred times; it felt like it anyway, and this wasn't any different. In St. Augustine, we stayed in a haunted B&B; in Eureka, we camped out in the library. Sure, I had those weird Pippa dreams that put me off the idea a bit, but Dex didn't know about those dreams. I had to wonder if he was the one who was scared then.

"Well, good," Rebecca said with a loud clap of her hands, trying to diffuse the strange tension. "Let's take over this joint."

We headed back outside to the Highlander and started unloading our gear. I couldn't help but glance up at the top floors again, as if expecting to see a little girl's face or rivers of blood streaming from the windows.

There was nothing there, just the glare from the windows, reflecting slices of the foggy sky.

And still, I knew something was there.

Watching me.

And waiting.

CHAPTER SEVEN

Our new sleeping quarters didn't get any less sterile once we started to unpack. For some reason the cloth partition between the beds wasn't movable, so when Dex and I picked our beds, it seemed like we wouldn't be able to push them together.

"You can still squeeze in with me here," he said, patting the middle bed. He gave me a wistful look that I found downright charming. "I don't like sleeping without you."

I smiled but said, "Dex, it's a single bed. My ass barely fits on it as it is."

"You might change your tune later."

"And you'll be the first to know about it."

Rebecca peered at the third bed then looked over at us. "You know what, I really don't feel like having a repeat of Eureka. Please try and keep your hands to yourself."

"You are absolutely no fun," Dex told her while I blushed furiously. One night when we were camped out at the haunted library, Dex broke out the Jack Daniels. One thing led to another and we ended up having sex in the library stacks—and not too far from Rebecca. Poor woman was probably traumatized from that.

After we'd put our bags on the shelves and Rebecca brought out her planner, discussing our goals and objectives for the shoot, the school bell rang and Davenport came to see us.

"I trust you've made yourselves comfortable," she said with nary a smile. "You're free to use the break room anytime you'd like. There's a microwave, a hot plate, and a fridge. I know heading into town can be quite a pain, so I suggest you stock up at the Fred Meyer in Tillamook and have all your meals here."

Great. A week of ramen noodles and microwavable mac and cheese. My thighs were going to love that.

"Please, no alcohol," she added. "This is a school, first and foremost."

Actually, it's a sanatorium, I thought to myself. I looked over at Dex, knowing what he thought of that. His mug was tellingly impassive. I knew he had beer and whiskey under the bed already like a rebellious teen at a sleepover.

"When do we get a tour?" Rebecca asked. "I'd like to start getting as much footage as we can."

"I'm afraid you'll just have to be patient," she said with a cock of her scary penciled eyebrow, not even picking up on her own pun. "Originally I thought I'd do it myself, but I'm running out of time today. All you need for now is to know this first floor, and I'm sure Kelly showed you that well enough. Tomorrow morning at nine o'clock I've arranged for a local historian to stop by. Patrick Rothburn. He runs the maritime museum here and comes from a family who used to run the post office for Sea Crest. He'll show you the rest of the building. Hopefully you can get some good footage." She lowered her voice. "To be frank with you, as much as I'd love to believe Ms. McIntosh, I'm not entirely convinced she is telling the truth. I hope the three of you will at least prove her wrong or right."

She drummed her fingers anxiously along the side of the doorway, her attention off in the halls as a few students straggled in the background, heading to the main doors and the way home. She looked back at us after a few moments. "I'll be working in my office for the next hour. I suggest if you're going to get food, you go now. We lock this place up at night and I don't feel like entrusting the keys to you. No offense, of course."

"None taken," said Dex. He turned to me. "Well, kiddo, what say we get some provisions before we get locked up in The Overlook Hotel?"

"Very funny," I muttered. Images of the twins from The Shining were the last thing I needed in my head.

We bid goodbye to Davenport and hopped into the Highlander. We were halfway down the mountain when Rebecca exhaled noisily.

"What?" I asked, twisting in my seat to face her. She had rolled down the window, the cool air messing up her black curls. Her face looked paler than normal and her eyes were closed, exposing the perfect lines she'd drawn on her lids with liquid liner.

She kept her eyes closed. "I don't know, I was just feeling I was going to be sick back there. Didn't realize it until now."

"Altitude sickness?" I suggested.

"It's only 400 meters above sea level," she said. "That doesn't make sense."

I looked over at Dex. His lips were pursed in thought. He eyed her in the rear view mirror. "You know, Becs, if you ever feel, uh, creeped the fuck out, you know it's okay to admit it, right? Perry and I know the feeling better than anyone."

"I'm not scared," she said through clenched teeth, her eyes still closed and head back on the seat rest. "I'm not creeped out. I just feel sick."

"You're not preggo, are you?" I asked her.

Finally, her eyes flew open. Man did she look pissed off, considering it was an obvious joke.

"Really, Perry," she said.

I shrugged and sat back in my seat. I also felt a million times better now that we were away from the school and back on Highway 101, winding south toward Tillamook. After we stocked up on simple groceries—frozen meals, freeze-dried coffee, health bars, and some fresh fruit—we pulled into a local diner to catch a quick cup of coffee before we headed back up.

As soon as Dex parked the car, I realized where we were. It was the same diner that we had gone to when we first met. The faded orange awning, tired-looking patrons, and peeling graphics all looked exactly the same.

"Wow," I whispered, feeling the past rush through me.

"What? What is this place?" Rebecca asked as she peered at the aging café.

"Where Perry and I had our first date," Dex answered with a grin. I looked over at him and smiled.

With his newsboy cap pulled low on his brow, his light black jacket and scruffy face, the Dex of now—my Dex—could have been the Dex back then. Of course, that Dex would have been nervously chomping on Nicorette or breaking a toothpick in his mouth, his hands fidgeting, his face thinner and drawn into a mysterious scowl. Oh, and now he had hard, tight muscles to fucking die for.

Once again I was reminded about how far we'd come in such a short amount of time.

Rebecca eyed the both of us. "This was your first date? I thought that was at Zekes."

Dex sighed. "If you want to be technical, then this was more our first...real chance to talk."

I frowned and folded my arms. "If I recall correctly, we didn't get much talking done. You were being an asshole."

"That's right," he said playfully, "and you stormed out of here like I lit a fire up under that bouncy ass."

"You said I was faking it," I countered.

"Well you could have been a famewhore for all I knew."

"You guys," Rebecca spoke up. "This is really sweet and romantic and all—in a twisted way—but are we going to get coffee here or what?"

I ignored her. "And then when I came out here, that's when I saw Pippa. Where she talked to me for the first time."

At the mention of her name, their faces became drawn. I continued, "She warned me about Dex, told me to watch out. Then she said I'd need him."

Rebecca looked over at Dex. "She was kind of right."

"And after that," I added, "she went into the diner. Next thing I knew, Dex was coming out of here like *he* was the one with the fire under *his* bouncy ass. He nearly drove us into a tree before he admitted to me that he'd seen Pippa before."

Rebecca clucked her tongue. "All right then. You two definitely win the award for the most fucked up history. It still blows my bloody mind that your grandmother used to be his nanny."

I was barely listening to her. I was staring at Dex, deep into his dark, brooding eyes, wondering if he was feeling what I was, the full circle of everything—that feeling that no matter what happened to us in the future, there was this aura of destiny about us. Okay, that was a pretty cheesy analogy, but I had nothing else. There was just this indescribable feeling that every little step in our lives had been a lead up to us meeting each other. I could only hope that the same fate would continue. After all we'd been through, that's all we could really hold on to.

"Have you seen her lately?" Rebecca's voice came into focus.

"Huh?" I said, snapping out of my daze and tearing my eyes away from Dex.

She snapped her delicate fingers in my face. "I said, have you seen her lately. Your grandmother?" When I didn't answer her right away, she looked at Dex. "Is this a sensitive topic?"

I shook my head. "No. Sorry, I haven't. Not since New Orleans." It was a lie of course, but sometimes it wasn't worth getting into my dreams, especially when I knew Rebecca couldn't understand them the way I did. It was hard enough for me to figure out if my dreams were something to consider or not.

The image of the little girl and the bouncing ball flashed into my head. If I ever ended up meeting this Shawna I'd be a little bit closer to the truth.

She nodded and walked to the door of the café. "Well, shall we go in? We don't have much time before we have to go back."

We went in together with Dex putting his hand at the small of my back, a gesture I found so enticingly protective.

"Are you all right, kiddo?" he asked gruffly in my ear, his breath tickling the hairs on my neck.

“I’m okay now,” I told him. We found a booth at the back—it wasn’t hard since the diner wasn’t very busy—and the waitress came over with some menus. It wasn’t quite the same waitress as we had before—this one had severe bangs and a crooked smile—but Dex flirted with her just the same.

While we downed the tarlike coffee, we quickly went over the plans for the coming week. I wasn’t too keen on staying at the sanatorium for that long, but Rebecca shrewdly pointed out that we should take advantage of the free accommodations.

“Besides,” she said, sipping from her cup of green tea, “I don’t want us to pull the usual get in and get out.”

Dex snickered at that and I kicked him under the table.

She smiled mischievously at him. “That is what you call the Dex Foray Special, right?”

He gave her a stern look. “Hey now.”

“What’s the Dex Foray Special?” I asked, suddenly intrigued. Sometimes the two of them had these inside jokes that drove me nuts. I just hoped it wasn’t something that involved Jenn.

“Baby, you’ve already had the special,” he said with a wag of his brows. “And you liked it. Anyway, I agree with Rebecca, but only if it’s what everyone wants.”

"And by everyone you mean me," I said, starting to feel the slightest bit annoyed. "Seriously, don't treat me like my head might start spinning around at any moment. We'll do what we have to do for the show."

He opened his mouth but I cut him off with the raise of my hand. "It's been almost six months since all that...shit happened. We've been taking it easy, and when things have gotten too scary or risky, we've gotten out. We'll do the same here. There's a difference between having our lives at risk and being scared. I know I'll be scared every second we spend there this week, that's just the way it is when you see fucking ghosts every day. But please don't start treating me like I'm some special case. The three of us have been through a lot already—I don't see how this is going to be any different."

Yet the minute those words came out of my mouth, I knew it was a lie. Whether it was the warnings from my dreams, the look of utter fear in Brenna's eyes, or the fact that Rebecca—our rock, our island—was being affected by the place, I didn't know. But I knew we'd find out.

***

The plan for the next few days seemed simple enough at first. We would start filming tomorrow with the historian and take in an actual tour of the place from top to bottom. Then, depending on what we felt about each floor, or if there were any particular areas that stood out to us from the tour, we would start concentrating our efforts there. Rebecca wanted to make sure every corner of the place was covered, from the playground at the back of the building to the roof where Dex saw the paper planes come from, with the most haunted sections getting the most attention.

Once we got back to the near-empty school and put our meager groceries away, the plans changed. Like usual, it was all Dex's doing.

While Davenport was bidding us farewell, she noted that Carl, the custodian, would be the last one in the building and locking up when he was done with his shift in a few hours. Rebecca, feeling her claustrophobia come back in full swing, was happy to know that the emergency doors at the ends of the first floor wings opened up from the inside.

"Remember, it can be very unsafe for you to investigate the upper floors without being supervised. I'll have you know that I do have security cameras monitoring the first floor, turned on by motion detector," Davenport said as she was ready to go out the main doors. She seemed to direct her eagle gaze at Dex, who didn't squirm under her scrutiny. "Just keep that in mind. Of course, as long as you stick to your rooms, the break room, and the washrooms, that shouldn't be a problem." She finished that off by eyeing a place on the wall behind us.

We turned to see a tiny video camera mounted just above the grand staircase that led to the upper floors. Big brother was watching. We didn't have to voice it to know that we weren't expected to go anywhere else in the building except for the first floor.

And I didn't have to look at Dex to know what he was thinking. I could just feel it. He was already plotting ways for us to get around that camera. As soon as we saw Davenport get in her Lexus and drive off into the darkening fog, he turned to us and said, "There's more than one way upstairs."

Then he grinned impishly, the dimples sticking out on his stubble-flecked cheeks, and turned to head back to the nurses' quarters. I looked at Rebecca and sighed. She shrugged, apparently not expecting anything less.

"Okay, so what exactly is your plan?" Rebecca asked as we followed him into our new bedroom.

He sat on the edge of my bed, his weight nearly lifting the whole thing, and looked up at us, completely devious. He really was something else when he was in this mode. His attitude was infectious, even when it proved to harbor a terrible idea.

"The way I see it, Custodian Carl is probably here for another two hours tops. I say while he's here we film a bit of the first floor. I mean, that motion sensor camera is going to be activated anyway. Then when he leaves, we hunker ourselves down in the break room where I'll whip up my patented mac and cheese and hotdog special, we break out a few contraband beers, relax a little. Then, when it's dark as sin and we're sure Carl and anyone else are miles away from here, we pick up the cameras and go upstairs."

"By this secret other way that you know about?" Rebecca repeated sardonically.

He stroked his chin. "Yep. The one elevator in this building doesn't work anymore. I saw it just past the washrooms. It's boarded up, the power probably cut a long time ago."

I put my face in my hands. "Please don't suggest we're climbing up an elevator shaft, because I'm not doing it."

"Relax, kiddo," he said. "This ain't *Speed.*" I watched him carefully to see if he was going to launch into another Keanu impression. He didn't. "Anyway, that normally would be the only way upstairs. But I've done my research, just like Becs here has done, and I know there's one more way. We may have to search for it, but it's there."

"Hold on," I interrupted. "Before I find out what this way is, what do you propose we do? Go upstairs and film? Alone? The three of us? Sure, we won't trip the camera and it's not like Davenport explicitly said we weren't allowed upstairs but...you know she's eventually going to see the footage. She'll know we went up on our own."

"So?" Dex said, looking at me as if I was crazy. "By the time this episode airs, we'll be back in Seattle and she'll be stuck down here with her Sharpie eyebrows and her shitty haunted school. No harm, no foul."

Mmmhmm. I hated burning bridges, but he did have a point. It's not like we were trespassing since we'd already been invited to stay on the property. "So what's the way?" I asked with trepidation.

Dex wiggled his lips back and forth and looked at Rebecca. She stared blankly back at him for a few beats until she groaned. "Oh dear, I think I know what bloody way you're talking about."

"Bloody is right," he said. "Unless the bodies had been drained already." He read my puzzled expression. "The body chute."

"The what?" I asked.

“Almost every sanatorium has a body chute. It was a way to get the bodies from the morgue or autopsy areas out of the building and into the hearses outside. Think about it...a hospital like this had at least five hundred deathly ill patients at a time. Thousands died, right here. How could you instill hope in people, the hope to survive, if you were wheeling out dead bodies in front of them on a daily basis?”

Shit. This was a lot bigger than I’d originally thought. Usually when we did a show, we went to where one or two people had died. Only in very few instances was it a group of people. I think the leper colony at D’Arcy Island was the largest amount, about thirty to fifty of them. But thousands of people—children—died here over the course of Sea Crest’s operation; right in the very building I was in. Thousands. This was so damn different from just one ghost. It was so different from just worrying about Elliot or Shawna or a few suicidal nurses. There would have been dead upon dead upon dead here.

“Perry?” Dex asked. “If you don’t want to come, you can stay behind.”

I nearly laughed. “Stay here? Alone in the room? And do what? Knit you guys some socks?”

“It might be less scary,” Rebecca offered. At that moment I kind of wanted to hit her. She was never scared, what the hell did she know about anything being less scary? She was barely even right. Yes, staying in the room seemed like a better idea than going up to the other floors, but being alone was being alone. I'd rather see horrendous gore with someone else by my side than hear the giggle of a child on my own.

"I'm good," I said firmly. "So where do you think this body chute is?"

"I'd think there would have to be access on this floor considering all the nurses were staying down here. We just have to do our usual try every door and see which one is a winner."

None of them are winners, I thought. "And this chute..."

"If I'm right," Dex said, "it's just a tunnel with a steep incline. Stairs on one side, a slab on the other where you can wheel the gurney."

"You do realize I'd rather trip Davenport's security camera and deal with the consequences tomorrow," I said.

"And where is the fun in that?"

So we decided to go with Dex's plan. While Carl—a quiet and small-eyed senior with the unruliest ear hair I'd ever seen—mopped the hall, we started filming the first floor. Rebecca operated the light while Dex filmed, and I tried to look both scared and pretty on film. Considering Carl was watching us at times, I'm not sure I succeeded at either.

Then when I ran out of interesting things to say and we'd filmed every single classroom, trying to find cold spots or weird sounds or unexplained breezes and coming up empty, we acted like we were done for the night and retreated to the lounge for Dex's redneck special. Carl eventually got in his beater of a car and drove off into the night, leaving us feeling completely and utterly alone.

"So," I said as I washed down a bite with a mouthful of warm beer. "It's just the three of us."

The isolation wrapped its cold arms around me. Outside, the fog was lifting but the sun had set and the sky was turning a purplish bruised color, darkening by the moment. Though the lights in the lounge and the outside hall were on, it still felt dark as hell. The only sound was from the hum of the fridge and from the clank of our forks against the plates. Everything else was quiet, deathly quiet. The kind of quiet that became a character of its own.

Rebecca gathered her frilled cardigan around her. "If I admit that the whole situation is a fair bit unnerving, will the two of you laugh at me?"

Dex took a swig of his beer before asking, "Do you want us to laugh at you? You know I'm always game."

She glared at him. "Here I am, admitting that I'm borderline scared and you're taking the piss."

"Ignore him," I told her. "I won't laugh. This place is like its own entity. I swear if you listen hard enough, you can hear the walls breathing."

"Perry," she admonished, giving me a dirty look. "That was something I didn't need to picture."

It was true though. Even though the lounge was tastefully furnished, resembling a trendy waiting area for a downtown office more than a staff break room, there was something in the air that reminded you where you were: miles above sea level on the Oregon coast, locked in an old sanatorium where thousands of children died, spending the night and hoping to film at least one of the many ghosts who were rumored to live here. I was hit again with that overwhelming urge to flee. I guess that fight mechanism of mine petered out from time to time.

I glanced at Dex, who seemed to be acting normal, eyes dancing slightly in anticipation of the night. "How many beers did you bring, by the way, because I think I might need another," I told him.

"I'll have some tea," Rebecca spoke up, pushing her plate toward us. "I can't eat anymore."

"Feeling sick again?" I asked her. I leaned in more to observe her face. Like earlier, she still looked more tired than normal, her skin taking on a lackluster bluish tone that looked vampiric against her dark hair and brows.

"Nothing tea won't fix," she said as she got up to put on a pot. Dex pulled another lager out of the fridge and handed it to me.

It wasn't long though before he started cleaning up and suggesting we get ready. I know it was my job as host to look as attractive as possible, but when your face was filmed in grainy, green night vision and you were usually making the stupidest expressions, I'd learned it was kind of a lost cause. I brushed my hair back into a ponytail, added some powder to my nose and liner to my lids, but the jeans and Kyuss hoodie stayed and I was ready to go. Or at least ready as I'd ever be.

With Dex taking the small camcorder, Rebecca with the external light, and me with...well, me, we headed out the door and down the hallway. I was immediately creeped out. The hallway was completely dark down the wing where the classrooms were. Our wing was only lit by the occasional wall sconce, giving off a romantic but dim light. The whole place must have been on timers.

"Do you know if there's power upstairs?" I asked as we slowly walked down the hall of the administrative wing, Dex and Rebecca peering at every door or wall paneling we came across.

"Probably not," said Rebecca. She walked along the wall, her fingers trailing beneath intricate white molding. "There would be no point if no one ever used the space above. Which reminds me, we have no idea what the physical state of this supposed tunnel will be, let alone the floors above. What if some places are out of bounds for a reason?"

"Relax," Dex said as he looked through the camera, aiming it around us. "We're just going to the second floor for now. We'll take a peek and if anything looks unsafe, we'll turn around and head back."

I licked my lips nervously. If we did have to turn back in a hurry, I knew I'd be sprinting down that main staircase, two steps at a time.

The thing about the building that made things extra eerie in the darkness was the way the floors were laid out. The main hall, where the nurses' room was, the offices, the lounge, the showers, it was all one straight shot up and down. If you stood in the absolute middle of the building—where the staircase was—and looked down past Davenport's office to the end, it looked like that was it, ending at a distant room. But the hall actually veered sharply to the left, so that if you were viewing the building from above, it would look like angular bat wings. We were almost where the hall turned down the wing when Dex let out a satisfied sigh.

"What?" asked Rebecca, shining the light where he was looking. There was the faint outline of a door in the wall in front of him, wider than normal, and though it had no handle or visible way of opening, it was obviously an entrance to somewhere.

Dex handed the camera back to me to film, and as I did so, he reached into the pockets of his cargo pants and pulled out a Swiss Army knife. I pretended I didn't notice the way his large forearms and biceps were flexing as he stuck one end of the knife into the door's edge and tried to pry it open. After a few frustrated grunts and failed attempts as Rebecca and I watched helplessly, he found purchase and with extra leverage, the door began to part from the wall. It let out a low groan and we were all hit with a blast of stale, frigid air. It wrapped around me and chilled me to the very core.

"Oh, man," I said, taking a step back but remembering to keep filming.

"What is it, Dex?" Rebecca whispered.

He took a small flashlight out of his other pocket and stuck it in his mouth as he pushed the wooden door open the rest of the way. He grabbed the edge of the wall and poked his head into the cold abyss. I could only see the light from his flashlight bobbing faintly against stark cement walls, and I had this fantastic urge to reach forward and pull him back, as if something was going to come out of the darkness and take him.

He pulled the flashlight out of his mouth and turned his head to look at us. “Looks like we found the body chute,” he said just as a loud smacking noise resonated from the tunnel, echoing loudly and making my heart thump.

He aimed the flashlight back inside in time to illuminate a lone bouncing ball roll past him and disappear into the rest of the darkness.

“Holy fucking fuck!” I screeched, my voice catching in my throat. “No. No! Bad!”

“Shit,” he swore, now frantically trying to light up the tunnel. ”Did you guys see that fucking thing? Holy shit!” He waved at Rebecca. “Quick, bring the fucking light here.”

Though my heart was in my mouth, I watched Rebecca as she stepped forward and handed him the light she was holding. In the dim glow of the hallway, she didn't seem scared at all.

“You did see that, right?” I asked her, my eyes begging for sanity. “Please tell me that wasn't just for me and Dex again.”

She gave me a half smile. “The ball again? Oh, I saw that. I just don't believe we're truly alone here after all. And I don't mean in the supernatural way, either. Who knows who Davenport has upstairs, playing tricks on us?” My mouth dropped slightly at her resistance to believe. She nodded at the camera and continued, “By the way, I really hope you got all that.”

As it was, I had gotten all of that, albeit a little shaky and peppered with our obscenities. But it was there. Despite how Rebecca saw things, it did feel good to actually capture something like that on film. It wasn’t proof by a long shot, but if it scared the shit out of Dex and I, it would scare viewers.

I looked up from the footage to see Dex staring at me impatiently.

“What?” I asked.

“Do you want to go in or not?”

Honestly, after seeing that ball go past, my answer was hell to the fucking no. But since Rebecca was so certain that everything was a set-up, a cruel part of me hoped we could prove her wrong. Besides, when you were with a skeptic, it made things a little less scary.

Well, in general. Probably not this time.

I took in a deep breath, trying to steady my nerves against the idea of going inside some long, closed up tunnel that some ghost child was playing ball in. “You lead the way,” I said. Then for good measure, I added, “Rebecca you can take the rear.”

I half expected to hear Dex make a joke about that, but he was so wrapped up in the moment that he didn’t even notice.

He pointed the flashlight into the tunnel and very carefully stepped down into it, me holding his upper arm for balance. Once he was in, he looked up at me. "It's just about a foot or two lower than where you're standing. It's kind of slippery in places though, so watch your step. I've got you."

Before I could say anything, he reached out and grabbed me around the waist. My weight was no match for his brute strength, and he picked me up and gently placed me in the tunnel so that my feet were on the step just below him.

"Thanks," I said, never tiring from the feel of his strong hands around me. It definitely tried to take my mind off the current situation, but really, there was no getting around that I was now standing in a long-forgotten tunnel that was used to transport dead bodies. As Dex helped Rebecca climb in, I looked all around us. There wasn't much to see except a few feet in front and back, as far as the light would reach. The stairs we were standing on were worn cement, splattered with dried stains that I hoped were dirt and rust. Beside the steps was a smooth incline for the stretchers to wheel on. The walls were cold and grey, and with a strange bit of relief I could see the remnants of a graffiti tag where someone must have left their mark back when the place was abandoned. If the vandals could brave it, so could I.

As Rebecca shined her light around, it seemed like the tunnel went on forever in both directions. “Should I prop the door open with something?” She looked genuinely concerned which threw me off for a moment, until I remembered her claims of claustrophobia.

Dex gently took the camera from my hand and the light from Rebecca. He eyed the door with consideration. “It’s heavy and has traction on the floor, see?” He gestured to the bottom of the floor in the hallway where the door scraped along. “There’s no draft in here either. We should be okay.” He slid his eyes to me, giving me a silent chance to back out.

“Well, let’s go,” I said. “We don’t have all night.”

He nodded and aimed the camera in front of him. “I’m assuming the tunnel runs diagonally along the length of the building. The very top probably lets out above the far corner of the west wing.”

I felt the darkness sitting on either side of us, the coldness of the tunnel seeping into my clothes. I quickly jabbed Dex in the back. “Hey, we’ll worry about that later. Let’s just get to the second floor.” It never left my mind for one second that the ball had rolled somewhere behind us, at the end of the chute, and there was no telling if the ghost that kicked it there had gone after it or not.

In other words, I didn't know what was worse—the void in front of us or the black emptiness behind us.

Thank god I was sandwiched between the two of them as we very carefully made our way up the passageway. I felt all my senses on fire as we went, my eyes happy to be watching my feet instead of the unknown that lay in front of Dex and his camera. The only sounds were our footsteps that echoed faintly from the closed-in walls and the raggedness of our breaths.

"Everyone holding up back there?" Dex whispered. As if he couldn't feel me hanging onto the back of his jacket like a little kid.

"Uh huh," I managed to say, my mouth dry.

We waited to hear Rebecca's response but she didn't say anything, though I could feel her breath and presence at my back.

"Feeling claustrophobic yet?" I prodded her for an answer. When she still didn't say anything, I dared to look behind me.

Despite feeling her breath a second ago, I could barely see her. She'd stopped in the middle of the tunnel, about ten feet away, her figure backlit faintly from the residual light of the hallway.

"R-rebecca?" I asked, my voice shaking. I stopped and pulled Dex back. He immediately shined his light on her.

"Are you all right?" Dex asked. "Why are you being creepy?"

"Shhh," she said softly. "I'm listening."

"To what?" I whispered as goosebumps prickled my arms.

She didn't say anything but remained absolutely still. I could hear my own heart thudding in my chest, Dex's breathing, the whir of the camera as it tried to focus.

I was about to ask again what on earth we were listening for when I finally heard it.

It was a few notes of music. But more specific than that, a xylophone, like the kind I used to play around with as a child. I held in a gasp as my brain tried to recognize the faint melody in it. The notes would come and go, as if being swept away by an imaginary breeze, so the song never felt fully formed.

"Ring around the rosy," Dex said in a low voice. I turned to look at him, wincing at the light he was holding in his other hand. "Listen."

He was right. I could pick out the tune, and once I did, I got pummeled with that *get the fuck out of here* feeling. We'd made it about fifteen feet into the tunnel and I'd already had enough.

Of course, I didn't tell them that. I could feel Dex watching me closely.

"Let's keep going," I said quickly. I looked over to Rebecca who slowly nodded. I could see the music was intriguing her and that her rational mind was trying to attribute it to something logical. I wished she could pass some of that logic on to me because her mind seemed like a safer place to be.

We resumed walking, and as we did, the tune began to fade until we were left again with the sound of our own breathing and blood pumping within us.

"Okay," Dex said slowly, coming to a stop. He shined the light forward, illuminating nothing but the never ending tunnel as its greying walls disappeared into the black. I was terrified of the darkness that lay ahead, getting that same peculiar feeling I'd gotten earlier in the day when I stared up at the building. Seeing nothing, but feeling—*knowing*—that something was hidden in front of your eyes and watching you.

He looked over my head at Rebecca. "Do we want to try communicating in here or on the second floor?"

"Communicating?" I repeated, my skin dancing with raw nerves. "In here? No way. Not tonight. We should do that after the tour tomorrow so we know what the hell we're dealing with."

"There's obviously something in this tunnel with us," he said, his voice an octave lower. "Don't you feel it?"

At that, a loud, gritty scraping sound rushed up from behind us. Dex immediately shined the light down the chute, illuminating the door to the first floor.

It was closing on us. Slowly.

As if someone on the other side was pushing it shut.

"Oh god," I gasped as the door closed with a groan, sealing us inside the tunnel.

CHAPTER EIGHT

With the door closing with such heavy finality, Rebecca suddenly sprang into action. She started walking down the stairs as quickly as she could until Dex and I had to run after her in order to keep illuminating her way.

"Rebecca!" I called out as we caught up to her. She was frantically running her hands along the walls, looking for the outline of the door. As on the other side, there was no door handle or anything to indicate it was a door at all.

"Here," Dex said, handing me the light and the camera. He told me to shine it on the wall dead ahead and he started running his hands over it. When he found a groove in the cement, he shoved his shoulder against it and the door budged open a crack. We expected the light from the first floor hallway to come seeping in, but everything was dark. Terribly dark. The timer must have turned the lights off.

"I'm getting out," Rebecca said as Dex pushed his palms flat against the door and got it fully open. Though Dex made it look easy, I could tell how heavy the door was. Just how the hell did it close on us?

"Getting scared?" Dex asked.

Rebecca gave him a sharp look before he helped her step up and into the hallway. "Scared? If you think I'm going to chance getting trapped in that bloody tunnel again, you've got another thing coming." She stood a foot above us, wiping her hands on her capri pants. "Now, are you two still going to go for the second floor or do you want to save that for some other time?"

Dex shrugged, far too cavalier considering what had just happened. I mean, once again, hello, how the hell did that door close?

"Aren't you concerned about the fact that someone pushed the door shut?" I asked her, suppressing a shudder as I said it. "Someone that's probably on the first floor."

She gathered her cardigan around her and quickly smoothed her hair behind her ears. "It was probably the wind." I exchanged a look with Dex that said "what wind?" but we let it go.

"Well, kiddo,"Dex said, taking the camera from me and putting his hand in mine. He gave it a hard, comforting squeeze. "Do you want to pack it up and try again tomorrow, or do you want to see what's on the second floor?"

I want to go back home to Fat Rabbit and laze around on the couch drinking wine and watching Netflix, I thought. I don't want to be standing in a death chute, heading to the second floor with one person less than we started with.

Time for me to put on my brave face. "Can we do, like twenty minutes? When the time's up, we head back?"

"We can do anything you want, baby," he said, taking a step closer until he was pressed up against me. Even in the dim light I could see the warmth in his eyes, his desire to protect me above everything else. "You know that." He bent down and kissed me softly.

Rebecca cleared her throat. "All right then, I'll leave you two be." We broke apart in time to see her take out her iPhone. "I've sent my alarm for twenty-two minutes from now, two minutes extra because I assume you might want to have a quickie in the death tunnel there. I'll give you a call then, sound good?"

"Production manager of the year," Dex said, raising his hand in a false toast. "Can you prop the door open this time, just in case?"

She smiled as if it was her idea in the first place. "I'm already on it. See you in a few."

Then she walked off down the dark hall, happier to be by herself than with us. I took in a deep breath and looked at Dex. He was giving me the eye and I could tell he had an erection from the way he was pressing it firmly against my hip.

"Don't even think about a quickie," I warned him with a sharp shake of my head. "I couldn't come in this place even if you had two dicks."

He grinned. "That sounds like a challenge. You know that can be arranged." Considering he packed a fucking dildo to New Orleans, I wouldn't have been surprised. But I just punched him in the chest. Actually, I was glad for the topic and our fun banter. It was easier to forget where we were and what we were doing.

"Time is running out," I reminded him.

He bit his lip and let his eyes rake over me. "Have I ever told you how hot you look when you're scared out of your mind?"

"You're an ass."

"You love it."

"I love *you*, stupid. Ass or not. Now either we go to the damn floor or we're going after Rebecca and I'm going to bed and pretending I never came in here."

Dex made a slight bow, gesturing up the passageway. "After you." Since I was frozen to the spot, he put his hand on my shoulder and gently turned me around so that I was facing in the right direction. "Unless you want to be behind me."

No way. I steadied the light and walked forward determinedly, finding it easier to find my footing on the steps this time around. They were long, so they had that spacing where you could walk a stride on one step until you stepped on the next. Now that I was in front, I kept my eyes focused dead ahead, at the approaching nothingness beyond the light.

My eyes wanted to see shapes, shadowy human figures that flattened against the walls. In fact, I could almost see them; they were almost real, but they had to be tricks of the eye with the light provided. Scratch that—I *wanted* them to be a trick, you just never really knew with me.

Dex suddenly stopped, and I let my eyes focus on the shadows for just a moment longer, trying to stay absolutely still and fix my vision so that I'd notice any movement.

One of the shadows came off the wall.

"Found it!" Dex exclaimed in a ragged hush.

I put my hand on my chest, nearly letting out a yelp, and looked over at him. He was running his hands down the wall, obviously needing more light. Before I could give it to him though, I stole one last glance at the tunnel. The shadows were still there, but they were static—nothing more than the absence of light.

I steadied my nerves and put the light on the wall where Dex started pushing, ever so conscious of the darkness behind me, just nipping at my heels, an imaginary finger at my shoulder blades. My heart was thumping so loud within my head that it sounded like shitty dubstep.

With a grunt, he pushed in as hard as he could and the cement started to give way, a plume of dust rising up from the cracks and disappearing in the tunnel.

He poked his head into the void, staying silent. I watched his back rise and fall as he breathed. I was about to ask him what was wrong, but before I could he pulled his head back and looked at me with an excited grin. "So this is the second floor. You want to go first or should I?"

"You go," I said. I'd rather be left behind in a tunnel that I had a feel for than to step into the unknown darkness of another level. Though we saw the bouncing ball go off into oblivion, the tinkling of "Ring Around the Rosy," and a door closing on us, things could have been worse. For all the death that passed through the tunnel, it could have been a lot worse.

"Hold this," he said, putting the camera in my other hand. While I held the light steady with the other, I filmed him as he grabbed the edge of the door and hauled himself up. As it was with the first floor, the angle of the tunnel slicing upward meant it wasn't quite level with the floor of the hallway and was about a foot below it.

"Wow," I heard him slowly breathe out as he got to his feet. Whenever Dex said wow, it was either something awesome or horrible. I assumed it wasn't going to be awesome.

"What?"

"It just..." He trailed off. With the shadowy light illuminating the bottom of his face, I watched him stare at nothing. "It feels so different. Come up here."

I breathed in deeply, wishing for that extra shot of courage. It didn't come. I forced it. Dex held out his hand for the camcorder, and after I gave it to him, I let him help me up.

Once I was standing in the hallway of the second floor, I realized how right he was. Though we could only see a few feet in front of us from the light, that few feet was enough. In fact, it wasn't what we saw that made a difference.

It was just a hallway, fairly clean though covered with a layer of grit and dust. Beyond the glow, you could see rooms stretching out on either side, some doors still intact, others gone. Patients' rooms, empty skeletons in the darkness.

But aside from that, it was the *feeling* that got you. It held your chest, like a cold dark hand reaching in. While the whole building had given me the creeps so far, this was the part that told you that you were no longer safe. You were no longer at home.

"This ain't Kansas anymore," I murmured out loud, my breath visibly rising up into the air. It was cold, much colder than the tunnel.

Dex turned to look down at me and handed me back the light before putting his hand at my waist. "It's something, right?" he asked. "Even if I brought Rebecca up here, she'd have to say that things weren't right. The alignment is off. I wouldn't be surprised if the toilets ran backward." He looked away, surveying down the darkened hall as far as the eye could see. "It's just all wrong."

I could only nod. There was no other way to describe it.

We stood there for a long moment, perhaps thinking about the next steps. I know I was thinking about the blackness around me. I was thinking about the tunnel, about everything in there. I was thinking about what lay around us, the unknown. Sometimes I wished we didn't have to put ourselves through so much inner turmoil to just get a show.

"Perry," Dex said, looking at me over his shoulder with a furrowed brow. "Are you with me?"

"I'm here," I said. I lifted the light so it was illuminating everything in front of us in a ten-foot radius. "Let's see what we can do."

He nodded, and after I shined the light down the hall both ways, he decided to head toward the east wing, toward the section that would be right above the administration offices. I supposed it was easier to stick with what we knew, and knowing Rebecca was directly below us would give us some comfort.

I walked to the side of Dex and just ahead enough to be captured on camera, taking in careful, frozen breaths. I spoke in a voice just above a whisper, enunciating properly so it would be picked up by the mic. It was my on-camera voice.

"We're now on the second floor of the Sea Crest Sanatorium," I said, "after coming up the so-called 'Death Chute' where they used to take the deceased." I paused, knowing Dex would cut in with shots of the tunnel. "While we didn't see any ghosts, we observed a bouncing ball, thrown down the passageway by an unknown entity. We also heard music that sounded like Ring around the Rosy."

"What do you think about this floor so far?" Dex asked in *his* on-camera voice.

I stopped and looked around. So far I'd just walked straight down the hall, only briefly passing the light over the open rooms on either side. "It's different. It feels...unreal, in a way. It's very cold here. It could be because there is no power or heating above the first floor, but look." I breathed out in front of the lens so you could see my breath rise in the air like a burnt-out cloud. "It's probably fifty-five degrees outside at least. It's May and we're in Oregon. There's no way it can naturally be this cold in here."

"But supernaturally..." Dex noted. I almost smirked at that cheesy line but I just didn't have it in me. I wanted to get to the end of the hallway, come back to the tunnel, and call it quits.

He lowered the camera slightly and gestured at one of the empty rooms. "These were the patients' rooms. Maybe we can find something in there."

I sighed, not really wanting to find anything, and headed to the closest room to me. The doorway was extra wide and from the rusted hinges, it looked like the door had been taken off long ago. The room itself was long, big enough to fit a bunch of beds, and the windows that lined the wall were either broken or missing entirely. Cobwebs swung lazily in the breeze, white wisps in my light.

There was a strange, almost foul smell in the air and a faint sound that I couldn't quite place. Suddenly Dex jumped toward me and yelled, "Jesus!"

"What?" I cried out, automatically jumping too.

"Something touched my foot," he said, taking the light from me. My heart was racing a mile a minute and I held on to his arm, my fingernails digging into his coat. He shined the light at the doorway behind us just in time to see a large rat scampering out of the room and out into the hall.

I exhaled noisily, feeling as if I'd almost had a heart attack. "This is ridiculous. I think we ought to head back."

Dex frowned. "Rebecca hasn't called yet. Come on, let's just keep going until she does."

"Are you going to scream like a girl every time you come across a rat?"

"You're asking for a spanking, missy," he warned, raising his palm as a threat. "And for your information, that rat came across *me*."

We went back into the hallway and continued in the same way as we had before. My pulse still hadn't slowed, and all I could think about was how cold and dark it was in this place where thousands of souls lost their lives. I think part of the reason—other than being scared out of my wits—that I wanted to pack it in was because I wanted to know more about the sanatorium, the way it was run, the people who were there. I wanted to know the history so I could give meaning to the things we were seeing. For all we knew, the second floor was a happy place and posed no harm to us.

Once we reached the end of the hall, we came to a washroom and then the rest of the wing as it veered off at an angle. Dex reached out for the washroom door, the faded symbol of a woman in a dress on it, but I quickly grabbed his arm and stopped him.

"Can we just leave it for now?" I asked, looking at him with pathetically sad eyes. "Good things never happen to me in bathrooms."

"Not true," he countered, though he took his hand back. "What about when I fucked you in that bar washroom a few months ago? From the way you came, you can't possibly tell me that wasn't a good time."

I managed a smile, remembering. Jenn had been just outside the door too. "Okay, I'll give you that. But still. No way am I going in there. I'm having enough trouble in the washrooms downstairs. I keep thinking I'll see, like, someone standing on the other side of the door when I'm in the stall. Pippa did that to me once. Scared the hell out of me."

He adjusted the camera in his hand and raised a brow. "When was this?"

"Oh, a long time ago. Back when we first met."

"That wasn't so long, you know." From the way his voice dipped, I could tell that Uncle Al probably had talked to him about the same thing.

I swallowed thickly. "Feels like it's been ages."

"Yeah?" he asked. "Me too, baby. It feels like I've known you my whole life."

He was looking at me with such intensity, the light reflecting off of his dark eyes in hard specks, that I started feeling strangely anxious. I rubbed my lips together and looked around us. "I guess when two people are constantly placed in situations like this, you go through a lot together."

He took a step closer to me. Despite the chill, I could feel heat radiating off of him. "And we've been through a lot together. And I certainly don't mind a future of this, as long as you're at my side."

Okay, he was getting oddly mushy considering our circumstances. It really wasn't the place to start reflecting on our relationship. In our bed, in each other's arms, yes. Standing in the freezing cold dark, trying to find ghosts...um, no.

Dex stared at me relentlessly until I was tempted to ask him if I had something on my face. Then he bent down to put the camera on the floor and straightened up, his hand going into his pocket.

"What's wrong?" I asked, because now I had the impression that something was wrong. His forehead was creased with worry and he was biting his lip.

He closed his eyes and breathed in through his nose, his hand still in his pocket. "Nothing is wrong," he whispered.

"Then why are you acting weird?"

He opened his eyes, looking at me in the softest way. "Perry," he said gently.

My heart did a thumpa-thumpa and missed a beat.

"Yes?" I whispered back, his tone of voice contagious.

Just then I noticed the area behind him lighten up slightly, providing a faint outline of his silhouette. I looked around his body and let out a small gasp. At the very end of the hall, in the west wing, a single light had come on in one of the rooms.

A wave of nausea rolled through me. "Shit."

Dex turned around to see then quickly scooped the camera back off the ground. With vague curiosity I noticed he hit record and started filming, which meant he'd turned off the camera just seconds earlier. He cleared his throat a few times and then said for the sake of the recording, "We were just standing here talking when that light down there suddenly came on. We don't know what it is since we haven't explored that end of the second floor. From here it appears that the light is coming from one of the rooms. The odd thing is, I'm pretty sure there is no electricity up here."

"The other odd thing is that lights just don't turn on by themselves," I added. "Electricity or not."

"Could be a motion detector," he said. "Solar paneled."

"Now you're pushing it."

"Well then, why don't we go down there and see?"

"Because...a million reasons," I said. My eyes were glued to the light, the way it splayed out from the room with a chilling white glow, illuminating the area around it and deepening the shadows. "Because I don't want to know what turned it on."

"I do," he said, staring at it before looking back at me. "Come on. You'll never sleep not knowing what it was."

He was right about that, but I figured I wouldn't sleep either way now. He walked a few steps then stopped to look at me expectantly. I knew if I told him I wasn't ready or felt...at risk, we'd head right back downstairs. But the thing was, some sick part of me wanted to know what was down there. That sick side always popped up at the worst times.

But curiosity hadn't killed me yet.

I adjusted the light and joined him. He shot me this wicked, adrenaline-fueled grin.

"Now, if you think I'm going first, you're crazy," I told him.

He grabbed my free hand and held it with a vice-like grip. We were going like this, as if we were carefree young lovers out for a midnight stroll.

We walked down the hall, my eyes trained on the light ahead. Each step we took, I felt my pulse racing faster, my heart beating louder. The air grew colder, each inhale burning down into my lungs like I swallowed dry ice, until it felt like I couldn't breathe at all. We didn't even dare utter a word. The only sound other than the dull patter of our footsteps was the rustling of leaves blown in through open windows or the distant scurrying of a rat.

We crossed the center of the building, where we both looked over to the staircase that led to the first floor. I had to remind myself to breathe and then I almost had to laugh. It was funny how easy it was to just get to this floor via the grand staircase instead of the body chute. If we weren't on a mission, I would have popped my head over the edge and called out to Rebecca.

And that's when it happened.

We both looked back down the hallway, making our way to that eerie white light, when something moved in the shadows between us and the lit room.

It *was* a shadow.

At first.

Where the black inky space began to move, my eyes suddenly focused on a large, long-limbed creature, like a skinny human on all fours, crawling *down the wall.*

It paused—long enough for me to see an oblong head and stark white eyes, long enough for me to feel the life being sucked out of me—and quickly scampered across the hall, disappearing into another room.

The scream ripped out of my throat, leaving me raw. Dex cried out, "Holy fuck, did you see that, did you see that?"

And yes, I saw that, but oh god I wish I hadn't.

Oh god, we had to get out of there.

But Dex wasn't moving, stuck as if in mud, and he kept mumbling, "What the hell was that, what the hell was that?" He was losing his mind. My mind was already trucking it down the stairs; it was just waiting for me to catch up.

Whatever the hell that thing was, it crawled across the hall and was in some other room, waiting for us. And that's when I knew it was the thing in the darkness, the thing I always felt watching me when I couldn't see it.

The bad thing.

Brenna had some explaining to do.

With a blast, Dex's phone went off with his *X-Files* theme song ringtone which sounded like death. I cried out, tears springing to my eyes from so much fear, my body assaulted by nerves that would not let me be. Dex quickly pulled out the phone and put it to his ear, his eyes still trained on the doorway where the bad thing disappeared.

"Rebecca," Dex shouted into the phone, "you need to fucking come up here." He paused. "Rebecca, are you okay?"

"She's not there," said a boy's voice from behind us.

We whirled around, my hands shaking uncontrollably as I shined the light forward. There was nothing in front of us but the swirl of dust motes.

"It's not her," the young voice said again, even though we couldn't see where it was coming from. "Don't leave her alone."

"E-Elliot?" I whispered, my voice breaking.

"We have to go," Dex said. He pulled at my arm and I snapped to attention. We ran to the staircase and went racing down it, two steps at a time, not caring if we tripped the motion detector cameras or not when we reached the first floor.

I slid on the shiny marble floors, almost falling over, but Dex held me up, and we scampered down the hall, nearly colliding with Rebecca as she stepped out of the nurse's office.

"I was just about to call you," she said. She frowned at us, stepping closer. The lights on the first floor were working again, giving off a warm glow. "What's wrong? What is it?"

Dex waved his phone at her. "You called. You were...I heard you crying."

I shuddered. Crying?

She shook her head, her face paling. "No, my alarm went off just now. I hadn't had the time to call you yet."

"It doesn't matter," Dex said, even though I thought mystery phone calls from people who weren't Rebecca *did* matter. He shot me an agitated glance. "We saw something up there."

She pushed her hair back behind her ear. "What?"

"I don't know. A light in one of the rooms went on."

At that her eyes grew to be saucers. "What? Where? How?"

"I don't know. It was down the other wing. We headed over there to check it out and then some black...form, like a black dog or something, it ran across the hall."

I gave him an odd look. "Dog? It was definitely a person...or something like it."

I didn't want to say the bad thing; I didn't want to acknowledge its name. "It crawled down the walls," I added to quell his dubious expression.

He rubbed at his chin. "No, it went across from the room with the light to the room across the hall." I stared at him and he shrugged uneasily. "What? That's what I saw."

"But you heard the voice, the little boy."

"That I did, kiddo."

"All right, hold on," Rebecca said. "You said a light turned on upstairs and there might be a dog loose, and you heard the voice of a young boy but you didn't see him."

"More or less," I conceded, even though it sounded a lot tamer than it was.

"Well, bloody hell," she said, hugging herself. She looked down the hallway to the staircase. "I don't exactly feel safe staying here if there's someone else in the building with us."

"Are you talking ghosts now or people?" I asked carefully.

"People," she said loudly. "Ghosts don't bother me but people do. How do we know there isn't some homeless person, some vagrant, living in the building? They could have a dog. They could set up a nice little area for themselves upstairs and no one would know."

"I know what I saw," I said. "It wasn't a dog."

"But you don't know for sure," she said. "Your eyes play tricks on you, you know that. That's why you and Dex didn't see the same thing."

"I also know ghosts play tricks on me too."

Dex waved his camera in the air. "I have the footage, we can take a look and then figure out what to do. Either way, it's eleven o'clock at night. If we wanted to, we could leave this place and go stay at the motel."

"No, we can't," I reminded him. "We're locked in here, remember? Carl has the keys, we don't."

"Baby, there are emergency exit doors on either end. We *can* leave. We'll just probably get in major shit for it."

"We'll probably get in major shit already for tripping the motion detector," I muttered. I pushed my fingers into my forehead and then looked at Rebecca. "Okay, boss. What do you suggest we do? I can tell you what I'm not doing and that's going back upstairs. But I'm also not staying down here by myself. If you want to go explore with the camera and the light by yourself, you go right ahead."

"Okay," she said, holding out her hands. "Give those to me."

I held the light to my chest and out of her reach. "Rebecca...I was kind of kidding."

"Well, I'm not. You guys saw something. I want to see what I can find. They'll already know tomorrow that we were upstairs so we should try and abuse it while we can. I want to go upstairs. Alone."

I looked at Dex. "She's crazy." She was crazy.

"I know," she said smartly, looking at both of us. "I really am not in the right frame of mind now, let alone lately, but dealing with this sounds preferable to thinking about other things, so if you two will please indulge me." She made a grabby motion with her hands.

"It could be dangerous," Dex said, though I could tell from his tone that he was relenting.

She pursed her lips. "Maybe I feel like living life on the wild side." She snatched the camera out of his hands and then took the light from me. She fixed a few settings on the camera then nodded at us. "If I'm not back in thirty minutes...just wait longer."

We watched as she walked off down the hall.

"I should really go after her," Dex said, making a move to follow.

"Don't you fucking dare, Dex," I said as I grabbed the back of his coat. "Don't you dare leave me here alone. You can't do that to me."

His expression softened as he saw how panicked I was. "I won't. I'm sorry. I'm just worried about her."

"Well, so am I!" I said. "We know what we saw. We'll kind of." The more I started thinking about it, maybe it had been a trick of my eyes. Maybe it really was a dog. Maybe there really was some squatter upstairs. Funny thing was, I hoped it wasn't. When it came to Rebecca, ghosts were less of a threat.

"This has been one hell of a first night, hasn't it," I muttered.

"You can say that again." He grabbed my arm. "No use waiting for her out here. Let's get ready for bed and by the time we're ready to fall asleep, she'll be back."

And if she isn't? I thought. *What then?*

Even though sleep was almost unheard of, Dex and I did get into our pajamas and settled in for bed. He walked me over to the washroom where he stood guard as I did my business because I was too chicken shit to go alone. By the time we got back to the nurses' quarters and settled into our beds—I decided to squeeze in with Dex on one bed that night—Rebecca returned.

Naturally she appeared in our doorway like a shadow figure, nearly prompting me to scream before I realized it was her.

Dex and I sat up, and I nearly fell off the bed in doing so.

"What happened?" he asked.

She sighed and came into the room, shutting the door behind her with a click. She plopped down on a wheelie chair across from us and put the camera and light on the counter. "Well, I didn't see anything weird. Unusual, maybe. The light was on in the room when I went. It was a room with an old, moldy desk and a desk lamp. The lamp was on...no idea how, I guess they do have electricity up there after all. I didn't see any signs of habitation though. Maybe that's on the other floors, I don't know. But there were no moving shadows or children's voices."

"But you believe us," I reminded her.

She nodded, staring off into space, her eyes looking tired. "Again, yes Perry, I believe you. I heard the music in the tunnel earlier. I believe there's something about this place....you can definitely feel it on that floor, too. It's like the air pressure has changed or something. But did I see anything, experience anything weird aside from that lamp? No. Shall we watch the footage?"

"You know what," I said, "I don't think that's the last thing I should see at night. How about we look it over when it's daylight?"

I had to admit, the fact that nothing unusual happened to her made me feel a million times better. Still, even after she got settled in for the night, I got out of bed and shoved a chair under the doorknob. If something, or someone, really wanted in the room, it wouldn't keep them out. But it made me feel saner. As did Dex's strong, protective arms around me.

I just wished I had something similar to apply to my head, some way to prevent my mind from dwelling on dark figures crawling on all fours, or ghost children chasing after a ball.

It felt like the sun was coming up by the time my weary body finally found sleep.

CHAPTER NINE

It's funny how different things can feel by the light of day, let alone look. Our alarm clock was Davenport rattling the door and trying to get in. I actually fell out of bed and onto the floor, trying to get up in a panic, my body confused from lack of sleep and the terror fresh in my mind.

Yet the moment I opened the door to sunlight streaming in through the halls and Davenport's disapproving face, I felt like whatever we dealt with last night was nothing compared to this woman's wrath.

"Pardon my intrusion," she said, disdainfully eying my clingy t-shirt that my breasts were high beaming through. "But I need a word with the three of you. Since you're staying on my property, I take it you won't mind."

She pushed past me and walked over to the beds where a shirtless Dex was sitting up, his crazy bed hair pointing every which way, and Rebecca pulling her covers up to her collarbone.

"I don't want to say this more than once, but it's too late for that," she said.

"And good morning to you too," Dex said with a groan. "Are you sure we can't have coffee before the lecture?"

She put her hands together. I noted she was wearing another brown suit that made her look like a giant Hershey's Kiss. "So then you know what I'm about to talk to you about. This morning as I was getting ready for work, I got an alert to my email saying that the motion detector on the camera had been tripped. Imagine my surprise when I saw footage of the two of you," she looked from Dex to me as I rubbed my bruised tailbone, "careening down the staircase like you were on fire."

I gulped. "We're sorry, we—" Rebecca started.

She raised her nose in the air and went on as if Rebecca hadn't said anything. "I don't even know how you two managed to get up there without tripping the recording the first time. I never got an email about that." I shot Dex a look to keep quiet. We didn't want to tell her we'd been in the body chute. "What on earth were you guys doing up there without my permission?"

"We are so sorry," I said, coming forward with my arms across my chest. "We were only on the second floor, We just thought we heard something, like someone was here. We just wanted to look around."

She cocked her ugly eyebrow. "And? Did you find anything?"

"Sorta," I said, though now I could see Dex was giving me a look to keep my mouth shut. I guess he didn't want us sharing our footage with her just yet. "We thought we saw a dog."

"A dog?" she repeated. She seemed to mull that over. "I don't know anything about any dogs. But this building does house raccoons on occasion. I'm sorry if it gave you a fright."

That was no damn raccoon, I thought, trying to convey my thoughts to Dex. *We* knew raccoons.

"Still," she said, clearing all the sympathy out of her throat, "you know I don't want anyone up there without a staff member present. This could be a large liability for us. Do I make myself clear? Those floors are off limits unless I give you permission otherwise."

Dex raised his hand straight up into the air like an eager school kid.

She narrowed her eyes. “What is it?”

“Can we have permission?”

She sighed like her patience was near depletion. “You have your tour with the historian in two hours. I suggest you film what you can. If you want to do more after that, then we'll talk.” She marched across the room toward the door then looked over her shoulder at us. “Coffee is in the teacher's lounge.”

She left the room just as I remembered something. “Dex,” I hissed. “Did you remember to get all the beers out of the staff fridge?”

“Fuck!” he exclaimed and popped out of bed. He ran out the door and down the hall in just his boxer briefs. His hard, beautiful body got a cry of surprise and look of admiration from an early-bird teacher who had just walked in the main doors. I could only hope he wasn't sporting his usual morning wood, though I'm sure our encounter with Davenport had officially frozen his balls.

I looked over at Rebecca. “How did you sleep?”

“Why, do I look tired?” she asked almost defensively.

“No,” I said, coming around to sit on the edge of her bed. She did have dark circles under eyes and this sense of weariness to her, but I was no better off. “I just barely slept at all. Doesn't help that these beds aren't made for two." I observed her, pondering over her words from last night, that she wasn't in her right frame of mind. It had been at least two months since she and her ex-girlfriend broke up and I wondered if she was still deeply affected by it.

Before I had a chance to ask her though, a breathless Dex appeared in the doorway, a six-pack of beer cradled in his arms like he'd just stolen the holy grail, and quickly shut the door. "That was close," he said, opening the cupboards under the nurse's sink and sliding it in there. "Let's hope Kelly doesn't like beer."

"Did anyone see you?" I asked.

He grinned. "With the beer, no. In my underwear? Let's just say I gave a few teachers something to dream about tonight."

I snorted while Rebecca's eyes sought the ceiling.

With the school slowly coming alive, it became easier to go about the morning without that ever-present cloud of dread hanging over me, enough that I was able to use the showers by myself and not freak out that someone was going to trap me in the stall or pull a *Psycho*. The events of last night seemed far away, and even though I was a bit nervous about the tour, I was excited to hear some of the truths about the place from a trusted source and not "Dikipedia."

Just before nine o'clock, as bleary-eyed students were shuffling into their classrooms and occasionally looking at our motley crew with curiosity, the three of us waited outside Davenport's office for Brenna and the guide.

"Hey guys," Brenna said, waving at us as she came down the hall. She looked bright-eyed and bushy-tailed and I had no idea how she was able to work at this place day in and day out without going absolutely crazy, especially given the things she had seen.

Dex smiled, adjusting the camera in his hand. "Does your boyfriend ever sing 'Hot for Teacher'?" He glanced at me. "Man, if you were a teacher, I'd be singing that to you every night. Maybe pull your hair back into a bun, put on some sex kitten glasses, and carry a large ruler..."

"Dex!" I admonished him, jerking my head at Brenna.

She only laughed. "It's no bother. And yes, he sings 'Hot for Teacher' all the time. Makes a nice change from Raffi."

Rebecca leaned in closer to her and lowered her voice. "So what can you tell us about the man who will be giving us the tour?"

"Patrick?" she asked. "He's legit. Lived in Gary his whole life. His mother or grandmother used to work here."

"But does he know about what you've seen?" I asked. "Will he think we're nuts if we start talking about what we saw last night?"

Her attention sharpened. "What did you see last night?"

Dex patted the camera. "We have footage. We haven't looked at it yet, but I think it picked up most of the anomalies. When do you have a break today?"

"Just at lunch," she said. "Noon."

"We'll come by your room then, if that's okay," I said. "I personally have a few questions for you my-self."

She nodded with trepidation. "Okay."

The doors to the school opened and in walked a man in his mid-forties with thick brown hair and glasses. He was hunched over a bit from bad posture and wearing a khaki jacket that looked too warm for the sunny day we were having.

"That's Patrick," she said, gesturing to him. "I'll see you at noon."

While she walked off, Rebecca managed to catch Patrick's eye.

"You're Mr. Rothburn?" she asked.

He gave her a shy smile and walked over to us. “I am, but please call me Patrick. Are you...?” He had quite the low, raspy voice.

We all introduced ourselves, which went well until Dex added “Ghost hunters” to the end of his introduction.

Patrick brought a toothpick out of his front pocket and stuck it in his mouth. “Oh, I don’t care much for ghost hunters.” He eyed Dex’s camera warily.

“Weren’t you told why we’re here?” Rebecca asked.

He nodded slightly. “I was. But I thought you were from a paranormal society, not for an actual show.”

“We don’t have to film you,” Dex told him. “And if we accidently do, we can blur you out.”

“I’d like that,” he said appreciatively. His eyes softened beneath his glasses. ”Sorry, I work at the museum and don’t want to be associated with any sort of show or entertainment. I’ll gladly show you around though. It’s much better this way than it has been in the past.”

“What happened then?”Dex asked.

“Ghost hunters or paranormal researchers have broken in on their own, trying to film. So, I guess we can all appreciate you taking the official route and respecting the history.”

I exchanged a loaded glance with Dex. It was probably a good idea if we left last night's rule-breaking shenanigans out of it.

"No problem," Rebecca filled in quickly. "Shall we get started? Do you want a spot of tea or coffee from the break room?"

He raised his palm. "No. Thank you though."

"Are you still offering, Rebecca?" Dex asked. "Because you know I'd love one." He batted his eyes at her.

"Get stuffed," she told him. She and Patrick turned and headed for the stairs.

Dex looked so stunned at her comment, as if he was genuinely let down, that I had to kiss him on the cheek. "Nice try," I teased.

"The nerve," he said. "She does it for this Gary Oldman impersonator but not for good ol' Dex."

I put my arm around his waist, loving the feel of his abs beneath his thin t-shirt. "Tell you what, I'm not going to get you a coffee either but when we get back to Seattle, you can put on Van Halen and I'll dress up like the bad, bad teacher that I am."

"Fucking hell," he groaned, turning so his body was pressed up against mine, his eyes becoming seductive. "Don't tease me because I'll seriously pull you into Davenport's office right now and bend you over her desk."

I grinned, sticking the tip of my tongue out through my teeth. "I told you, I'm not having sex in this place even if—"

"I had two dicks," he supplied. "Yeah, so you say."

"Ahem," Rebecca said, clearing her throat. We looked over to see her and Patrick (who *did* look freakishly like Gary Oldman) standing at the middle of the staircase and waiting for us.

"Sorry," I apologized. I looked back at Dex, covering him from their unamused eyes while he adjusted the erection in his jeans.

We caught up to them just as the morning bell rung and I nearly flew out of my skin in surprise.

"Got the creeps already?" Rebecca asked.

"I guess in some way I know what things might lie ahead," I said carefully.

"Actually," Gary Oldman said as we climbed the stairs, "Sea Crest was a hopeful place. My grandmother was a nurse here, just at the end of the administration when the cure for TB had been found, and she said that most of the children were happy. Sick, yes, but not all of them died. Many of them went home, and until then, they had their friends here to play with. Have you seen the playground out back?"

We stopped on the landing and he nodded out the large bay window that faced the back of the property as he fished another toothpick out of his pocket and placed it in his mouth. I had no idea where the other toothpick went.

Outside there was a large play area—a small grassy field lined with flower beds, a baseball diamond, a woodchip flecked jungle gym complete with swings and slides. Everything looked brand new, if not unremarkable.

"That's where the playground used to be back when Sea Crest was operating," he said. "See that grassy area there just before the trees? The students often go there to paint nature scenes. The forest, the flowers, the clouds. In the old days, that grass stretched along the length of the building. The nurses would wheel the patients out there for fresh air and leave them there for hours. If they were well enough, they'd play on the old swing set which is where the new swing set is located now." He let out a sad sigh. "Being outside was important for these kids—they believed fresh salty air was the cure. On the fourth floor, where they had the deathly ill, they had the windows open all the time, even in the dead of winter. Sometimes the nurses would come in the morning and find them dead of hypothermia."

"My god," I said, putting my hand to my mouth. "That's horrible. You said this was a happy place."

He gave me a wry look. "Happier than you'd think, yes. But like any hospital back in the day, there were horror stories. It didn't mean it was the norm for these kids, though."

We started back up the stairs to the second floor. Dex was already filming. "And these horror stories would be..." He trailed off.

"You want to hear some of them?" Oldman asked.

"A floor by floor rundown would be great," Dex said. He looked over the camera to see Oldman wincing, toothpick in mouth. "Don't worry, I'm not filming you, just past you."

He nodded and stopped in the middle of the hall, the same place where Dex and I had been when we saw the thing. "The second floor," he announced without flourish. "This floor housed the majority of the children. To our right here, down this wing, they kept the lower-class children. Over to our left is where they housed the upper class."

"And the difference?" Dex asked.

"Minimal differences now," he said with a wave of his hand. "Let me show you."

He took us down to where we were last night, near the room where Dex saw the rat. We poked our heads into one of the rooms. In the daylight it was still creepy, but a little more morose; the walls were a stark grey, the floor hard and austere. Dead leaves and yellowing newspaper littered the ground, along with rat droppings. You could see the broken glass of the windows, jagged edges glinting against the sun. I walked across the room and peered out. From this floor you could just see over the tops of the trees, the Pacific Ocean glinting on the horizon.

"They had a nice view," I said.

"They did when it was sunny, like today," he said. "But most of the time, the fog rolls in and gets stuck here on these hills. When they first built the hospital back in 1912, they were having good luck with the summer. This spot never saw a lick of fog. Then, a year after it was built, the fog rolled in around Gary and never left. The patients were caught in the clouds." I turned around to see him addressing Dex, who was filming me. "That's something to note for your show. On the fourth floor people report seeing fog in the hallways, no matter what time of day or what the weather is like outside. Sometimes the fog gets so thick you can't see your hand in front of your face."

"What have you experienced?" Rebecca asked. "If you don't mind me asking."

He stuck another toothpick in his mouth. Dex nodded at it. "Can I have one? I used to chomp on these fuckers myself."

Oldman raised an eyebrow but took a container of them out of his pocket and offered one to Dex, who confidently popped it in his mouth. He shot me a cheeky look. “Just like old times, kiddo.”

Oldman waited patiently for Dex’s attention to return to him. Once he did, he continued. “My experiences have been all over the map. If you believe in ghosts, they would frighten the hair off your chest. If you don’t...I’m sure you’ll find some way to explain it scientifically.”

“And do you believe in ghosts?” I asked.

He smiled quietly, eyes glinting beneath those glasses. “All historians believe in ghosts.” His toothpick bobbed from his lips. “Let’s see. On this floor I’ve seen the little boy. Many people have seen him, including previous ghost hunters.”

“Elliot,” I said.

“Is that his name?” he asked curiously. “Suits him. I often see Elliot when I’m here, day or night. He’s usually going after a rubber ball. I’ve seen ghost hunters place toys around on this floor, trucks and the like, and I’ve seen them move as if he is playing with them.”

“Anything else?” Dex asked.

Oldman eyed Dex in surprise. “That isn’t enough? No, I suppose it isn’t really. But the boy is a kind soul, never playing tricks or doing anything malicious.”

"Do you know if he plays the xylophone?"

His lips crooked upwards. "Ah, you've heard the music. I have never seen evidence of him playing any instrument, but you must understand there were so many children here over the years, so much energy in one place. No one knows where the music comes from, but we at least know it comes from this floor. You can sometimes hear children giggling and laughing too, or the sound of footsteps and children running past, though you can't see them. I've experienced all of that on this floor."

With that we left the room and walked down the hall back in the other direction. Toward the room with the light. My heart started racing as we neared it. I had to find a way to point it out.

Oldman showed us one of the rooms, saying, "As you can see, these rooms are smaller. They were private or semi-private, while the other rooms for the lower class were bigger, having sometimes twenty children squeezed into one room. The rich could afford privacy and space. Sometimes the kids were older, in their teens, and they were kept separately."

While he spoke, I kept walking down the hall, trying to ignore the pounding in my chest as I neared the room. Once I saw a glimpse of the desk and the lamp, I stopped. I didn't dare poke my head inside.

"Hey, why does this room have a desk and a lamp?" I announced, thinking I sounded totally fake. I kept the questioning look on my face as Oldman, Dex, and Rebecca came over. Oldman walked in the room which gave me the courage to do the same.

The lamp was turned off, the desk covered in a thick layer of dust. The window behind the desk was boarded shut for unknown reasons. There was a crooked picture on the wall, a painting of a girl that caught my eye.

"This would have been an office," he said. "Perhaps one of the doctors who was stationed on this floor." He went on to tell the history of some of the doctors who came to work at the hospital but I stopped listening. I was totally fixated on the painting.

It looked exactly like the girl I saw in my dreams. Brown hair, dark eyes, and a smile that seemed more wicked than joyful. Was this Shawna? I felt myself staring deeper and deeper at the painting until I heard the voice of a young girl whispering "Perry" in my ear.

I jumped and turned around. There was no little girl behind me. The three of them were ignoring me while Dex was trying to turn on the lamp.

"No electricity up here," Oldman informed him just as the lamp's switch went click and nothing came on. I looked at Rebecca as if to say I told you so but she just shrugged in return.

"Hey, what's this painting about?" I asked, motioning to it. "Kind of weird that it's just hanging here."

"Perhaps it was a favorite patient or the daughter of one of the doctors," Oldman said without much interest. "Shall we move on? If you folks are really interested in the horror stories of this place, this floor isn't the one to give them to you."

We all nodded and followed him out of the room, me being the last one out. As we went, I absently glanced into the room across the hall, the one that I'd seen the bad thing go into.

The little girl in the painting was standing in there, her pale hand holding onto a leash.

She smiled at me with cold black eyes and menacing teeth.

I screamed bloody murder and stumbled backward, trying to run away, just as the girl vanished before my eyes.

Dex was at my side in seconds, holding me at the waist, while the rest of them ran over.

"What happened?" Dex asked, brow furrowed with concern as he looked me over and then the empty room.

I shook my head, my mouth Sahara dry. "I...I just saw a girl. A little girl. Like the one in the picture.

She was standing right here." I looked over at Rebecca who was pursing her red lips. "I'm serious. I know what I saw."

"I believe you," Dex said. "Are you sure it was the one in the picture? The one right in there?"

"Yes!" I cried out, my chest feeling squeezed. "Yes. She looked the same. She smiled at me. She was holding onto a leash."

"A leash?" Rebecca asked, her voice rising.

I nodded meekly. "Uh huh. But I couldn't see around the corner to see what was at the end of it." I looked at the historian. "Have you ever heard of people seeing a little girl before?"

"Yes," he mused, sticking his hands in his pockets. "But she's usually on the fourth floor, not this one. I didn't know what she looked like either, but if she's like the girl in the painting...perhaps I should take it to the museum and do some background work on it."

"No offense," Dex said, "but that picture is probably there for a reason. I don't think removing it would be a very good idea. We have to live here for the next few days, if you catch my drift."

He nodded. "I do. I guess it's not really helping that I'm telling you these stories then."

"Occupational hazard," Dex said with a quick smile. "We're all used to shitting our pants."

"Lovely, Dex," Rebecca said coolly. She slid her eyes over to me. "Are you okay to continue?"

I exhaled. "Yes. I'm fine. Obviously that just scared the shit out of me."

"Hey, come here," Dex murmured, pulling me into an embrace. "You stick by me, okay? I don't want you seeing anything without me."

I nodded and we started for the third floor, Rebecca throwing me looks of concern—or pity—as she and Oldman walked ahead. Gah. I'd like to see how she reacted if she saw a dead girl.

As we climbed up the staircase to the next floor, Dex whispered in my ear, "Do you think that girl was Shawna?"

I swallowed hard. "I think so," I whispered back. "She's at least the girl from my dreams."

He paused on the step we were on and stared blankly at me. "What dream?"

I glanced up the staircase to Rebecca and Oldman who were almost at the third floor. "Oh, it's nothing."

"Perry," he said sternly, his eyes turning dark. "You know it's never *nothing.* What dream?"

"I'll tell you later," I said, and then continued up the stairs after them. I really didn't want to get into a conversation about my crazy dead grandmother in front of a stranger.

He let out an annoyed grunt before running up after me, loose coins and keys in his pockets jingling.

"So this is the third floor," Oldman said, voice slow and measured. "This was where the dirty work happened."

"Dirty work?" Rebecca repeated.

"This is where the morgue is. Where the operating rooms are. Some of the rooms were used as a barber and a dentist office for the staff. I'm sure you know by now that if you worked for the hospital, you weren't allowed to go home until there was a cure. No one could risk infecting friends and family members in the town below. Everyone was truly isolated up here."

We looked down the hallways. They looked the same as downstairs except there were fewer rooms and many had metal doors with the white paint peeling off. It was also a few degrees colder. I voiced that to Oldman.

"You're correct about that," he said. "But I've been here when it's cold enough to see your breath, cold enough to freeze water. That's something you can't really explain."

"So tell us something about this floor," Dex prodded him. "What have you seen here? What have others seen here?"

"Do you want me to show you something?" he asked. "Follow me."

We went down the hall to the left, pausing in front of a closed door. He put his hand on the knob. "This is the autopsy room. Or as some people have called it, the room of blood."

He pushed the door open and it groaned on its hinges like a wounded animal. There was nothing but dust and darkness in front of us. He turned to Dex. "Do you have a light on that thing?"

Dex nodded seriously, flicking it on. Rebecca and I stood in the doorway while the men went into the room, Dex's light illuminating the walls in a harsh glow. To my surprise, the room wasn't empty, not by a long shot. Somehow this made things even more disturbing.

There were counters and a couple of sinks, closets, and large metal storage cabinets all along the walls that were decaying with splotches of rust. In the middle of the room were three tables, all spaced well apart and bolted to the floors. Large operating lights hung above them, looking like a doctor was about to switch them on at any moment. To the side of all of this was a giant compartment with six slots—the body cooler.

Every bone in my body felt frozen. There was no way I was going in that room. I looked over at Rebecca, who was biting her lip and watching as Dex and

Oldman walked over to the operating tables. I knew she felt the same, even if she didn't say it.

"Shine the light here," Oldman said, pointing to the middle table. "You see this ring around the edge? That acted like a moat to catch the blood. The doctors had little understanding of tuberculosis and how it was transmitted. They thought if they could study it, they could find a cure. Of course, as time went on, they did fewer autopsies. What was the point? You'll notice the cooler there." He waved at the metal block with its compartments. "Only six bodies could fit in there at one time. Because the disease was so highly infectious, the dead were moved out of here right away."

"Down the body chute," Dex said.

Oldman eyed him. "Yes. You've heard about that, no doubt. I believe the doorway to it is somewhere in this room, but I haven't bothered to look. I don't like to push my luck."

"So this was called the blood room because of the way they bled the patients out?" Rebecca asked. She sounded slightly disgusted.

He shook his head. "Yes, and no. There were also a lot of surgeries done in here—experimental surgeries. One involved collapsing a lung to get the fluid out. That was the most common one, done to probably half the patients that came in here. Others involved removing ribs or muscles in their chests in order to expand the lungs. Sometimes they would insert balloons into their lungs and fill them with air." He grimaced and looked at the walls, and I realized the rust might have been blood stains. "It got messy."

"They actually did that to children?" Rebecca asked.

"Not all," he said. "But some. They rarely survived the procedure. If they did, they were usually worse off, walking around like their chests had been scooped out."

"Jesus," Dex swore under his breath. "I just can't imagine it."

"The horrors of history," Oldman said slowly. "And I'd love to say that a visit to this room was as bad as it got for a youngster. But with rumors of abuse and crumbling standards in Sea Crest, I hate to think of what could be worse."

"Was there abuse?" I asked.

He cocked his head, considering his answer before saying, "My grandmother never reported anything like that. She was a good woman, saintly almost, who loved to help others in need. But they weren't all like her. It was hard to be up here, isolated, in constant fear of death while constantly surrounded by it. The nurses had rules too. They couldn't get emotional over patients, they had to act like everything was fine all the time. It was hard. Many nurses killed themselves. And some nurses, we'll if you believe the rumors, some went crazy. Took it out on the children. But they are, of course, just rumors. None of this has ever been documented. I should know."

My body felt like it was getting colder by the moment. This floor had fewer windows than the others, making it darker. If Dex thought we'd explore this floor in the night, he was absolutely out of his mind.

"We should get going," Oldman said as he came toward us with Dex in tow. "I need to get back to the museum soon and we've one more floor to go."

"But you haven't told us what you've seen here," Dex pointed out.

Oldman grunted and stopped in the middle of the hallway. "Personally, on this floor, it's not what I've seen but more what I've heard. What I've felt. I've had the feeling that someone was behind me when there was no one there. I've heard screams coming from the blood room. I've heard wet coughing, like someone is coughing up blood, the sound of wheels going past, and footsteps. I've seen a doctor in a white coat standing in the corner of one of the rooms." He shuddered at that thought. "And I hope I never see him again. Can we get going?"

I picked up on how noticeably agitated he was acting, which in turn made me feel queasy. If the historian wanted to get going, we were definitely going.

"What have others seen?"Dex asked as we climbed the stairs to the final floor.

Oldman gave him a grave look. "It depends who you ask and what their beliefs are."

"Beliefs?" I repeated.

He nodded as we stopped on the landing. Below us was the darkness of the third floor, above us was the contrasting light of the fourth floor. And yet I felt the fourth floor held more secrets, more animosity than any of the others.

"People have reported seeing the same...creature...on the third and fourth floors."

"Creature?" I felt icy trails going down my spine. I didn't want to venture what the creature looked like.

"The fourth floor, as you'll soon see, was used to house the patients who were close to death and the ones that had gone insane. There used to be a metal gate right here," he pointed across the stairs, "that prevented them from escaping. As weak and skinny as they were, they were always a threat. Some people say that with all the bad energy, the lost souls, the mistreated patients, the experiments gone wrong, the mass grave—"

"Mass grave?" I interrupted.

He gave me a sympathetic look. "Many bodies were never claimed by their families. They feared the disease would get them, even in death. Superstitions, you know. The dead had to be put somewhere."

This place couldn't possibly get worse.

"So what was the creature?" Rebecca asked.

"Many that have seen it believe it's a demon," he said. "It looks like a human but isn't. Crawls on the ceiling and walls."

And it totally just got worse. That was what the bad thing was. A demon.

A motherfucking demon.

I started to think that maybe Pippa's warning hadn't been a figment of my imagination after all.

"Does it ever hurt anyone?" Dex asked in a low voice.

Oldman shook his head and stuck a toothpick between his teeth. "I honestly don't know. I've never seen it. That doesn't mean it's not there but...as you can tell, this place will play tricks on you. There's too much history, too many people who have passed through these walls. You never know what you're going to get here. And I find that fascinating." He looked up at the fourth floor. "On second thought, do you mind if we skip that floor? You're welcome to take a quick look but that whole thing I said earlier about not pushing my luck…"

"No, that's totally cool," I said a little too gratefully.

"Do you mind if I just shoot a few seconds?" Of course Dex had to ask that.

Oldman shook his head and sauntered over to the window on the landing, hands behind his back. "Go ahead."

Rebecca decided to go up with Dex while I stayed at the historian's side as he looked out the window.

"You know," I admitted, hoping that talking would calm my heart rate down, "before I knew about this place, I had no idea that sanatoriums existed."

He smiled quietly. "That was the same back then. Despite these hospitals all over the country—despite the fact that hundreds of thousands of people came to them to die—everyone liked to pretend that this didn't exist. But it did. You can shuffle people away into isolated buildings and lock them up with false promises of a cure. But the patients, the ones that never saw their families again, they didn't forget. It's no wonder this place is haunted. All the ghosts here just want someone to talk to, someone to recognize that they exist, even when they don't."

"And the demon thing?" I said, my voice shaking slightly.

"Maybe some ghosts don't want attention. Maybe they just want to inflict the pain and terror that they felt every day. Maybe some are too far gone in their hate and revenge that they cease to be ghosts and become something else." He spoke quietly as he leaned in closer and speared me with a shrewd gaze. "Have you seen it?"

I felt like my throat was closing up. I nodded slowly.

He made an "ah" face, then said calmly, "You've got a nice energy about you. They like that."

"Okay," Dex said loudly as he jogged down the stairs with Rebecca at his side. "There wasn't too much to see up there. Looks pretty much the same as the second floor, although I think I located the door to the body chute."

"Dangerous thing," Oldman commented. "You know they found a runaway girl in there one year. She'd snuck in by the post office and then got stuck for a few days."

"Post office?" I asked.

"There's an abandoned one down the road. The body chute actually goes all the way in. It's a real long walk in a very dark place."

I shot Dex a look to warn him to not even think about it, but Oldman went on, "After that, they boarded it up around the post office so you couldn't get in. Or out, I suppose." He glanced at his watch."Well, I'm afraid it's time for me to go. I hope you've enjoyed your tour of the Sea Crest Sanatorium."

We walked down the stairs, and with each landing we reached, my shoulders felt lighter and lighter. Once we got to the main floor, the first bell rang and teachers began scurrying about, and I started to feel like I was back in my own skin again.

"And I hope you be extra careful while you're here," Oldman said to me just before he walked off into the sunshine.

"What did he say?" Dex asked.

I shook my head. "Nothing I wasn't already thinking."

CHAPTER TEN

After we'd gone through the tour, the last thing I wanted to do was talk to Brenna about her experience with the bad thing. In fact, I was so close to suggesting we head out into Tillamook to get some food while we could, just to be in the sunshine and see the freedom of the waves, when Kelly came looking for us while we were sprawled in the teacher's lounge.

"Hi there," she said in her quiet voice, her hair gathered delicately around her face. "Brenna wanted to let you know that she had to go home sick and that she'll take a rain check for tomorrow."

"Oh no," I said, straightening up in my chair. "Is she okay?"

She nodded. "I took a quick look at her. It's probably food poisoning or a 24-hour bug. She'll be fine."

"What about her students?" Dex asked. "What do they do if she's not there to teach? Is there a sub?"

I gave him a look. "You better not be thinking about teaching art, Dex, because I've seen your drawings." Nude drawings, I wanted to add. Like, Anime porn.

"There's no sub for her class on such short notice," Kelly said. "The kids get an extra hour of recess with either me or one of the lunch ladies supervising. I'll just take them out in the front yard where it's sunny, let them run around."

"Can we come watch?" Dex asked, getting off the couch, mug of coffee in his hands.

"Dex..." Rebecca said in a warning tone, not getting what he was doing.

Kelly shrugged with one shoulder and smiled shyly. "Sure. I bet you guys need some sun after being in here all morning."

She was right about that. After she left, I got up and poked Dex in the side. "What's your deal, mister?"

He eyed us both like we were morons. "If Brenna isn't there, then we can talk to the kid. Jody."

“I’m not sure if that’s the right thing to do,” Rebecca cautioned. “I think we need permission.”

“It doesn’t have to be on camera,” Dex said adamantly. “And besides, you’re losing your touch, producer lady. You need to be thinking about the big picture here. Roll with the punches, turn disappointment into opportunity.”

“I think you’ve gone mad,” Rebecca said, swiping his coffee out of his hand. “But I see what you’re saying.”

I didn’t really care either way; I just wanted to be outside in the sunshine.

Though the playground and small sports field was in the back of the building, the amount of trees kept the sun from reaching the ground. Out in the front there were wide fields on either side of the driveway, with picnic tables scattered about. We plunked ourselves down at one with microwaved meals and tried to eat all the while wondering which kid was Jody.

Eventually, however, she found us.

“Are you the ghost hunters?” a little girl asked as she walked toward us. I noticed an orange rubber ball in her hands. The sunshine in her blonde hair and the green freshness of the grass made everything look so wholesome, but that damn ball was a weighty reminder of what was always present at this place.

"That we are," Dex said with a wide, welcoming smile. "And who might you be?"

"I'm Jody," she said, rubbing at her nose. She was a cute kid with big blue eyes, a little on the short side for her age, dressed head to toe in a matching pink leopard sweat suit. "Miss Brenna went home sick today."

"We heard," Rebecca said. I was surprised to see how warm her features became as she addressed her. "But the nurse Kelly said she would be fine. She'll probably be back tomorrow, feeling as good as new."

Jody shrugged and started twisting back and forth at the waist. "I guess. I was sick for a while."

"Were you?" I asked, even though Brenna had told us.

"Yes," she said. "I had consumption."

I nearly spit out my orange juice. Rebecca recovered faster than I did.

"Consumption?" she repeated. "I don't think you had that."

"I did," Jody said like it wasn't a big deal. "The nurse said it wasn't and my doctor Willard said it wasn't, but Elliot said it was. I was coughing up blood. He said that's how it happened to him." She stopped twisting and looked me right in the eye. "Shawna told me I'd never see my family again."

She kept staring at me to the point where Dex and Rebecca glanced over to see what was going on.

"Who is Shawna?" I asked gingerly, trying to keep my voice light and breezy.

"Shawna isn't my friend. She doesn't like that Elliot pays attention to me. And she doesn't like you."

I felt like walls were closing in on me. "She doesn't like me?" I barely got out. "I've never met her. We just got here yesterday."

"She says she saw you earlier when you were looking in her room," Jody said matter-of-factly. "She's looking at you right now."

Oh, Jesus. Oh, just *no*. "What?"

Jody pointed at the building. I followed her finger to the second floor windows. I didn't see anything there; the sun was shining off the broken panes. "I...I don't see anything," I told her.

"She's there," she said assuredly. "You just have to look for her."

Fuck that. I leaned forward, looking at Jody more closely. "Why doesn't Shawna like me?" I whispered.

She shrugged again and went back to twisting. "I dunno. Maybe you won't play with her. Or maybe the bad thing is telling her not to like you."

My eyes flew over to Dex. I could see his Adam's apple bob as he swallowed, worry in his eyes. I looked back at Jody. "What is the bad thing?"

"I dunno," she said again. Then her face brightened. "I used to be afraid of it, but then one day Shawna said it was her pet, and she had it on a leash. I was more afraid when it was running around loose. That's how it got Miss Brenna one day."

I was speechless. Speechless and scared absolutely shitless, sitting here on a picnic table in a sunny fucking meadow.

"Jody," Rebecca said delicately. "You know it's wrong to lie about things."

"I know," she said. "But I'm not. If I lie, I'll go to hell. So I tell the truth. I don't want to go to hell. Shawna says the bad thing will take me there if I misbehave."

I pictured Shawna standing in the room, the way her smile didn't reach her eyes, the way the leash went off and I couldn't see what was on the other end of it. But my brain wanted to go there. It wanted to fill in the blanks. It wanted to see the bad thing.

I had to get fucking out of there.

"You're an awfully morbid little kid, aren't you?" Dex said to Jody.

Jody stuck her tongue out at him. "No, you're morbid."

"Do you even know what morbid means?"

"Dex," I said sharply before he could start an argument with a child. I hopped off the picnic table. "You know, I think I'm done here."

He looked at me in shock. "What? For good?"

"Perry..." Rebecca cautiously.

I rubbed my arms, feeling a sudden chill, and eyed the building. "I don't know. But if I don't get away from this place for a few hours, I'm going to lose my mind."

Rebecca looked at Dex. "Why don't you take her into town," she suggested. "I'll stay here and talk to some people, film some things."

Dex gave her an odd look, then nodded as if he was just realizing something. "Sounds like a plan, boss." He got up and came over to me, taking my hand in his. "I'm just going back to the room to get something. Need your purse?"

I nodded. "Can you bring me my sweater too?" I figured it was warmer down by the water but the chill had its sudden hold on me, so that even in the sun I couldn't imagine warmth.

I looked back at Rebecca who was smiling at me.

"What?" I asked, frowning.

"Nothing," she said, still smiling.

"Did you want to play a game with me?" Jody asked her.

Rebecca hesitated. I thanked my lucky stars that I wasn't staying behind to play a game – it was probably hide and go seek out the dead kids.

"Of course," Rebecca said.

"Do you know any?" Jody asked, putting her hands on her little hips.

"Well, in England I used to play a game called 'What Time is it Mr. Wolf.' Do you fancy you'd like to play that?"

I rolled my eyes. Of course she had to choose one of the more disturbing children's games but Jody seemed game.

Soon enough though, I was in the Highlander with Dex and we were cruising down the road toward the coast. I hated being trapped in my head but all I could think about – all I could see – was Shawna's face and the black shape of the bad thing.

"Baby?" Dex asked gently. "Are you okay?"

I shook my head, staring out the window as the trees went past. "No."

"Do you want to quit and go home?" I turned my head to look at him. He looked so damn sympathetic. "You know I'd understand. I just want to make you happy."

Ugh. My heart started to swell like a warm balloon. I gave him a small smile. "I don't know what I want, Dex."

He swallowed. "Do you still want me?"

Everything inside me melted. I twisted in my seat to face him and reached up to touch his cheek. "Of course I still want you. Dex, I love you. You know I do. I'm just...really freaked out. Everything that's going on in that place is..."

"Too much?"

"Yes. Too much."

"Tell me about the dream you had. The one where you saw the girl."

"Oh, I don't want to think about that now," I said. "Really, I just want to pretend for the next while that the sanatorium doesn't exist. Pretend I'm back in our normal life."

"You're right," he said and suddenly he was pulling the car over by a scenic lookout. He put it in park beside a low stone wall that overlooked the cliff and the town below. It was so clear you could see the tiny cars making their way on 101 through Gary, see the shimmering ocean and the endless blue sky. I immediately felt better just seeing that, feeling the warmth of the early summer air that was blowing through the open windows.

Dex reached over and unbuckled his seat belt, then he unbuckled mine. “Come on,” he said, lifting it over me. “It’s too nice to be inside the car.”

Though we were halfway down the mountain-side and not in civilization like I wanted to be, I got out of the car. He took my hand and led me over to the low stone wall and sat me down. He glanced out at the bright horizon, his eyes squinting, the eyebrown ring on his dark, arched brow shining in the sun. Like I had so many times before, I was struck dumb by how handsome he was. Sometimes it really snuck up on me.

“This coast, kiddo,” he said, voice low and rough. “This coast is where we first met. All because I had this strange feeling that I had to go visit that lighthouse. I just had to. And then I saw you. And that was it. I knew why I’d been brought there.”

I couldn’t help but smile. I didn’t know why Dex was reminiscing so much lately, but I liked it a lot. “You’re turning into quite the romantic lately.”

He raised his brow coyly. “That’s a new one. Do you prefer that Dex or the crude Dex?”

I put my hand on his. “It doesn’t matter. They’re all the same. They’re all you.”

He turned my hand over so that my wrist was facing up, the anchor displayed. “This is looking real good, baby. Real good.” He took in a deep breath and glanced up at me with intensity. "You still don't regret it?"

"No fucking way," I assured him, unable to look away from his gaze.

"You know that's going to be on you forever."

"That was the point."

He squeezed my wrist. "We don't know what the future holds for us. I see you here, now, you're scared, you're frightened. I don't want to keep doing this to you."

I watched him quizzically. "What are you saying?"

He licked his lips. "I'm saying...I want you around for the long haul. By my side. But I don't want to keep doing this show. I think I want out. For the both of us." My mouth dropped slightly. He went on, "What you said the other day about this show not going on forever, about doing something else instead. I think you're right."

"Well what would we do?"

"I don't know, kiddo," he said. He reached up and cupped my face in his large hands. "I don't know. But I guess we'll just sort it out along the way, together. I have money. I will take care of you – take care of us – until we figure it out."

His words coated me with a heady mix of relief and apprehension. “So this is the end of Experiment in Terror?”

“I think this should be the last episode,” he stated. “And I think we should commit to it, go out with a bang. But yes, I think it should be the end.”

He let go of my face and bit his lip anxiously as he gauged my reaction. “So? What do you think? I can’t make this choice alone.”

The end sounded so final. I’d only known Dex through this show. I didn’t know what our lives would be like without it. The unknown – whether with ghosts or with life – scared me.

He leaned in and brushed his lips against mine and I breathed in that comforting, familiar musk of his, the mint and Old Spice. “This is only the end of the show,” he murmured. “This is the beginning of us.”

“You promise?” I purred back.

“I’ll do more than promise, baby.” He kissed me softly, my mouth opening against his, our kiss wet and hot and pulling me under into waves of honey. I moved in closer, my hand sliding up his shirt and feeling the tight lines of his stomach underneath.

But to my surprise, he pulled out of the way, then smiled and brushed my hair behind my ear. “Perry,” he said. His eyes were alive with emotion, his breath heavy. “Perry…I…”

I was entranced by what he was going to say that I wasn't paying attention to the car that was pulling up alongside us.

"Hope I'm not interrupting anything," a familiar voice said, breaking through the spell between Dex and I.

Dex's eyes sparked with anger. "Fuck!" he muttered angrily under his breath before fastening his death gaze on the intruder.

I looked over to see Patrick Rothburn/Gary Oldman in his Prius, the car running, his arm hanging out the window.

"No, it's no bother," I said to him quickly before Dex could blow up at him. I wasn't sure why his fuse was suddenly so short, but being on Dex's bad side when he had a temper was a dangerous thing.

I squeezed Dex's hand and got up, walking over to Oldman. "What brings you back?"

He put his car into park and adjusted his glasses. "I'm just on my lunch. I just wanted to let you know that the girl in painting? Well, I did some research back at the museum. I'm not 100% sure but I think I was right. She was the daughter of one of the doctors. That's why he started working there, to be near to her. Doctor Ridley was his name. His daughter was Shawna. He died about a year before she did, when she was moved upstairs to the terminal floor."

"How?" I asked.

"He fell," he said simply. "Probably a suicide, maybe because he couldn't find a cure and she was going to die. I don't know."

"Do you think he's the man in the coat that you saw that one time?"

He didn't say anything but reached into his file folder on the passenger seat and pulled out a photo. "I drove up here to show you this."

I took it from him and looked it over. It was a smiling picture of a man and his daughter. The man had slicked back hair, tanned skin and a fancy suit with a pocket watch. The girl, who was in fact the girl I'd seen, had her hair done up in long ringlets, wearing a dress that looked like it was made out of metallic threads. A stately Christmas tree in the background placed the photo around December. I flipped it over where someone had scrawled "Doctor Timothy Ridley and his daughter Shawna, admitted May 15th, 1933."

"Eighty years ago tomorrow," Oldman said. "Do you mind if I have that back?"

I fervently shook my head and thrust it back into his hands. Like hell I wanted to hang onto that.

He craned his neck around to look at Dex. "Sorry to interrupt. I just thought you guys should be on the lookout. I don't know if tomorrow would mean anything in the grand scheme of things but history has a way of hiding events that were truly important."

He raised his palm in farewell, then took his car into a U-turn and disappeared back down the hill.

I exhaled noisily, feeling that tension creeping back into my shoulders, and walked back over to Dex.

"That was weird," I said, shoving my hands in the back pockets of my jeans.

Dex glared off into the distance. "The guy sure has fucking bad timing."

I frowned. "What do you mean?"

He sighed and got up from the wall. "Nevermind, kiddo. Let's go back."

"Back to the school?" I asked, remembering all too well why we had just left.

He nodded, pausing by his door and shielded his eyes from the sun with his hand. "Yeah. If this is the end of the show, for real, then this is our last episode. We should get serious about it, I mean really work on getting as much as we can. I guess we have to tell Rebecca, too."

"Do you think she'll be mad?" I asked as I opened my door and climbed in.

"She might be disappointed, but she'll understand. She's been telling me to grow up and get serious for a long time."

As we drove back up to the school, I asked him, "You're not doing this because of me, are you?"

"Ending the show? Of course, I am," he said seriously. "You're my world, Perry, that's all there is to it. There are bigger and better things out there for us. Something legit, or, as you said earlier, meaningful."

I know I said it, I just didn't really think Dex had been listening to me. I hated the idea of the show ending just because he was scared for me, just because I wanted something more. I didn't want to live with that ball of guilt.

"Don't feel guilty," he said, his mouth twitching into a smile. "This is what I want. And now I know it's what you want too."

I was unnerved. "Did you just hear my thoughts?"

The handsome devil didn't answer me, he only grinned to himself. "And by the way, I'm always listening to you."

Once we got back to the school and nosed the Highlander into a parking space, Rebecca came trotting over from across the field, Jody running behind her.

"Perry!" she exclaimed, her smile cracking her face in two. "Oh, let me see!"

"See what?"

She frowned, looking over my shoulder at Dex, and then quickly put her hand on my arm. "Let me see your tattoo!"

"Uh," I said, holding it out for her awkwardly.

She took my wrist and showed it to Jody. "See Jody, this is a tattoo. I told you that, erm, girls can have them."

Jody looked at Rebecca as if she had two heads. "You're going to hell now."

"Okay, okay," Dex said, coming around the car with his hands in the air. "Enough with the hell talk, young lady." He dropped down into a crouch so he was at her level, looking her in the eye. "I don't care what this Shawna girl said, but it's not exactly polite to keep saying hell."

"What word should I say?" she asked, bright eyes sparkling with curiosity. I could tell she was enthralled with Dex. I couldn't blame her.

"Well, you can always do what I do and make up a word. Like, twatwaffle."

"Dex," I cautioned.

"Or douchecanoe."

I sighed.

He straightened up and smiled down at her. "How about duckspunk? Ducks are cute."

I slapped him on the arm, while Rebecca asked us, "You weren't gone very long. What happened?"

"We ran into Gary Oldman," I said.

"Gary Oldman the actor?"

"Sorry. I mean the historian, Patrick Rothburn."

"I guess he does look like Gary Oldman."

"Duckspunk." We all looked down at Jody who was staring at Dex proudly. "I didn't say a bad word." Then she giggled and ran off to her friends who had started a game of dodgeball.

"Great, Dex."I glared at him. "I'm sure her parents will be thrilled when duckspunk comes up at dinner."

He shrugged. "Duckspunk comes up everywhere. You should watch where you step next time you're by a pond."

Rebecca wrinkled her nose. "Anyway, what did Patrick want?"

I quickly explained to which she crossed her arms and looked up at the massive façade of the school. "So he thinks something could happen tomorrow."

"Maybe," I said. I looked over at Dex, trying to signal that it was time for the talk.

"Hey, Becs," Dex said, taking a step toward her. "You know we love you, right?"

Her eyes widened. "Are you guys breaking up with me?"

"Noooo," Dex assured her in a soothing voice. Then he cocked his head. "Well. Yes."

We went inside and explained to her as best we could our thoughts on the end of the show, my desire to do something more with our life. It wasn't until Dex started talking about plans for the future and keeping my safety and happiness as his top priority that I started to melt all over again. And Rebecca began to understand where we were coming from.

She wasn't mad, but Dex was right, she was disappointed. And worried.

"What am I going to do?" she asked as we sat around the breakroom table with a giant pot of tea. "Not to make you feel badly about it all, but I was kind of depending on this job for money."

"Don't sweat it,"Dex said earnestly. "Jimmy loves you. You know he'll have a million opportunities for you to jump on board."

"But he only wants me in front of the camera," she whined.

"It could be worse," I said. "He could only want you *behind* the camera."

"Look," Dex said, folding his hands in front of him. "You're a hot, striking woman who made men eat Taco Bell until they were shitting fire. You can do anything."

I tilted my head at him. "You ever think you could get into motivational speaking?"

"Next career choice, baby," he shot me a wicked smile.

"So this is really it. You just decided and...," Rebecca trailed off.

Dex and I gazed at each other. We were in it together. And as much as it felt spur of the moment, as much as it would seem that way to Jimmy, it was also a long time coming. To say goodbye, to move on and do something else – that felt right. It felt good. We all knew that we weren't going to be ghosthunters forever. Seeing the supernatural, that was something Dex and I had to deal with for the rests of our lives, but it didn't mean we had to seek them out – not in this way, not for entertainment, at any rate.

He nodded gravely and I said, my eyes still on him, "Yes. I think it's the right thing to do."

She sipped her tea delicately and appraised us over the cup. "All right. Then it is the right thing to do. I'm going to miss working with you guys."

"Oh don't get mushy, Becs," Dex chided her with disgust. "We still have an episode to make and like dick I'm going to let it go to waste. Now that we know everything that Rothburn told us, I say we spend tonight and tomorrow making the best of it. Are you with me? Or against me?"

Rebecca and I managed to roll our eyes in unison.

"We're with you, mate," she said, raising her tea in the air. We cheersed her with our own mugs and though she was smiling pleasantly, her posture was rigid. She was probably more worried about losing her job than she was letting on. Of course, I knew she'd be all right in the long run but I guess she didn't see it the same way. It was Dex and I that I needed to worry about.

I knew someone, though, that would be happy with this news.

As soon as the two of them started going over the freaky shit that Oldman had told them, I took my phone and excused myself into the hallway.

Though I'd texted Ada just yesterday to tell her about Uncle Al, I hadn't called her in a while. It was no wonder then that she sounded shocked when she answered her phone.

"Perry?" she cried out.

"Hey," I said, leaning against the wall with the phone cradled to my ear and smiling absently at a pair of teachers who were walking past. "How are you? This a bad time?"

I heard something muffled, then she said, "No. I'm fine. I was just exercising."

"Exercising?" My sister did not exercise. She was thin as a rail and never needed to.

"Yeah," she said. "You know, you break a sweat, move your muscles and shit like that?"

"Smartass," I muttered. "I mean, why are you exercising? You're fifteen and look like a model."

"I'm sixteen next month," she said. "And it's not about weight-loss, you douchecanoe." I nearly snorted at her choice of word. Her voice dropped a register. "Exercise helps your brain. It makes you feel better – happier."

I frowned. "Happier? Are you okay?"

"Yeah, fine."

"Ada. Come on, you can tell me."

She sighed. A moment passed on. "I don't know. I just...I really wish you were here, Perry. I really need someone to talk to. Someone that understands. Sometimes I think I'm going crazy and I get so fucking scared and then I get angry because you're with Dex. Don't get me wrong and stuff, I like, like the guy. But you guys both have each other. You both *understand* each other."

I had to read around the lines there. "Are you seeing ghosts?"

Another weighty pause. "Just one. Just sometimes. It's an old man. He's not scary and I only see him on the walk home from school. Once I get my license I'll be zipping past that floaty fucker." She let out a nervous laugh.

Suddenly, I felt for my sister. I felt everything that I did at her age, all the shit that I went through and the way I buried it all with food and drugs and everything bad for you. I could only hold onto the hope that if I could be there for Ada, that she wouldn't turn to that and turn to me instead. I mean, it's not like either of us could ever go to our mom or dad about our affliction.

"Hang in there," I told her. "I'll see you in a few days and then we can really talk."

"You better not be bailing on us."

"I'm not. I promise. Anyway, I called because I have good news."

"Shut the front door!" she squealed. "What, what is it?"

She sounded way too excited already. "Why, what do you think it is?"

"Either you're moving back to Portland or Dex proposed to you."

I nearly choked on my own spit. "What?" I hissed, my eyes flitting to the door to the breakroom as if he'd hear her over the phone.

"No?"

"No!" I whispered harshly. "Are you crazy?"

"Whoa, dude, why so defensive?"

I rubbed at my forehead. “I don’t know. Uncle Al said some stuff to me that kind of rubbed me the wrong way.”

“Like what?”

I wanted to tell her but unfortunately I didn’t have the time for it. “I’ll tell you later. But no, no one is getting...*that.* And we aren’t moving to Portland. But we did decide to end the show.”

Another pause. “EIT?”

“Yes, Ada.”

“Is that what you want?”

I pursed my lips, wondering why she was trying to sound rational. “Yeah, it’s what I want. I’m tired of this Ada. I need something more.”

“And Sexy Dexy?”

“Please don’t call him that,” I groaned.

“Why not?”

“It’s weird. Anyway, Dex agrees. He worries about me as much as you do.”

“Well, if you’re happy Perry, I’m happy. It’s one less worry for all of us. I know I never tell you this, but you’re pretty awesome and you can do anything you want with your life. You should hang out with the living more often.”

“Thanks, sis,” I said, my heart warming over.

“It’s too bad he hasn’t proposed,” she mused thoughtfully. “The two of you would make beautiful babies and I could be the kick-ass fashion designer aunt."

"We've only known each other eight months," I reminded her with a sigh.

"Is that what Uncle Al told you?"

"Well, yeah."

She scoffed. "Old people. They don't know shit. This generation is moving faster. Just last week my friend Amber slept with Cole Phillips on the first date. I mean, hello, way to welcome him into your hidey hole so soon." And then Ada went off into a rant about these people I didn't know. When she was finally done I told her again that we'd talk more as soon as I got to Portland and we hung up.

I put my head back against the wall and took in a deep breath. I thought about what Ada said, that Dex and I would make beautiful babies together. Hopefully they'd have all of his genes with my hair and eyes. Actually, they could all just look like Dex and I would be happy with that.

And once again I was getting ahead of myself. He hadn't proposed and, aside from the fact that we'd known each other less than a year, I wasn't really sure if Dex was the marrying type. After seeing the devastation of his parent's marriage, the way his father just up and left one day and never contacted his sons again, the way his mother went crazy – I couldn't imagine that was something he wanted. Not to mention his former man-whore ways and his fly by the seat of his pants personality. I just didn't see it. Not saying I didn't want it but…it takes two. And I couldn't set myself up for disappointment.

Just then, Dex appeared in the doorway, his arm above his head, lazily leaning against the frame. "You all right here, kiddo?"

I stuck my phone back in my pocket and gave him a smile that felt stiff. "Just talking to Ada."

"How is Little Fifteen?"

"She's fine."

He pointed inside the room. "Do you want to see the plan for the next couple of days? It kind of involves you."

I nodded and followed him back into the room where Rebecca had her planner out. In the short time I'd been on the phone, they'd managed to make progress.

I peered over the table and saw the terms "room of blood", "demon on the ceiling", and "Shawna's ghost" scribbled on the pad of paper in Rebecca's elegant cursive.

A blanket of unease came over me. Perhaps the best time to quit the show would have been before we came to the hospital of death. Still, I pulled up a chair and let them talk me through the game plan.

One last time.

CHAPTER ELEVEN

"Okay, stay right there, face the camera, and look more scared," Dex said as he adjusted the settings. Rebecca flashed the light on me.

I was standing in the middle of the death chute. I was already fucking scared.

After the two of them came up with a shot by shot plan for the rest of the stay at the sanatorium, the three of us heated up some microwave meals, Dex and I started sneaking shots of Jack Daniels, downing them in the break room well after school was dismissed for the day.

I'd like to say there was a lot of boredom involved between then and when Carl the custodian left, but we managed to keep ourselves occupied with card games. Dex blatantly cheated during all of them and I didn't care. Rebecca had turned sullen though, her once smiling face replaced by a glacial expression. It lasted all through the evening, and I wondered just what the hell was going on with her. Could it be that she took more stock in the show than we realized or was there something else at play?

Once Carl left, it was time for business. Since we couldn't go back up the main staircase without Davenport finding out and kicking us out too soon, we had to go back in the body tunnel.

Luckily, our plan for the evening wasn't anything too pee-your-pants inducing. Dex noted that though Oldman said the body tunnel eventually opened up down at the remains of the old post office, when he was looking out the window into the back of the school he could see a little mound of grass coming off of the edge of the building that looked like it might house an opening to the tunnel. The hearses had to park somewhere and they probably weren't taking bodies out by the post office.

I looked up to see Dex appraising my supposed scared face.

"All right, that's better," he said, smiling at me with boyish charm. I swear, if he wasn't so darn sexy I'd be hitting him a lot more often and not in a pleasurable way. Though, knowing his penchant for spanking, he'd probably like that too.

"I'm sure I'll be screaming in a few minutes," I muttered as Rebecca came over and stuck a wireless mic on my shearling-lined jacket.

"You scream, I scream, we all scream for my cream," he sang. He had that look in his eyes, that devious, excited look that he always got pre-filming. Fuck. I had to admit, I was really going to miss that. "Okay, right, Perry, all we're going to do is head down the tunnel in the opposite way than we did last night and look for the door out. Rebecca will keep the door open, and you and I will go around the children's playground, hoping to interact with the wee dead ones. Sound good?"

I scowled. "Not really."

He nodded at the door leading out into the lit hallway, the normalcy of the first floor. "We might as well leave it like it is," he said. "If it closes I'm sure we can just push it open like we did before."

Not exactly the kind of thing you wanted to assume, but okay.

I sighed and rubbed my clammy hands on my jeans. I was cold and sweating at the same time. “Can we get started?”

Dex raised a brow at my tone. I know I was supposed to be more relaxed knowing everything we filmed was going into our last episode ever, but still, he did say we wanted to go out with a bang and I really hoped that bang wasn’t literal.

“No problem, kiddo. We’re all ready.” He put the camera on his shoulder and made the gun symbol. “And you’re on.”

Here we go. I looked into the camera, holding my face at a flattering angle and said, “We’re back here in the death chute at the old Sea Crest Sanatorium. And yes, for those who are watching, I have had the Metallica song in my head for days.”

Dex broke into a wide smile behind the camera. I went on, “Last night we explored the first floor and experienced supernatural occurrences such as lights coming on where there is no electricity and shadow people. Tonight, however, we’re going to explore the chute and the playground area where many of the children used to play.”

I motioned for the camera to follow me, like it was my idea, and we went down the damp chute, the darkness ahead waiting like a trap. Every time I thought I was doing it for a show though, that I was playing host, that I was acting a part, it almost made it easier. I was Perry Palomino the host and nothing bad could happen to me on camera...

We walked for several yards, more than I anticipated, just the sound of our breath in the cold night air and the whisper of our feet down the steps, until we came across a door to my right. Rebecca shone the light further down the tunnel to see where it would go, but it just petered off into the dark.

"I guess this is it," I said. I stood to the side while Dex handed me the camera and pushed his body against the door until it finally opened with a moan into the damp chill of the night. Sometime after lunch we lost our clear skies and the fog came rolling in like a massive dust bunny intent on suffocating us all.

Dex went first into the white mist, beckoning me to follow and film. It was probably too late to appreciate, but I liked the way we had traded on and off lately, like we were both sharing duties and both responsible for the show.

I straggled forward across the wet grass after him while Rebecca planted herself in front of the door, keeping it from closing on us. She gave us the nod to say that she was okay.

Dex joined me at my side. We looked around.

The sanatorium was just as creepy from the outside and especially so from the backyard. The fog that moved in covered everything in a layer of moving gauze while the building glowed from the faint moonlight that penetrated it. I could barely see the playground in front of us, and the structures that did stick out looked like charred, skeletal remains in the mist.

Lovely.

"Well," he whispered to me, away from the mic, "let's see if we can contact Elliot or any of the other kids out here."

"You know I'm not the ghost whisperer," I hissed at him.

He stared at me steadily before saying, "You don't give yourself as much credit as you should."

Then he nudged me in the back and I walked forward, in front of the camera, and looked around me.

"Elliot," I said, projecting my voice to him and the camera. I walked toward the jungle gym, pausing near the slide. "Elliot, if you can hear us, please give us a sign. We know all about you but would love to talk to you ourselves. We mean you no harm and understand you feel the same."

We waited, air in our throats, trying to hear anything unusual, for our eyes to pick up anything in the dark.

Nothing.

I tried again, saying I wanted to make contact and that we just wanted to say hello. But whatever trace of Elliot there was, whatever boy was warning me last night to run away and see Rebecca, he didn't seem to be on the playground.

I looked over at Dex, feeling slightly frustrated. Our next two days were strategic. We all knew we could stay a few extra days if we needed to record more, and that was the original plan, but I insisted we leave the place as soon as we could. Like Gary Oldman, I also wasn't someone to push my luck. It was now our last show, but the sooner we got out of it, the better it was for us in the long run.

I decided to pretend I wasn't being filmed and stopped asking anything from our supernatural hosts. I walked toward the edge of the playing field, where potted garden beds turned into scraggly wildflowers and the wildflowers turned into the trees.

I inhaled the dewy breeze, feeling the sharpness sink all the way into my lungs.

That's when I heard the giggle.

I froze in place and slowly swiveled around. Dex was in the middle of the field, filming me from far away, and beyond that was Rebecca in her vintage coat, still holding the door to the body chute open.

A movement at the playground caught my eye. I squinted, trying to focus on the swings just in time to see one of them swing back and forth by itself.

Oh man.

I gestured to Dex to turn around and film it. I was just about to join him and go over when I heard another giggle from behind me.

I shifted to see a young boy standing beside me.

The scream that wanted to rip out of me was stuck in my throat.

"You're Jody's friend," the boy said, plain as day. Aside from the sickly transparent quality he had, he looked absolutely real, from the shininess of his hair to the freckles across his nose, to the plushness of the toy teddy bear he was holding. The way he held his hat in his other hand reminded me of Oliver Twist asking if he could 'have some more.'

I swallowed painfully, trying to find my voice. "I met Jody today. You must be Elliot."

Elliot look at me for a moment, sussing me out, and in that one blinding instance, I was reminded of how fleeting the glimpse between life and death was. He was looking at me like I was real and I was looking at him as if he were the same, and yet we could never really coincide; we never belonged in each other's world.

"Elliot," I began, an idea building through me. "Why are you here?"

He stuck out his lower lip in thought. "Why are you here?"

"Do you know where you are?"

"At Sea Crest."

"Do you know what year it is?"

He began to flicker before me, like the light was going out of him. I started to panic. By now my eyes went over to Dex and I could see him filming me, though being careful about being too obvious and keeping his distance.

"Elliot," I quickly went on, "what do you want?"

He looked down at the hat in his hands. "I want to see my family. I want to go home."

"Why don't you then? Go see them. I'm sure they'd love to see you. You have no reason to be here."

He was staring past me at the swing set. I glanced at it over my shoulder to still see the swing moving.

"I can't. Not until she lets me." His eyes were white-rimmed with fear. I looked at the swing set again and when I turned back, Elliot was gone. I called after him into the forest but only heard the faint rustle of pine needles. The trees suddenly looked as if they wanted to envelop me in their darkness.

I spun around and ran across the field to Dex. "Did you catch all that?" I asked breathlessly.

He gave me a wary smile. "I did. But the camera didn't," he said, patting the side of it. "This time it looks like you were talking to yourself. Sorry, kiddo."

"But you saw it with your own eyes, right? You saw Elliot."

"Of course."

I nodded, as if that's all that mattered. In some ways, that was true. As long as I looked sane in Dex's eyes, I wasn't doing half bad. I looked at the swing set. "Well, that's still moving, and from the way Elliot was looking at it, I'm guessing that there is someone there."

I stalked off toward it, knowing in my heart that it was Shawna on that swing. She was dead, didn't like me, and I was frightened to death of her, but I had to push that all aside.

"Shawna," I said carefully as I approached the set, the metal chains glinting in the light of the camera. "Shawna, are you there?"

The swinging slowed down. Then stopped. The gravel underneath the swing began moving, crunching under unseen weight.

It stopped right in front of me.

I held my breath. I felt tiny fingers grasp my one hand and turn it over. What felt like teeth grazed the top of my anchor tattoo.

I gasped and snatched my hand back. The air filled with a girlish, malicious laugh, then a growling, drooling, snapping sound.

I cried out, the noise working its way into my bones, and staggered back into Dex's grasp.

"I have you," he said gruffly. He looked out at the playground, at the gravel that kept moving. "Hey, little bitch, you wanna come back and try something with me?"

I kept my wrist to my side and shook my head. "Dex, don't tempt her."

His eyes were on fire as he looked at me. "Yeah well, maybe I don't like it when they keep going after you. This is exactly why we have to end this show."

"And we are," I said. "We are."

He held me close to him, lowering the camera. "I fucking hate it when I'm filming and this shit happens to you. Hate it. Makes me feel so powerless."

"Jealous of the attention?"

"It's not funny, Perry," he said.

I managed a smile. "Well we can stay out here and find out what else they have in store or we can go back inside and try something else."

"To be honest, I'd rather just go back to our rooms and save the rest for tomorrow," he admitted. "I have the footage of the swing going by itself, that's a powerful enough image, especially with this background at night."

I eyed him closely. "What about me talking to Elliot?"

"That seemed more like a private moment. Even if the cameras don't pick him up, it's obvious he's there. I think it's better if we keep the kid out of it."

I nodded, completely besotted with Dex's protective side.

We turned back to head into the building when we saw Shawna standing between us and the door.

And Rebecca was no longer holding it open.

Dex's hand tightened around my waist and I heard his breath hitch. He saw her too.

"I asked you to play with me and you never did," Shawna said in her melodic voice. She pulled at the sides of her plain white dress as if she were trying to look weak. I did not buy it for a second.

"Where's Rebecca?" I asked.

She gazed at me blankly. "I do not know what you mean." She took a step forward, the grass looking like dark blades around her white shoes. "Why didn't you play with me?"

She was addressing me. I licked my lips and said, "You were in my dream."

"That woman scared me away," she noted. Her fine eyebrow rose. "Who was she?"

"No one," I said quickly, even though I could tell Dex was looking at me for an explanation. "She was just part of my dream."

"I don't reckon I liked the way she talked to me," she said, her voice rising. "She reminds me of the nurses. You do know what they did, don't you?"

Dex and I both shook our heads. I felt feeble and stupid.

"I think they tried to remove my soul," Shawna said, her voice becoming deeper, wetter, more guttural. More inhuman. She looked down at her chest where a red stain suddenly appeared on one side and started spreading outward. "I think they succeeded."

Oh shit. All Dex and I could do was stare at her, at the gaping hole that began to form in her chest, until the fabric of her dress burned away and we were left with a bloody view of her open chest cavity. Her lungs shrank and expanded as if she were breathing.

"Jesus H. Macy," Dex gasped.

"Look what my father did to me," she said, her voice back to being breathy and sweet. "He tried to give me new lungs. But it didn't work." Her black eyes narrowed into slits. "Perhaps if I had yours."

She took a step forward with an outstretched hand, her nails looking like claws, and Dex and I stepped back, holding onto each other. She paused then smiled wickedly. "I can always get my creature to get them for me. He would be better at it than I. He owes me for letting him *loose*."

She glanced over her shoulder at the building, where the fog was starting to lift. The *bad thing* was crawling out of an open window and for once we could see it all in its entirety.

I wished I could bleach my eyes out.

The bad thing was just as disturbing as I thought it was when it wasn't hidden by the shadows. It looked human, except for its black skin that had a sickly sheen to it and its watermelon shaped head. It had no nose, no features, except a razor-toothed slit and ghostly white eyes that protruded from the face. It crawled down the side of the building, moving like a giant spider, reaching forward with stick-thin limbs and extra-long fingers, making a skittering, snapping sound as it moved like a cockroach.

I couldn't move, couldn't do anything but stare at the bad thing until it disappeared into the bushes that lined the bottom of the building. I slowly brought my eyes over to Shawna, who was smiling again so broadly I could see her canines.

"What is that thing?" I found myself whispering.

"It eats hate," she said. "It devours fear. It has promised me things."

The bushes at the base of the building rustled and a long, spindly arm came out, digging needle fingers into the grass.

A second arm followed.

"Guys!" Rebecca's voice suddenly rang out across the field.

We both looked over Shawna to see Rebecca back at the door, removing a rock she had placed to keep it propped open. "Can we go? I don't feel so well."

She obviously didn't see Shawna standing in front of us. If I wasn't so terrified out of my mind, I would have found it fucking frustrating.

Shawna didn't seem to notice or care. But her smile dropped from her small, white face and she skipped off toward the bushes, the blood from her open chest trickling on the grass. We watched as she went into the bush. The bad thing's arms retracted and they were both gone from sight.

"Did you get any of that?" I whispered to Dex, almost afraid to raise my voice.

"No," he said slowly. "I forgot to film everything except that last part. Rebecca snapped me out of it."

We looked over to her where she was now waving at us. "If you don't hurry up," she shouted, "I'm going back inside and locking you out here."

No thank you. We scurried across the field over to her. Close up, she looked paler than normal and her lipstick was rubbed off.

"Are you okay?" I asked.

She shook her head and grimaced. "I was sick around the corner. Maybe it was something I ate. What were you guys doing?"

"You didn't see the little girl or the creature on the walls? The demon?" Dex asked.

"You saw the demon? The one that the historian was talking about?"

We nodded. She exhaled sharply through her nose. "Bloody hell. What happened?"

I gestured to the open door. "I'd feel a whole lot better if we could discuss this inside."

"Right, right," she said. We went back into the body chute, and for the first time, the tunnel of death almost felt safe. At least compared to the outside, where Shawna and the bad thing might still be. Sooner or later, it seemed, there would be no safe places left.

Maybe there never were.

CHAPTER TWELVE

After we filmed outside, we went back into the break room to review the footage while giving Rebecca the rundown on what we saw. It was true that once Shawna appeared, Dex dropped the ball on the filming. I couldn't blame him—the show was the last thing on my mind too. I was more concerned about, oh, I don't know, not dying or having my lungs ripped out of me.

But as soon as Rebecca called out to us, snapping us back to reality, Dex did start to film. He caught a few seconds of me asking, "What is that thing?" and though you couldn't see Shawna, per se, you could see an orb of light flickering past the camera and hear a garbled voice whisper, "It eats hate." Even though I was there when Shawna said it, the playback cut me to the core.

Even Rebecca looked impressed. Well, at least she momentarily stopped looking like she was going to puke. And then at the very end of the tape, you could actually make out the droplets of blood as they appeared on the grass as Shawna skipped away. Again, it wasn't everything that we saw, but for a ghost hunting series, that was some pretty good evidence. The three of us were practically giddy as we realized that the show itself was shaping up to be something pretty special.

And then of course, I think it made us all a bit sad. So Dex brought out the rest of the whiskey and we had a merry little time at that table, enjoying each other's company and not thinking about the horrors that were waiting for us on the floors above us.

When it was time for bed, I wanted a good night's sleep instead of cliffhanging off the side of the bed with Dex's body taking up most of it, so I went for the middle bed. Even though the immovable plastic partition between the beds meant that I couldn't see them properly except for their outlines and couldn't be close to them, being in the middle made me feel safer.

Dex was closest to the door as well, plus I'd propped the chair under the handle again, just in case.

I actually fell asleep for what must have been a couple of hours, something I never thought possible in this terrible place. When I woke up from my dreamless sleep, the first thing I heard was Dex snoring lightly from his bed.

He must be on his back, I thought. Normally I poked him in the side when he did that in order to get him to roll over and shut up.

I lay there, my eyes adjusting to the light, and pulled my covers up to my chin, feeling a chill set in. I turned my head on the pillow to look over in Rebecca's direction.

She was sitting up in bed. I could see her silhouette through the curtain.

"Can't sleep?" I whispered.

The outline of Rebecca's head moved, as if to face me. She didn't say anything.

"Are you awake?" I whispered again. Maybe she was dreaming or sleepwalking or something. "Rebecca?"

I could feel her staring at me through the curtain, still remaining silent.

Honestly, she was starting to freak me out.

I slowly got out of bed and walked toward her, trying to keep as silent as possible and not really knowing why. I put my hand on the edge of the curtain and pulled it back as far as it would go.

Her bed was empty.

No one was there.

I swallowed hard, my scalp prickling.

Just then I heard a muffled sob and the sound of crying. Now that sounded like Rebecca. She rarely cried, but the few times I'd heard her, all of it post-Emily, she sounded elegant even when she was breaking down.

I padded down the room, glancing over at Dex as I went. He was still snoring, eyes closed, deep in sleep. I decided to leave him be for now. The chair had been removed from under the door so I opened it and stepped out into the hall. The crying continued, coming from the bathrooms.

Not that I wanted Rebecca to be crying, but I really, really hoped it was her and not Shawna luring me to my own doom. I tried to keep my heart from pounding out of my chest as I carefully crept down the hallway, the lights above me flickering.

I stopped right outside the woman's washroom and took in a deep breath. Then I flung the door open and poked my head inside.

The washroom was empty and the crying had stopped.

Oh shit.

"H-Hello?" It was Rebecca's voice, coming from one of the stalls.

I let out a huge breath of relief. "It's me," I said.

"Oh." And then she started crying again.

I raced over to the stall she was in and knocked on it. "Can I come in, or are you, um..." What was the polite way to say "taking a dump?"

The stall door slowly swung open and Rebecca was sitting in her silk pajamas on top of the toilet, dabbing at her tear-soaked face with rolled up tissue paper.

"What's wrong?" I asked her, my voice softening.

"Oh, it's...I can't even say," she said with a sniff. "You'll judge me."

"Me?" I exclaimed. "Judge you? Rebecca, come on. It's Perry. I have no right to judge anyone and I'd never judge you. Believe me, I've been there, done that."

She gave me a sad look. "I guess you're right." She sighed.

"Well? What's wrong? Did something happen to you?"

"Something did happen. Recently. Before we got here."

I cocked my head, having no idea what she was going to say. "Well? You can tell me. I'm here to listen. I'm your friend."

"I know you are," she said quietly. "I haven't told anyone yet."

"Not even Dex?" I asked, knowing she was closer to him than she was to me.

She shook her head and a teardrop fell on her pants. She quickly wiped it off with her hand. "No. I can't tell him."

"Well, I won't tell. What is it?"

She took in a long breath and held it for a moment before she exhaled. Then she looked at me with regretful eyes and said, "I'm pregnant."

Whoa.

Whoa.

I was absolutely floored. "Pregnant? How could you be pregnant?"

She stared at the tissue in her hands. "It was almost a month ago. I went out to a club with Dean and Seb. You know, the night you guys took that cooking class. I got drunk...I didn't want to be alone. One thing led to another," she trailed off. "I had sex with a guy."

"I don't know what to say," I said, still flabbergasted. "I mean, how?"

She gave me a wry look with her red eyes. “You want a demo?”

“But I mean, why? You’re a lesbian. Why are you sleeping with men?” Maybe it was a stupid question on my behalf, I don’t know.

She let out a long, tired sigh. “It wasn’t the first time for me. It’s happened before. Similar circumstances. Too much booze, just got out of a relationship…”

“Wow,” I said slowly, letting it all sink in. “I had no idea. So do you have a type of man you sleep with? Ones that look like girls or…?”

I half-expected her to give me a snippy remark over that but she just stared at me, her forehead creasing with worry. “No, not at all,” she stated gravely. “Perry, there’s something that’s been weighing on me…promise you won’t get mad.”

My eyes widened defensively. “If you’re starting something off like that, I can probably promise I will get mad.”

She nodded a few times, licking her lips. “All right. But please don’t get mad at Dex.”

This conversation was definitely heading in the wrong direction. A direction that was making me feel sick to my stomach, considering what we had just been talking about. I shook my head. “Please don’t tell me what I think you’re going to tell me.”

She gave me a crooked smile. "I still can't read your mind."

"Then just stop talking," I pleaded.

"You really want me to?" she asked but the damage was already done. She put forth the bait and I was biting. I couldn't be left dangling like that over something I wasn't allowed to get mad at Dex over. I couldn't bring myself to say anything though, so I just stared at her.

She dabbed her tissue at her nose before taking a deep breath and looking me straight in the eye. "Remember when we first met? When we first had lunch together?"

I barely nodded.

"I had told you that when Dex first joined Wine Babes, before he was with Jenn, that he asked me out and I turned him down?"

Oh dear lord. No. No. No.

She continued, "And I'd said that he wasn't my type, that we were just flirting together but it didn't mean anything, because, hello, lesbian here."

I couldn't even breathe.

"Well, that was all true. But..." She looked away, eyes drifting to the ceiling as if there was something interesting there. "One night, around the time that all of this was happening, maybe the first week of filming the show...erm....stuff kind of happened."

This was not happening. I was not here. It was not the middle of the night in a haunted sanatorium and I wasn't in the bathroom with one of my best friends hearing her say what I feared she was going to say.

"What kind of stuff?" I asked, my breath hitching.

She looked back at me, chagrined. "Well, at least that time I didn't get pregnant from it."

My hand flew to my mouth and I gasped. "What the actual fuck?"

"Sorry," she said, swallowing hard. "We never told you because we'd pretty much forgotten about it."

"You slept with Dex!" I yelled, my voice surprising me.

She winced. "Ugh, yes, please don't be mad. It's really not what you think at all."

"How do you know what I think?" I cried out, my fists clenching at my sides. "I'm thinking about hitting you right in your face, did you know that?"

She looked uneasy. "I figured. But seriously, Perry, it was nothing. It was my fault. I got really drunk and Dex was there and I knew he was into me and it just happened." I gasped again, I couldn't help it. Now I felt like I was going to be sick. "It meant nothing, which is why we never spoke of it again. It was just...a bad time all around, even though I'm sure Dex thought he was brilliant."

I pressed the palm of my hand to my forehead and closed my eyes, trying to stave off the coming headache. "Oh god, please shut up."

"No, you have to know," she said, getting off the toilet seat. "You have to know that it was something we put past us as a stupid silly thing. I like pussy, not dick. And Dex, well I knew he could tell."

"Oh god," I mumbled. "Why are you still talking?"

"We were better off as friends, both of us knew that. A few days later he started shagging Jenn. This was so long ago."

Finally I snapped my head up and looked at her. "Will you please just shut up? Why the hell are you telling me this now if it didn't mean anything? Look, I get that the past is the past and I have no control over it but...Jesus Christ, Rebecca, you've made everything really fucking weird for us now."

"I know!" she exclaimed in a shaky voice. "I know I have, but that's why it was weighing on me. Because you didn't know. And it probably should have stayed buried but I just thought..."

"You just thought what?" I asked, folding my arms. "That because you're having a shitty time now that you're pregnant, you thought I should have a shitty time too? And Dex? Because believe me, if you think I'm not going to have it out with him over this, you have another thing coming!"

"Perry, please listen to me."

"I did listen to you. I've had enough."

"I just thought you guys should...have no secrets at this point in your relationship."

"No secrets?" I repeated. "That's really none of your business, you know. And this point...what point is that, exactly? All this does is prove how little I actually know Dex. You think I didn't have enough to think about trying to ignore what Uncle Al said to me, that we've only known each other for eight fucking months?"

"That wasn't my intention," she said, angrily brushing her hair behind her ears. "It was the opposite. You guys are in this for the long haul, I know this. You know it too."

I groaned and turned away from her. I couldn't deal with this anymore. Dex and Rebecca had slept together. Suddenly every single time he acted like he was hitting on her or hinting at a threesome seemed less like an endearing joke and more like something he had prior knowledge of. Fuck, I hated this. Hated it. It changed the way I saw the both of them forever. I couldn't believe that all this time they never said anything to me about it.

"Perry," she said again, her voice cracking a little.

I walked over to the door and glanced at her over my shoulder. "I'm sorry that you're pregnant and everything," I told her. "But I just need some time to process this."

What I really wanted was time to think. And considering it was the middle of the night, I had it. But the last thing I wanted was to go back to bed beside Dex—I just couldn't do it. On the other hand, I didn't exactly feel like going for a stroll on the first floor. With my luck I'd see Shawna again and this time she wouldn't be as coy.

"I'm going to spend the night in the teachers' lounge," I informed her. "Okay?"

She sniffed, looking absolutely forlorn, but nodded. "Okay."

I started walking away but she called out to me. "If you're staying up, do you mind rolling the camera? You know, just in case? It's our last show and all, and..."

I sighed. It was a good thing that Rebecca was a lesbian because the two of them were way too alike.

I headed down the hall, my pace quick, my eyes downcast, not wanting to see any shadow people in the walls, and went back into our room to grab a blanket and the camcorder.

"What the hell is going on out there?" asked a groggy-voiced Dex from his bed. "Are you having a pillow fight or a cat fight?"

With blood boiling in my veins, I switched on the small light by his bed and turned to face him. "A pillow fight? You'd like that, wouldn't you?" I sneered.

He raised his brow, eyes all squinty. "This is a trick question, I can tell, and as such, I won't answer it."

I glared at him. "Rebecca is pregnant."

His mouth dropped open. "What?"

"Oh don't worry, it's not your baby. I'm sure you used a condom when you fucked her all those years ago."

Oh yes, there it was. The look of utter doom on Dex's face. His wide eyes stared at me like he was caught in headlights and I could almost see his brain trying to make sense of what I just said, trying to figure out how to play it off.

For once, he was actually speechless.

Finally he licked his lips and said with a tilt of his head, "Perry…"

I rolled my eyes and moved over to my bed to get the blanket. "I'm sleeping in the teachers' lounge."

"Perry," he said more sharply this time and reached out to grab me by the elbow. "Seriously, don't go. Stay here. We'll talk. I'll tell you everything."

I wrestled out of his grasp. "I already know everything. Rebecca told me—she told me more than I wanted to know."

"Well why the fuck is she telling you this shit?"

"I don't know, cuz she's gone hormonal and crazy?"

"Oh god, come on, baby," he said, swinging his legs off the bed. "I understand you're mad, but it's in the past."

"Well what the fuck else is in your past, huh?" I asked angrily as I picked up the blanket. "Anything else you're hiding, any other affairs I should know about? Any secrets you've been harboring?"

He seemed to flinch at that before running his hands down his face in exasperation. "Baby, I don't even think about it," Dex said. "Seriously. Never. Just like I never think about any of the other women I slept with. Do you think about the other men you've slept with?" His voice became harder there at the end.

"All two of them? No, Dex, I don't."

His nostrils flared for a moment before he exhaled noisily. "Let's not fight here. We can fight back in Seattle, but not here, not in this place. This place is already fucking with us and it's our last show."

"I'll fight with you wherever the hell I feel like fighting with you." My stomach twisted like a hot knife was inside it but I kept to my guns.

“This is dangerous,” he warned. ”Please, stay here with me. Or I’ll go in the lounge and you can stay here.”

“With Rebecca? No thanks. I don’t feel like seeing either of you right now.”

I tried to walk away but he suddenly stepped in front of me, all hard lines and steely eyes. “You’re not going anywhere.”

“Get out of my way, Dex,” I told him, looking up at his face and matching him glare for glare.

“Sorry,” we heard Rebecca say and Dex turned around to see her standing in the nurse’s office, her face in shadows. “I didn’t mean to cause a fight.” She looked to Dex. “I just thought you’d want her to know.”

I took that opportunity to squeeze past Dex and head out to the hallway.

“Perry,” Dex called after me in frustration, but I was quick on my feet. I ignored Rebecca as I walked past her and headed straight for the lounge. I could hear him yelling at Rebecca now. “What the fuck did you do that for? What’s your problem?”

Rebecca yelled back at him, something about “having a clean slate going forward” and then I didn’t want to hear anymore. I went into the lounge, flicked on the lights, and immediately closed the door after me. I leaned against it and breathed in deeply through my nose. Okay, I was going to be okay. Eventually this sick feeling would pass and I would get over it. I only wished I was one of those people who didn't let everything bother them, who didn't feel everything. My mind knew that what happened between Dex and Rebecca was in the past, that it really didn't mean anything to a lesbian and a man-whore. But still. It was going to take some time to get the images of them having sex out of my head, let alone the fact that they had both kept it from me.

Now, of course, I could see why they did. This was going to be an awkward shoot for the next day. As if we didn't have enough to deal with already in this hellish place. A part of me wished I was a little less stubborn, so I wouldn't be holed up in the lounge by myself to make a point.

I sighed and stepped away from the door. I laid the blanket out on the couch and pushed the couch further down the wall so one arm was against the side of the kitchen counter. If I were to get any sleep, it had to be so that there was no space behind me so I could clearly see the door. I sat on the couch and looked around, feeling vaguely protected. I stuck the camera up on the counter above my head and then got up and pulled the two beers out of the fridge that I knew Dex had stuck in there earlier. Beer was my only way out of this night.

I went back to the couch, pulled the blanket up over me, and drank, staring intently at the door as if I were expecting it to open, and listened to the muffled sounds of Dex and Rebecca as they were fighting. As much as I didn't want to see them at war, their blurred obscenities were soothing, reminding me that I wasn't alone.

I drank until their voices faded.

Then I close my eyes and slept.

And I dreamed.

***

Everything was cold. The air whooshed past me, whistling quietly in my ears, and even before I opened my eyes, I knew I was someplace else.

I opened them cautiously, preparing for what I might see. In front of me were white swirls rising up from the ground, waltzing a ghostly dance in the night sky. It was snowing lightly, the air filled with that muffled, peaceful sound that comes with snowfall, and I was standing in the middle of an empty bridge. Only it wasn't just any bridge. It was the Brooklyn Bridge, and beyond the trails of snow, I could make out the lights and the glowing skyline of Manhattan.

"New York City," a voice said from behind me.

I whirled around, my hair swinging around me as if in slow motion, and I saw Pippa sitting on a chair a few yards away. Just sitting there in the middle of the bridge's walkway, the cables framing her on either side, making criss-cross shadows appear on her face.

Her face. My god, she looked even worse than the last time I saw her. She was hunched over in her coat, her hands in her lap looking as breakable as twigs, her legs nothing but bone under her long skirt.

"Pippa?" I said gently.

No need to speak, she said weakly. *I must save my energy.*

Why are we in New York? I asked, hugging myself against the cold. It was amazing that even though I knew I was in one of my dreams, I was feeling everything like it was real. The damp smell of snow, the cutting chill of the wind.

It all started here, she said. *Everything. For both of you.*

Me and Dex? I asked.

And me.

Pippa had moved to New York after she left Sweden and became a nanny to Dex and his older brother Michael, but I wasn't sure how I came into it.

She gave me a sly look with her tired, hooded eyes. *You come into it because that's where I saw you, Perry. When I first used the Veil to look into your life.*

It's where Dex and Michael were born, brought into this world. Where both Dex and I were put away. It's the beginning of so many horrors. And I believe it will be the end.

I frowned and wiped the cold flakes of snow off my face. *End? What do you mean?*

I don't know. It's a feeling.

You know what? I said angrily. I started stomping through the snow to get to her, the cold sinking into the tops of my Converse shoes. I stopped right in front of her, close enough to count the flakes nestling on the top of her thinning hair. *I am getting sick and tired of you and your feelings! Why can't you ever be sure of something for once? Why is it always a hunch? It's never real.*

Because I'm not real, my dear, she said. *And I can never be sure of anything. All I have is what I feel and what I fear, and it's better that than nothing.*

Well, what am I supposed to do about it? I shoved my hands in my back pockets to keep them warm. *I'm quitting the show now, didn't you hear? Didn't you feel that?*

I did. A timid smile stretched across her wrinkled lips. *And for that I am glad.*

Then what's the problem?

I think the problem is something you won't see coming. I think the problem will come in the form of someone who is trustworthy. And I think when he comes, he will bring you here. Where everything will end. She breathed out slowly, like her lungs were labored. *It will come full circle.*

He? I repeated.

She just stared at me, eyes dull. *There will be death. And in that, I cannot help you.*

"Death!?" I cried out loud.

The world is changing and I am growing weaker. The death may be my own.

"You're already dead," I tried to say as politely as possible.

She cocked her head and for once her eyes sparkled as if they belonged to a younger woman. "Death is never the end, only a transition. I have tried to stay here, in the Veil, for as long as I can, to look after you and Dex. But time here can run out. It can be used up. Just like the time in your hands. And when I go, I don't think we'll ever have contact again. So whatever I am able to pass onto you, even if it's a feeling from deep inside my lost soul, I will. While I can."

Her words seemed to exhaust her. She breathed in deeply through her nose just as the snow began to fall harder, thicker, until she was gone and all I could see was white.

CHAPTER THIRTEEN

I woke up with a start.

My eyes flew open and I sat straight up, trying to get my bearings. I wasn't on the snow-covered Brooklyn Bridge anymore. I was in the teachers' lounge at Oceanside Arts Academy.

But what the hell woke me up? I thought to myself, holding the covers close to my chest while my heart pounded as if set off by something else, something I wasn't aware of yet.

I tried to listen, keeping my breathing as quiet as possible, and surveyed the room for anything unusual. The clock on the microwave above the fridge read 3 a.m. It was always 3 a.m. when the scary shit happened, but the room looked normal to me. I'd fallen asleep with the lights on, naturally, and though the window above the sink showed the black sky outside, if I tricked my mind hard enough, maybe I could pretend it was morning and I was safe and I could fall back asleep.

I laid my head back on the armrest and tried to think of nice thoughts. I was drawing a blank. I kept thinking about my dream, about Pippa, trying to decide whether that was a figment of my imagination or if it was real. I kept thinking about Rebecca being pregnant and the fact that Dex stuck his dick in her all those years ago. I kept thinking about Ada and how alone she felt, then about my parents and how disapproving they were going to be when I showed up with Dex.

And then I thought about where I was and what I was dealing with. And it seemed pretty fucking futile to try and think about anything nice.

I sighed and watched with surprise as my breath hung suspended in a cloud. It had grown colder in the last minute, so much that my nose and chin and hands, the only things outside the blanket, felt partially numb. I hated cold spots.

They usually only meant one thing.

A mechanical noise by the door caught my attention, making my pulse jump. I carefully slid my eyes over to it. The doorknob was very slowly turning, almost so imperceptibly that you couldn't even see it happening.

I held my breath, paralyzed by fear, submissive by my lack of options. I watched as the door knob continued its long turn until it couldn't turn anymore.

The door jumped in its hinges as if someone on the other side tried to push it open.

The lock held.

I let out a little cry, bringing my knees up to my chest, as if shrinking away from it would help.

Suddenly, the door stopped jangling. The room grew silent. I knew this was probably a good time to turn on the camera and film whatever the hell was going to happen, but I didn't want to turn away, I didn't want to take my eyes off the door.

There was a knock at it. Faint, just three raps, but definitely there.

"W-Who is it?" I cried out softly. "Dex? Rebecca?"

I slowly got off the couch, tossing my blanket aside. The vinyl floor was ice cold underneath my feet as I crept over to the door.

I gingerly put my ear against it, hoping I could hear something on the other side.

And I could.

Whispering.

At first it was the harsh, ragged whisper of just one voice, male or female I couldn't tell. They were speaking nonsense, words I didn't recognize as any language, and yet they sunk into me just the same. The intent still came across.

They were the whispers of psychosis, of pure hopelessness and desperation.

And then they multiplied. One voice became many, all whispering their rough pleas, their nonsensical words getting under my skin, lulling me into their madness until the hundreds of crazed voices were all I could hear.

I pulled away from the door, and the minute I did so, the whispering stopped, leaving me in silence. I counted to ten, gathering the courage to do it again. I carefully put my hand on the knob and my ear back on the door.

There were no whispers.

Just one metallic voice, like it was speaking through a crackly radio.

"She's behind you," it whispered in its strained transmission.

My lungs felt like they were shriveling up, my heart seeming to stop. The fear was so strong, so wicked, I thought it might just consume me right there and reduce me to nothing.

She was behind me. I didn't have to guess who.

I straightened up and turned around to look.

Shawna was across the room staring at me intently, her posture stiff and her head angled down, creating shadows on her sickly white face. Blood dribbled down her chin and a red-stained rag was clutched in one of her small hands.

She didn't say anything. She just stared at me.

And ever so slowly smiled, displaying a mouth soaked with blood.

I wasn't about to hear what she had to say.

I pushed out the door lock and was ready to turn the knob when I looked down and saw eight long black fingers coming in underneath the door, wiggling up at me.

I screamed and staggered backward toward the couch.

"Dex!" I screamed. "Rebecca! Someone help!"

"I can scream louder than you can," Shawna said in her sing-song voice. She took two steps toward me and stopped, her gaze going over to the door, to the wriggling, stick-thin fingers of the *bad thing* as it tried to get underneath it. It was only a matter of time before it realized the door was unlocked, a matter of time before it was in the room with me.

"Dex!" I screamed again.

"Dex!" she screamed, high-pitched and piercing. Then she laughed, mocking me.

"That's right," she said. "Keep screaming. I screamed and I screamed and I screamed when I was locked in that space, locked in that cold box. I wasn't dead and they wouldn't believe me."

I eyed her with trepidation, not wanting to engage her but feeling I had to all the same. "What box?"

"The morgue," she said, smiling and twirling a strand of her hair around her blood-stained finger. "It wasn't my time, I wasn't dead. And they knew it. The nurses knew it. But they had to make room. And my dad wasn't there anymore. He couldn't tell them no."

"The nurses..." I trailed off, finding it hard to speak. My gaze kept going to the fingers under the door, now making long scratches in the floor. "The nurses killed you?"

Her eyes turned black as coal, her irises obliterated. "I was going to die anyway, we all knew that. My father couldn't save me. He couldn't save himself either." She came two steps forward, almost floating along the floor. "I wasn't the only one. Some of us burned in the incinerator. Some of us were left in the cold to die. My friend Elliot was smothered with a pillow. We were all tossed out to make room."

"What do you want with me?"

She eyed me curiously. "You're the only person who really sees me."

"What about Jody?"

She snarled contemptuously. "She doesn't have what I need."

I inhaled icy air into my lungs. "What do you need?"

She grinned. "A way to be alive again. He promised me I could have that if I let him eat."

I didn't have to look to the door to know whom she was talking about.

"And he can't do that without you?" I was afraid of the answer to this one, but I asked it all the same. "He can't *eat*?"

With a scraping sound, the bad thing retracted its claws underneath the doorframe. Shawna looked at me in shock. "What did you do?" she hissed at me.

I shook my head, terrified and confused.

Shawna ran over to the door and opened it, poking her head out into the hallway. She gave me one last blood-glazed snarl before she ran out the door and down the hallway. Her already faint footsteps faded into nothing.

Well that was just great. I posed one question and their whole dynamic came crashing down. I had to wonder here who was the pet and who was the owner.

The answer made me shiver.

If he was a demon like Oldman said some believed, and he fed off of hate and fear, he'd have an endless food supply at this hospital, especially if what Shawna said was true. Was there really patient abuse, nurses killing off young ailing TB victims in order to make room for others during the epidemic? It wouldn't have been the first time it happened, but to imagine sick children with no hope being tossed into a fire or smothered with a pillow, like Elliot was supposedly, it got me deep inside.

I looked around the teachers' lounge again, paranoid that maybe some other child would be in the room with me, another child like Shawna with a deal with the devil and an obvious vendetta, but everything looked normal again.

I couldn't stay in here. I didn't care about my pride or my point. With shaking hands I gathered up my blanket and the camera I'd never turned on, and cautiously made my way to the door.

I poked my head out. The hallway looked empty. I stepped out, looking both ways.

Down by the washroom I saw Rebecca walking toward it. She stopped halfway, looking over her shoulder at me for a moment before she continued and disappeared through the door. I walked back into the nurses' quarters, wondering if I was being selfish by being upset over her and Dex when here she was pregnant and feeling alone

Dex was lying on his side in bed, his eyes watching me and glinting in the low light. I couldn't look at him, not now. I wanted to ask if he had heard anything, heard me screaming for help, but I could only assume he didn't. Dex was loyal and protective to the core. If he heard anything wrong, he would have been there for me.

I ignored his stare and made my way over to my bed.

That's when I noticed the silhouette of someone in Rebecca's bed next to me.

Fuck.

Before I could think about it, dwell on it, get scared about it, I poked my head around the curtain and to my surprise saw Rebecca, in the flesh, sitting up in her bed and looking at me with sad, wet eyes.

"Sorry, Perry," she whispered. When I didn't respond and could only stare at her dumbfounded, she lay back down in her bed, turning over on her side.

What the damn ass hell was going on? One minute I see Rebecca going to the washroom, the other she's back in her bed. I stewed on that as I climbed into my bed, dragging the blanket up to my chin. This place really was fucking with me, and now I was in bed between my two friends and partners, both of whom were intimate with each other at one point, both of whom had kept something major out of my life, both of whom I was mad at.

And both of whom were the only people in this place that I could ever trust.

I didn't sleep a wink for the rest of the night.

I didn't think any of us did.

***

"Are you sure you're up for this?" Dex asked Brenna as she puttered about her classroom, putting art supplies away.

She waved at him dismissively, a big smile on her face. "Oh, don't you worry about me. I feel right as rain. Just a quick stomach bug, as nasty as it is. Speaking of rain," she turned to look out the windows where the trees were waving in the wind and dark, ominous clouds rolling in, "it looks like it's going to downpour any minute."

It was third period and Brenna was back at school teaching, but not without offering to accompany me, Dex, and Rebecca throughout the school to any of the floors we wanted to visit while she had a spare hour. Davenport was still being extra strict, and though she never knew we had gone into the body chute or the playground last night, we knew we only had one more night at this place and didn't want to risk pissing her off. Supervision it was.

That morning the three of us had woken up short-tempered and fuzzy-headed from lack of sleep. With dark circles under our eyes and a pasty pallor, we looked no different than Elliot or Shawna. I was still mad, or at least uncomfortable, around Dex and Rebecca, and they seemed equally awkward around each other. In short, it was pretty much the worst morning ever, made worse by the weather taking a nasty turn.

I never told them about my dream, nor what happened in the teachers' lounge after I woke up. Dex tried a few times to break the ice, and though I felt my defenses melting down every time, it still wasn't enough. We'd been to places before where it felt like outside forces were fucking with us and making us turn against each other, like D'Arcy Island, and it didn't seem wrong to say this place was doing the same kind of thing. Maybe all the years of death, anger, murder, and loneliness builds up and seeps into you. I looked around at the children who were going to and from their classes, and even though they looked to be okay, you could see the irritability in their teachers' faces, as if something was permanently hanging over them, a net waiting to drop.

In my opinion, the net was the floors above the school, the ones that housed all the horror. There could be no peace here, not while so many injustices happened, tragedies that were supposedly buried and never saw the light of day. I thought about Oldman and his grandmother, whom he knew would never hurt a fly. I wondered if that were true, and if so, if she knew of others that did do such a thing. The wrongs that were made in this place would have been insurmountable.

"Brenna," I said cautiously as she nervously tugged on the ends of her sweater. "Before we get started, do you mind if we ask you a question?"

I knew Rebecca and Dex had no idea about this so I quickly launched into it before anyone had a chance to say no.

"The other day when we were interviewing you, you were going to tell us about the time you saw the bad thing. You never did. Do you mind telling us now?"

"Now?" she questioned. "Right before we head up into its usual territory?"

"We saw the thing last night," I said simply without looking at Dex. "I don't think it has a territory anymore. I think it's off leash and running loose."

Brenna's face contorted pitifully. "Oh dear. I wish you hadn't said that. I'll never be able to get any work done. Sometimes I stay after school to work on projects and..."

"The sooner we know more about it," I said, venturing into unknown territory myself, "maybe the sooner the ghosts will be gone for good. Either the school will get recognition from the episode and parents will demand a new school, or we can help you."

"Perry," Dex warned.

I ignored him. I knew I was shooting my mouth off. I knew when we first met Brenna that she had assumed we were ghost whisperers and that we could get rid of the problem. I still didn't think that was true, but if we could, it was definitely worth a shot. And it all started with understanding what we were dealing with.

Brenna leaned back against the radiator heater and crossed her arms. She sighed, a piece of curly hair flying off of her face. "Okay. I'll tell you. But I'll make it quick because it's not something I like to relive." I gave her an attentive nod, trying to tell her that I knew exactly how she felt. "I was teaching my class how to do a multi-media collage, using paint as well as day to day materials such as paper, dirt, and twigs. I wanted to do something different though, something that would challenge their minds and mix up their environment. I decided we would pay a visit to the second floor. It was a week when Davenport was away, and I made sure that none of the teachers knew about it. The floors really can be a hazard. So much upstairs is falling apart or structurally unsound. But I figured the second floor would be okay."

She looked nervous but continued as rain began to pelt the windows and the morning light dimmed, making it look like evening outside. "We were only two rooms down from the staircase. I wanted the kids to take materials they'd found upstairs and bring them down here, and find a way to incorporate pieces of history into a project about this place. Well, it was going fine until Jody wandered off."

That damn Jody.

"It took me a second to realize she was gone," she continued. "I should have been watching her more closely; I knew that she'd probably find Elliot and try to play with him. I left the kids for a moment and went after her, searching down the hall. I came to one of the rooms that had a closet and I could see her tiny footprints in the dust, leading to there. The closet door was even open a touch. I called out her name, quietly, not wanting to alert the other kids, then I opened the door. The closet was somehow filled with coats of all different shapes and sizes. Old coats that had probably never been cleared out, belonging to the staff. One of the coats moved slightly, like Jody was in there, trying to hide behind it."

She took in a deep breath and pushed her hair off her face. "I called for her first. I told her I found her and if she didn't come out, she'd be in big trouble. But she didn't answer. And so I went into the closet after her. The doors immediately shut on me, locking me in. I was trapped and I knew, I knew that Jody had never been in there to begin with. I tried to open the door, pushing my weight against it, trying the handle, doing everything I could without drawing attention to myself. Then I felt hot breath on my neck, and long hands around my waist..."

I nearly swallowed my tongue trying to imagine that, the fear she must have felt. It was all over Brenna's face. She angrily wiped away a falling tear with her hand. "And then I started yelling for the children, all while this thing...had me. It was whispering in my ear all these words that I knew were cruel but I didn't understand, and I almost lost my mind. But then Jody yelled something from outside the closet, something like "leave her alone," and the door opened and I came falling out onto the floor. We immediately went back downstairs, and I was so shaken, I almost quit right then and there. To make matters worse, when we walked back into my classroom, one of the easels was standing in the middle of the room. I know it had been bare when I left, but now it had a painting on it. A black, human-like creature with white eyes and very long arms and legs. Jody pointed at it and said, 'Look, Miss Brenna. That was in the closet with you.'" She looked at us with worried eyes. "I never found who painted it, but I assume it was Elliot or Shawna. Anyway, I tore up the painting and lit it on fire. I never wanted to see it again. And I haven't seen it—the bad thing—since."

While I felt almost immobile from the fear, Dex said to Brenna, "Are you sure you want to take us upstairs then?"

She nodded. "I can't live in fear. The fear makes me sick, you know. I'm often getting terrible migraines or stomach aches. When I spend the day at home, even if I'm in the worst pain, I feel at peace. I feel safe."

I frowned. "Maybe this isn't a good idea."

She straightened up and put on a brave face. "No sense in hiding. Besides, if you guys are there, and you're more, um, ghost-friendly than I am, I don't think they'll be as interested in me."

She was probably right about that. If the bad thing or Shawna were to show up again, they'd be bee-lining it straight for me, Perry Palomino, ghost magnet. I was like the highly sought after call girl of the supernatural. A whore for the unhappily deceased.

With that, the four of us gathered our wits and left the room. As we approached the stairway, Dex pulled me aside.

"Baby, talk to me," he said gruffly. His brows were stuck in a permanent frown.

I looked at him as if he were nuts. "Later. We have work to do. This is our last show, remember?"

"This isn't fair."

"No, Dex," I hissed at him. "*This* isn't fair. You've had all morning to talk to me and you're choosing right now, as we're taking that poor woman upstairs to go look for the ghosties that traumatized her? What is with your shitty timing?"

"I don't know!" he exclaimed, then recovered once he realized that Rebecca and Brenna were both waiting for us and staring at us, totally unimpressed. "We'll talk later."

I rolled my eyes and followed them up the stairs. It wasn't as if I wanted to hold a grudge over him and Rebecca, but knowing me and my insecurities, coming to terms with it all was going to take time, and at the moment, all I could think about was the fact that we were heading up the stairs to our potential demise.

Or at least *my* potential demise. And no, I didn't think I was being overdramatic, considering what a dead child had said to me last night, that I had what she "needed."

I suppressed a shudder and continued on up the staircase. Luckily, none of us had any intentions of exploring the upper floors. The wind was blowing harder now, rattling the window panes and whistling through the gaps and parts of the ceiling that had started to leak with rainwater.

"Looks like we should just stick to this floor," Dex said, much to everyone's relief.

Just as we did before, we headed down the hall toward the room where we had seen Shawna's picture hanging—and near the room where she had been with the bad thing. We were silent as we walked, listening for anything out of the ordinary. It was amazing how quiet that floor could be considering there was an active school downstairs.

When we approached the room with the desk, we were all suddenly overcome by a nauseating stench. I knew what death smelled like, and that was it.

"My god," Rebecca said, covering her nose. "That smells wretched."

We peered around the corner and saw something that immediately made me want to vomit.

The entire floor of the room, as well as the desk, was piled with the carcasses of hundreds of dead rats, festering with crawling maggots and flies.

"Fuck me," I cried out as we all staggered backward from the disgusting sight. I looked over to

Brenna who was turning a shade of green. "Do you normally have rat problems here?"

She shook her head, her eyes watering, and walked a few more feet away so we were out of the range of stench. "We have some, I guess, because the building was abandoned for so long, but not like this."

"This isn't a job for the Orkin Man," Dex commented, still breathing into the sleeve of his jacket while filming us at the same time. "This is a warning of some sort."

As if we hadn't had enough warnings already. If this was how we were starting out our expedition, I didn't want to know how much worse it was going to get.

He looked at us all. "Shall we continue?"

We all nodded begrudgingly and followed Dex further down the hall as the wind swept in through the open windows. We went all the way down to the end where it veered off into a wing with rotted doorways and a lot of water damage.

"Look," Brenna breathed out. She pointed in front of her where an orange rubber ball was rolling toward us. It slowly came to a stop just a few feet away.

"Elliot?" she asked, her head cocked like she was listening, trying to hear through the creaking building and the howling storm outside. We all did the same until I realized there was a piece of equipment we hadn't used yet.

"You guys," I said, "I'm going down to the room to grab the EVP recorder." Normally we brought the recorder out when we were filming the show and Rebecca usually handled it, but I guess since everything had been up in our faces since the moment we stepped in the building, it kind of slipped our minds. But for communicating with Elliot and possibly other ghosts, it could come in handy. It was amazing the sounds and voices the device sometimes picked up.

Dex frowned while Rebecca said, "Be careful."

She didn't have to tell me twice.

CHAPTER FOURTEEN

I wasn't planning on casually strolling down the second floor to get the EVP recorder, anyway. I was going to get in and get out as fast as I could. Ignoring the warning look in Dex's eyes, I turned and booked it down the hallway, not looking into any of the rooms—especially the room of dead rats—nor looking ahead of me in case there was something I didn't want to see. I ran watching my feet, and as soon as I hit the stairs, I vaulted down them. Once I reached the school's floor, I relaxed and walked quickly over to the nurses' room without drawing attention to myself from the passing schoolteachers.

I knocked just in case Kelly was in there with a patient. When I didn't hear anything, I opened the door and peered in. She wasn't in her office, so I walked through all the way to our room. Now I had to remember where the EVP recorder actually was. I went through my bag first then brought out the one that housed the camera equipment.

"Hey."

I nearly jumped out of my skin and flung myself around to see Dex coming through the door to Kelly's office. He gently closed it behind him, then came in the room and closed that door too.

"What are you doing here?" I asked. "I was going to come right back."

"I need to speak to you," he said, his voice grave and rough. He walked over to me, standing a foot away. "You need to talk to me."

"I need to talk to you?"

"Damn it, Perry," he growled, reaching out to grab my arm, holding it tightly. "You can't ignore me forever."

My mouth flapped open. "I'm not ignoring you."

"Bullshit. *Bullshit.*" He pulled me closer to him. "So stop it. And talk."

I'd never seen him so distraught, so volatile before.

His eyes narrowed for a second as he observed me closely. Then he straightened up and said, "Fine. I'll talk. Look, Perry, I don't know what to say other than I'm sorry. But I don't think I should be punished for something that happened in the past, something that happened before I ever met you."

I looked away, feeling the bubble of disgust rise up in me. "I'm not punishing you. But how the hell do you think it makes me feel to learn that?"

"And that's why I never wanted to tell you!"

I put my hands on my hips and backed away from him, trying to reclaim my personal space. "By not telling me it looked like you had something to hide."

He grunted, shaking his head. "There was nothing to hide. Nothing. Don't you get it?"

"Sex isn't nothing."

He stroked roughly at his jaw. "Yeah, well sometimes to me, it is."

"Nice."

"Well, it's the fucking truth. Do you want to know how it all started?"

"Uh, no."

"I thought she was hot, okay?"

I grimaced, feeling stabs of pain in my gut. "I said I didn't want to know."

"She was hot," he went on while my eyes widened incredulously. "And I'd just started the show and I was nervous. And she was upset over a breakup, and at the time I had no idea she was a lesbian. She just seemed like a flirt."

I stuck my fingers in my ears. "La, la, la, la, la, can't hear you!"

He pulled my fingers out, his grip hot and hard around my wrists. "Listen to me. We got drunk and it just happened. It wasn't very good. It was awkward and I couldn't figure out why. I couldn't even come."

I shut my eyes. "Dear god, I am going to murder you in your sleep if you don't shut the fuck up."

"And," he continued, "the next day she fessed up and said she was a lesbian and that she was sorry for leading me on. And I told her it was fine, because honestly, even if she didn't turn out to be gay, I wouldn't have fucked her again. There was something missing from the start. So we obviously just decided to be friends and that was that. We never think about it, we never talk about it, because it was just that stupid funny thing that we once did. She's like my sister, Perry, you know that."

I glared at him. "A sister that you make all these inappropriate comments about. God, Dex, now I'm thinking back to all the times you talked about the three of us having a threesome."

"Baby, you can't possibly think I'm serious when I say that. That's why I say it. It would never happen, and it should never happen, so it's just funny. It's harmless. If it wasn't harmless, I wouldn't dare joke about it."

I glared at him, still unhappy. I tried to get out of his grasp but he held me firmly in place, his eyes blazing deep into me. "You should have told me," I said.

"When?" he cried out. "When should I have told you? It has no bearing on our relationship, and it's, frankly, none of your business."

I bristled at that. "You're an ass," I seethed.

"I know," he growled back. "You keep telling me. But even an ass deserves the benefit of the doubt from time to time. When would I have told you? Huh? When I first introduced you to Rebecca? Oh, this is my friend Rebecca. You should be friends with her. By the way, we once had terrible sex together. Or later on, maybe, when we started going out and she joined the show. Hey, now that we're working as a threesome, here's some interesting information that will make our jobs awkward as hell." He finally let go of my hands with an exasperated sigh. "No, I don't think so."

Now that I was free, I turned away from him and walked over to the opposite wall, trying to get space and think. I know what Dex was saying and he made a lot of sense. I didn't want to punish him over something he did prior to meeting me and I understood why he never told me. It didn't mean I had to like it though. And it wasn't the real reason why I was so upset. In the end, I didn't think it had a lot to do with feelings of insecurity or betrayal. It was that I didn't know this piece of information about Dex. And how could I expect to know everything when we've only been together for eight months? How well did we really know each other?

"Are you done being mad yet?" he asked.

I almost was, but then his callous words made me snap my head around and send him daggers with my eyes. "Hey, give me a fucking break, okay? Why don't you put yourself in my fucking shoes for once?"

He shook his head, his eyes burning, and stormed over to me until he was right up against me and my back was pressed against the wall. He put his hands at my hips, holding them tight, and leaned in so his face was just inches away. I could smell his sweet breath, count the gold flecks in his brown eyes, see the enviable length of his dark lashes. It was probably a bad time to have the thought, but sometimes there was nothing sexier than Dex when he was angry.

"Baby," he murmured roughly, staring at me fixedly with half-closed eyes, "I try and put myself in your damn shoes every single day. Because you're my girl. You're my woman. You're my partner. You're my lover. And if I can't try and fucking understand you and that complex, crazy head of yours, then I'm not doing my job. Then I'm not worthy of you. I want to be worthy of you, baby. I want to know how you work, how you function, how you think. I want to know you so I can be there for you and be there with you. There's not a day that I'm not trying to discover another one of your beautiful layers. So don't say that I'm not in your shoes. I've been wearing them more than you think."

Oh god. His words rendered me speechless and sent my heart into a tailspin. I could only stare back at him, my resolve melting into his warm hands.

"And I'm sorry," he went on, licking his lips, still gazing at me seductively, "if I didn't tell you about me and Rebecca. I wasn't trying to hurt you—I wasn't trying to do anything. All I think about is you, Perry. From the moment I wake up to the moment I go to sleep, and even in my dreams. I don't think about my past anymore. I only think about my future. And you're my fucking future."

Wow.

"You jerk," I blurted out breathlessly. "I love you."

He grinned at me as his eyes slid over to my lips. "That's all I needed to hear."

Then he kissed me. Hard.

Hard enough that the back of my head banged against the wall and I let out a cry of surprise that was buried by the intensity of his moan. His tongue was feverish, relentlessly fucking the inside of my mouth, his lips soft and violent. I closed my eyes, immediately succumbing to the delicious feeling of him wanting me, of his obvious desire, of his brute strength and masculinity.

My hands went for his jacket, helping him shrug it off while he pulled my sweater and t-shirt over my head. He put his mouth to my neck, biting me sharply, his hands going to my bra and unclasping it from behind. I moaned as he licked the sore flesh of my neck with his tongue then continued licking up to my ear. As soon as his lips enveloped my earlobe, his heavy, lustful breathing making my skull buzz, I was as wet as sin and famished, desperate for him to be inside me. As if knowing this, his fingers swiftly unzipped my jeans and thrust themselves inside me—one, then two, then three at a time.

"Fuck you're so wet," he grunted, his mouth covering mine again. "I've never wanted you so badly."

"You can fucking have me," I managed to say before I was overcome by his tongue again. He pushed his fingers further inside, making a motion that rubbed hard against my G-spot. I cried out, insane with pleasure, but still needing more. "Deeper," I told him breathlessly. "Harder."

"I'll give you harder," he said. I heard the unbuckling of his pants, and the stiff, solid length of his cock against my thigh. He pulled off the rest of my jeans, then grabbed the backs of my thighs and pulled me up. I wrapped my legs around his waist and he pressed me hard against the wall, the tip of his dick finding purchase within seconds, as if it was second nature. He pushed himself into me slowly and I widened for him, taking him in as deep as he could go without it being painful. I never felt better than when he was inside me, filling me up, making me feel whole.

He brought his head down to my breasts, biting and sucking them as he started thrusting deeper inside of me, his pace quickening.

"Harder," I groaned.

He hissed in a breath through his teeth and I looked into his eyes, almost startled by their madness and intensity, the pure hunger that was rolling through him. He drove himself deep inside until I gasped and then he kept hammering me, one thrust after another until my head was banging against the wall, the pain a complete turn on. He'd never wanted me so badly and I'd never been so fucking horny.

Pretty soon I was coming just from the feel of his cock inside me, of the crazed frenzy of our fucking.

But Dex had stamina. After my moans quieted down and I stopped clenching him from inside, he grabbed me around the waist and spun me around with a powerful cry. He slammed me down onto the counter, a bunch of medical textbooks and boxes of latex gloves clattering to the floor. The rest of the books and other items poked into my back as he tried to lay me flat, still pounding me with the same wild intensity. He looked like a man possessed by lust, and I had the perfect view of him, from his intense eyes and sexual sneer to his wide shoulders and hard, sculpted chest with those infamous words *And With Madness Comes the Light*. I loved the sight of his large, strong arms and skilled hands as they gripped the softness of my hips, the muscles in his forearms tensing as he ground in and out of me. His bronzed six-pack was taut with his movement and I knew his ass cheeks were flexing as he worked.

He smirked at me, the cocky bastard knowing I was gaping at him. He put his thumb onto my clit, and the slick pressure had me coming again. I yelled out his name, taken by shock with this orgasm, my eyes not leaving his as he kept my heady spasms rolling through me. I was flying fucking high, delirious and possibly insane, and yet he still drove deep inside me and I still wanted more.

"You're being a little greedy," he grunted as he stared down at me, his lips parted, chest heaving from the strain.

"You're being a little generous," I lazily said back to him. "Are you afraid of coming?"

"Baby, I could go all night."

"You know we can't. Let me finish you off." I tried to push back with my elbows so I could sit up and suck him off, but he just growled at me, wrapping his hands tight around the small of my waist.

"Oh, you will," he stated huskily. He pulled me off the counter and placed me down on his bed before immediately flipping me over and pulling my ass high in the air. "Just fucking perfect," he murmured as his lips and tongue trailed over the soft mounds, taking his time to try and lick me to death. I groaned, about to lose my mind as I felt the pressure inside me building up again.

He pulled his head away, and while stroking me softly with one finger, pushed himself inside me again. His grip on my hips tightened. "Sweet Jesus, you're so fucking beautiful," he whispered, his breath hitching. I could feel his eyes scanning over my bare body. "So beautiful. I'm so damn lucky, baby. You have no idea." His began to pick up the pace, both his thrusts and his finger becoming quicker. "I'm going to come now. Oh god, I just want to come."

"Then come," I growled at him. He started banging me harder, the bed moving back and forth, his balls slapping against my ass. The swirl of his fingers tightened, the pressure increasing, until once again I was reaching the brink. The result was explosive, violent. I came harder than ever—an out of body experience—before plunging deep into a wave that drowned me in pleasure. I cried out his name, expletives, and then I was just crying, a few tears leaking out while I tried to comprehend the feelings rushing though me and knocking me off my feet.

Dex came at the same time, his fingers digging sharply into my hips, holding on as if he'd lose me otherwise. He grunted loudly, gasping for air, letting loose the pressure inside as he pounded the last of himself into me.

I fell forward, flattening against the bed in exhaustion, and a spent, naked Dex tried to spoon me on the single bed, wrapping his arms around me, his ragged breaths at my ear.

"I love you," he whispered between exhales. "More than you know."

"I love you," I told him back, meaning every word.

And then the room went black.

As in, the lights just went out.

"The fuck?" Dex asked.

I tried to sit up without edging Dex off the bed. We had been plunged into darkness.

"Did the power go out?" he asked.

"I don't know," I said quietly. "But I'd really appreciate it if you kept your arms around me."

"Don't worry, kiddo," he assured me. "It's probably just the storm. It will come back on."

"You do realize where we are, right?"

I felt him smile against my cheek. "I do. A haunted school. And look who said she could only come in this place if I had two dicks. Well, guess what, baby. You came three times on just one cock. You should never underestimate my penis again."

"Believe me, I won't," I said. While it was obvious the power was out, we also weren't alone in the school. I could hear people in the halls walking, chattering loudly, their voices high and anxious. Through the frosted glass of the door to the nurse's office I could see a scarce amount of light shining in, just a dull glow.

"You'd think their generator would be coming on," I said to him, picking up on the anxiety of the staff and students in the halls.

Suddenly we heard the door to the office open and saw the moving beam of a flashlight. A wide silhouette paused outside our door.

“Hello?” Davenport’s shrill voice shot through us. “Anyone in there?”

Shit.

“Just a minute!” I yelped. Dex and I both tried to get off the bed at the same time, resulting in both of us tumbling to the floor. I landed half on his back and half on my side. “Fucker!”

I scrambled to my feet, trying to figure out where my clothes were. They were clear across the room with Dex’s clothes. No way we could find them in the dark without injuring ourselves.

“Kiddo,” Dex said, and suddenly I was enveloped with a blanket. “Cover up.” I felt him stand behind me, holding my shoulders. “Come on in!” he yelled.

The door opened and I automatically winced from the flashlight Davenport was holding in her hands and aiming right at us. Her mouth dropped open before she quickly snapped it shut and gave us an unimpressed once-over.

“I came to tell you that the power in the school is out,” she said. ”You may or may not have noticed.”

“We noticed,” I said, holding the blanket tighter around my boobs, hoping that naked Dex was well hidden behind me. Thank god for my wide hips.

Just then, Rebecca came inside, holding the camera and our own light.

"Oh," she cried out softly when she saw us. She raised her thin brow. "I see."

Just claiming back my man, I thought, which was totally petty. But whatever, I was still pretty miffed at her for telling me about her and Dex the way she did.

Davenport shook her head and clucked her tongue. "At any rate, I'm glad you three are here. The power has gone out because of the storm. We're sending everyone home. We do have a generator here, but it's not enough to power everything we need. Carl can keep it running for you, but it would just be in the cafeteria so the food doesn't spoil. You'd have to move yourselves down there—keep in mind I don't want anyone sleeping in the kitchen. That's unhygienic."

The cafeteria was one of the few places on this floor we hadn't really been in; we just had a little look when Kelly was taking us around. It also wasn't a place I felt like holing up in. Though it wasn't a big space, there was something extremely unsettling about empty cafeterias and kitchens at night. I think I developed a healthy fear of them after Jurassic Park.

"Well," Dex said slowly, "what do you think?"

"I find it hard to talk to you when you're naked, Dex," Rebecca said.

I kept my mouth shut, biting my lip hard. I looked over at Davenport. "Will Carl be staying to clean up?"

"No," she said with that patented brand of disdain. "He's being sent home as well, which is why I need to know now what your plans are. The generator will be going on for the fridges and freezers but he needs to know if it will go to the heat and lights in the cafeteria as well."

I looked over my shoulder and up at Dex. "It's up to you."

I didn't quite feel like staying in that place with the power all out, and I definitely didn't like the idea of the cafeteria. But it was our last show and it was our last night. No doubt we could stay at a motel tonight and come back tomorrow to film, but I knew once I was out of here, I wasn't coming back.

He nodded as if he understood what I was thinking. He looked to Rebecca. "How about it? Give it a shot?"

You could see she was less than thrilled as well and probably not for the paranormal reasons. Dex and I had very obviously made up, but things between her and me and her and Dex were still strained, leading to one awkward night.

Still, she was a trooper. Either that or terribly stubborn. Probably both. She smiled tightly. "I'm game if you are."

Davenport made an unimpressed noise. "Suit yourself." She walked over to the counter where we had made a mess and put down her flashlight. "You might need this to find your pants, Mr. Foray." She pivoted on her heel and left the room.

"I'll give you a moment," Rebecca said as she followed Davenport out into the hall. I shut the door then propped the flashlight up so it lit the room, putting my jeans and my Master of Puppets sweatshirt back on while Dex quickly slipped on his clothes.

"So how are you feeling about this?" he asked as he slipped into his jacket.

"About the hot sex?" I asked as I gathered my hair back into a ponytail.

He smiled. "About staying the night. You sure that's what you want?"

I nodded and rubbed my lips together. "Yeah. But I mean, if one thing goes wrong, I'm leaving and I'm not coming back. We're done here. Once I set foot outside, I never want to return to this place ever again."

"Right with ya, baby. And you won't ever have to do this show again."

My face fell slightly. I couldn't help it. "You know, I will miss it."

"So will I," he said, coming over to me and wrapping me into his arms. "But you're the best part of it. As long as I have you, I don't care what I'm doing."

"Same." I pulled away and looked at him carefully. "Except amateur porn."

"Aww," he said. "You're killing all my dreams here."

I punched him in the chest then quickly kissed him. "We should go see the ruckus."

We gathered up the flashlight and went out into the hall. There were only a handful of teachers loitering in the marble-tiled foyer and a few kids holding hands and being led by a teacher out onto the front lawn. Brenna was there on the front steps, typing something into her phone, Jody hanging by her side, while the wind blew violently, shaking the pine trees. Once Jody spotted us, her eyes lit up and she ran back inside.

"The power went out!" Jody exclaimed.

"We know," I said. "Were you scared?"

She shook her head. "Nah. It's just nature."

"Hey," Brenna said as she came over. "I just talked to Rebecca," she said, motioning that Rebecca was somewhere out in the parking lot. "She said you guys are actually staying the night."

"Squatting in the cafeteria," Dex told her. "At least we will have an endless supply of those really tiny ice cream cups. The ones with the tiny wooden spoon." He made the spoon motion with his hand.

"Nice try," Brenna said gleefully. "Our school has a gluten-free, non-dairy menu. Hope you like frozen soy milk."

He made a face. "Soy milk. Ugh. Tastes like jizz."

I gave him a curious look. "And how do you know that?"

"I have bad aim sometimes," he said. He looked back to Brenna and smiled lightly. "We might be gone by morning so we just wanted to say good luck and thank you for showing us around."

Brenna was still blushing red at Dex's bad aim comment but she smiled. "Thank you. And good luck to both of you. I'm sorry I couldn't be as much help as I wanted. When Rebecca and I figured you weren't coming back, the only thing we captured was the rubber ball moving slightly, but I think it was the wind. That's what she thinks anyway. Sorry the tour was a dud."

"Don't worry about it," I said, and thanked her. She gave us a wave and headed out the door, holding out her hand for Jody. "Come on, Jody."

Jody looked back at Dex and I. "Bye." Then she looked at Dex and raised her little arms for a hug. Dex crouched down, smiling broad enough that his dimples stuck out, and let Jody put her arms around him.

God damn it if my uterus didn't swoon. I'm sorry, but I needed to have that man's babies.

Then as Jody pulled away, I could have sworn she whispered something in Dex's ear, enough to make him frown momentarily. Then she grinned up at me and waved. "Bye, Perry. Bye, Elliot!" I followed her gaze which shifted to a spot behind me. Elliot was standing at the foot of the stairs, hat in hand, staring at us meekly. "Take care of them," Jody added before she turned and skipped away, joining Brenna.

Brenna gave us a wary look to say that she had seen Elliot too, then she turned and they both disappeared out into the storm.

I looked back behind me at Elliot, but he was gone.

"Did you see him?" I asked Dex.

He nodded. "Yep."

"What did Jody say to you?"

"Just now?"

"Yeah."

His expression became darker. "She said watch out for the ones that look like you."

"What?"

A teacher walked past us and both Dex and I smiled politely and moved ourselves away from the front door. He leaned into me, lowering his voice. "I think she might mean doppelgängers, even though she doesn't really know what they are."

"Doppelgängers?" I whispered back. "Why would there be doppelgängers here?"

He shrugged, eyes still dark. "Why not? This is a genuine house of horror, Perry. There are ghost kids and demons and who knows what else. Doppelgängers make sense. This amount of sadness and death and pain is going to bring in a lot of very bad things."

"I think I saw one last night," I admitted.

He shot me a sharp look. "When? Who?"

"When I left the break room and came back to you guys. I saw Rebecca in the hallway, heading to the bathroom. She even turned and looked at me. But when I got in the room, I saw Rebecca in bed."

"Are you sure it was the real Rebecca in bed?" he asked.

I shrugged. "I don't know. I didn't think you could interact with doppelgängers. You just see them."

"Did she talk to you? The one in bed?"

"Yes. She said she was sorry. You were awake. Didn't you hear her?"

"Yeah." He scratched his head. "She was probably legit."

I almost laughed at how blasé he sounded. "How else can you tell though?"

"I have no idea," he said. "I suppose the doppelgänger wouldn't know the real you, wouldn't know your thoughts. They're an imposter as much as they're a double. Funny that it took us this long to encounter one, don't you think?"

"Better never than late," I said just as Rebecca came back in the building, her normally coiffed hair in a mess around her face, the camera light in her hand.

"Stormy," Dex commented, pointing out the obvious.

Woo boy. The awkward evening had already begun.

Rebecca pushed her hair away from her eyes. "It's a real ripper. Maybe we should start moving everything into the cafeteria now. In fact, perhaps we should start filming as soon as possible. It's still light outside, which means there's at least some light coming in through all the windows. It'll be easier to see that way."

And less scary, I added to myself. With the last of the staff heading out of the building and into the storm, we headed down the hall to move our belongings and prepare for one last night.

CHAPTER FIFTEEN

Our new headquarters were just as creepy as I imagined. Seriously, school cafeterias are unsettling in the daytime when students are beating each other up under bad fluorescent lighting, and disgruntled lunch ladies are throwing down sloppy joes. Although in this school it was apparently wild salmon filets with quinoa. Whatever. Give me sloppy joes any day.

We picked three tables near the far end of the cafeteria, ensuring we had a full view of the door in case anyone (or anything) came in. Of course, there were the windows just above us that were enduring the wrath of the wind, rain, and flying pine needles, and I knew that if anything *really* wanted us in here, it would get us. But it was the little things that made you feel safe, even if you weren't.

Once we got everything sorted and Dex passed around the last of the bottle of Jack Daniels—no shock as to why Rebecca wasn't partaking—we took our pre-EIT shots for the last time. If I wasn't so damn freaked out, I would have shed a tear.

"Raise your cup and let's propose a toast." He sang a line from one of our favorite *Faith No More* songs.

I raised my plastic cup. "To the thing that hurts you most. To the paranormal and to never being normal."

He winked at me. "To us."

Then we gathered up the equipment and set off on our last shoot. Though the late afternoon light was coming in through the windows, there was a sense of urgency and dread with every step we took. It didn't help that we were starting with the fourth floor.

The worst floor.

The floor where they used to have a gate to keep out the terminally and mentally ill.

I understood why Dex and Rebecca thought it was a good idea to go up there. In the dim light of day, it was easier to stomach. Daylight had this way of making things less scary, though we all knew that monsters didn't care what time of day it was. I was all too aware of that.

We didn't need to use the flashlights much, which was a relief, since the windows that lined the staircase and the ones on the floors were letting in just enough gray light. I was nervous and on edge as we climbed the stairs, passing the second floor and the third until we rounded the corner where Gary Oldman had stopped. Everything after that was unknown territory for me.

I took in a deep breath and walked in front of Dex and Rebecca. Even though they were the last two to visit the floor, there was no sign they had ever been up there. The shattered windows had blown away the dust and covered the floor with pine needles and leaves. Up here, it was about ten degrees colder, and the difference hit you like a sledgehammer.

"Was it this fucking cold when you were up here earlier?" I asked, the air hurting my lungs, my breath frozen in a cloud.

Dex shook his head. "No, not at all." His teeth started chattering. "You know what, you ladies hold tight and I'll be right back." He thrust the camera into my hands and started running down the stairs.

"Dex!" I yelled after him. "Where the hell are you going?"

“Getting you guys your jackets,” he yelled back as he rounded the landing on the third floor.

I looked over at Rebecca, expecting her to say she was fine. Instead, she was slightly hunched over, holding her arms close to her, her face like ivory snow.

“Are you okay?” I asked her.

She swallowed hard and nodded. “I’m fine. I’m just cold too.” The she straightened up and walked down the hall, peering into the rooms, illuminating them with her light.

“What are you doing?” I asked, following her.

“Taking another look,” she said, her eyes darting from doorway to doorway as she walked. “When I was up here earlier I thought I saw something in one of the rooms.”

Of course only someone who never saw a ghost in her life—only weird lights, abnormal sounds, and strange music—would be brave enough to investigate this.

“What was it?’ I asked, keeping right behind her.

“A painting or a drawing on the wall,” she said. She aimed the light into one of the rooms and said, “Ah hah.” She went in and stood by the missing door, and I watched her as she ran her fingers over the wall. She was right, there was something. It looked like a mess of black and red, like someone was painting with charcoal and blood. Given the fact that the floor was where a lot of the mental patients were, I wouldn't have been surprised.

"What does it say?" I asked, not wanting to get any closer.

"Help me," she said grimly. "Help me, they're going to kill me." Her words put a block of ice in my chest. She slowly turned to look at me. "Who are *they*?"

I took a step into the room. "I think they are the nurses."

She straightened up. "How do you know that?"

"Because," I said, looking down at my sneakers, "last night, when I was sleeping in the break room, I saw Shawna again. She told me that she was killed, that though she had TB, she didn't even have a chance to die from it. She said that many were thrown into the incinerator or smothered with pillows to make room."

I could feel her eyes on me, deciding if I was telling the truth, if I were crazy or not. I finally looked up and saw in the weak light that she was wiping away a tear. "I'm sorry," she said with a sniff. It took me a moment to understand what she was apologizing for. "I'm sorry for telling you the way I did. I'm sorry for not taking your feelings into consideration…"

My grudge evaporated on impact. "Rebecca," I started.

“No, Perry, let me say this,” she said. “Please. I’m angry, alright? I was angry before I even got here. And then when I got here, I started feeling sick. Started feeling like this was real, I was actually bloody pregnant. Then I got scared and I got angry all over again. Because there you and Dex go, deciding you aren’t doing the show anymore. You’ve made me jobless.”

I felt like she punched me in the gut. “I’m sorry. It’s not that we weren’t thinking of you…”

“I know,” she said quickly, her eyes flashing, her liner spilled under her eyes in dark pools. “I know. You and Dex are the show, you are each other’s show, and what you say goes. I know that. I also know I wouldn’t have a job if it weren’t for you. But there you are, in love with each other, about to start a new chapter of your life together, and here I am. I’m pregnant. Joblesss. Alone. I’m bloody alone, Perry.” She started to sob but caught herself quickly. “I am so scared. So, so scared. I’m so good at so many things, so good at pretending. And yet I can’t deal with this imperfection. I am so fucking scared!” she sobbed.

I forgot my fears and immediately went across the room to hug her. I took her in my arms and held her tight as she sobbed into my shoulder. “It’s okay,” I whispered into her hair. “We’re here for you, you know that. You aren’t alone.”

"I feel alone," she whimpered, "and that's the scariest feeling of all."

"You aren't alone," I reassured her. "And I'm not even talking about Dex and I. You're keeping the baby...I can tell."

She pulled away and looked up at me with glassy eyes. "Yes. I want to. It was the thing that drove me and Emily apart, but god, that's all I wanted." She looked down. "I just wish it was with her."

"I know you do," I said, holding her tight. "But we have to deal with what we have. This is a blessing, you know that. A challenge, but in the end, it's a good thing. Maybe the best."

"Do you ever want kids?" she asked.

I found myself nodding. "Yes. As funny as it seems, I think Dex would make a great dad."

She smiled. "I think so too. I am happy for you, really I am. I'm just..."

"Scared?" I asked. "You're allowed to be scared. We all are. And I don't mean with ghosts. I mean with life."

She smiled gently and put her head on my arm. That's when I bit the bullet and asked, "So, who is the baby daddy?"

She stiffened against me before finally looking up. "Promise you won't tell Dex?"

"No," I said. "I tell him everything."

She managed a small smile. “Then…just don’t tell him until I do.”

“I promise.” I held out my pinky finger and she hooked it with hers.

She took in a deep breath and let it out through her nose. “All right. It’s…Dean.”

I’m not sure why my first instinct was to laugh, maybe because Dean was so totally not the person I was expecting. And it had nothing to do with the fact that Dean was black and Rebecca looked like Snow White. It was that Dean was Dex and Rebecca’s friend, not a lesbian and so totally not Rebecca’s type, even when you ignore the non-lesbian thing. Dean was a fucking awesome guy but he seemed really chill whereas Rebecca was well-manicured and slightly up-tight.

“What. The. Fuck,” I said slowly, examining her face as if she were lying to me. “Dean?”

Rebecca nodded, wiping her lips with the back of her hand. “Yeah. Dean.”

“Does he know?”

She shook her head and then looked at me with big eyes. “Please don’t tell him.”

I assured her I wouldn’t tell. It really was none of my business.

I sighed and told her, “Rebecca, whatever you and Dex did, it’s in the past. It’s a lot for me to handle but...I'm not mad. Let's just forget about it and move on."

"Are you sure? I never wanted to hurt you, Perry. I'm sorry."

"I know," I told her. I let go and straightened up, looking around the dimly lit room. "Weird how Dex isn't back yet."

She nodded and got up. We walked back into the hallway, looking up and down, but didn't see anything unusual.

"Maybe he's in the loo," Rebecca offered with a shrug.

"Maybe," I said as we went back the way we came. Suddenly, every single hair on my body was prickling. This wasn't good. This was very, very bad.

And whatever it was...was right behind us.

"Rebecca," I said carefully. "I know you're the wrong person to ask. But. If you look over my shoulder, do you see anything?"

I watched her as she craned her elegant neck around and looked past me down the hall.

A small, breathy sound escaped from her lips. Her eyes grew wider. Her mouth gaped open. The delicate muscles in her neck stood out as every section of her skin grew tighter.

She was seeing something.

Holy fuck.

Rebecca was seeing something. I knew that terror like a second skin.

I slowly turned my head and followed her terrified gaze.

Down the hall, lit faintly by the light that was spilling in the windows, was the *bad thing.*

It was upside down, crawling on the ceiling, long arms stretching out in front of it, and coming straight for us. The weird crackling, skittering sound filled my ears as its razor-lined mouth snapped open and shut.

Somehow, I managed to tear my eyes away and look at Rebecca. She was paralyzed by the fear. I pushed back on her shoulder and yelled, "Move! Run!" in her face.

It took her a few seconds—terribly long seconds—to realize what I was saying. Then she wasted no time at all. She whipped around, her dark hair flinging in my face, and together we started sprinting down the hall. We ran so fast, so desperate to get away that we ran past the staircase and were halfway down the next wing before we realized our mistake.

We both ducked into a room, trying desperately to catch our breaths, and I poked my head around the doorway.

The *bad thing* was no longer on the ceiling—I couldn't see it anywhere.

"I *think* it's gone," I told her, even though I had no idea how that could be. Like fear, it was never really gone, was it?

She cautiously stuck her head around the corner and looked to see for herself. She made a noise that I couldn't decide was agreeable or not.

"Wait, hold up," she cried out as I was about to turn away.

I looked back to see Dex running up the hallway at the other end, where we had been before, and start running down the stairs.

"Shit!" I cried out. "What the fuck is he running from?"

I pulled at Rebecca until she was running beside me, heading down the hall. We got to the stairs and I looked over the railing just in time to see him heading off on the third floor.

"Dex! Where the fuck are you going?" I yelled after him as I picked up speed and leaped down sets of stairs until I was on the third floor. I looked to my left and saw him running away, making a sharp left into a room.

I kept running while assuming that Rebecca was hot on my trail and ducked into the room that Dex disappeared into.

All it took was to see the faint metal glint of the operating light before I screeched to a halt.

Dex had led me into the room of blood.

And as the heavy door shut behind me, I realized that it hadn't been Dex that led me in there.

Oh shit.

I spun around, completely taken over by the dark, and ran forward until I smacked against the door. I felt for the handle, trying desperately to get it to turn, while pounding on the door with my fist and yelling for Dex and Rebecca.

The door wouldn't open. The thump of my fists died in the air.

I couldn't hear anything on the other side. No sign of the howling wind. No sign that someone was yelling to me, trying to assure me everything was going to be okay, trying to help me escape, to let me out of that room.

The room of blood.

I breathed in deeply, trying to keep my senses focused, my mind sharp, my heart rate under control. I wasn't going to cry. I wasn't going to succumb to the black room that nipped at my back. I was going to hold it together and find a way out.

I turned around and faced the void of the unknown.

"Hello," I cried out softly. "I'm here. Whatever you want with me, please, just show yourself."

I sucked air into my lungs and waited for a voice to set me free, for a shape to show itself.

Nothing happened.

Except there was a noise, in the far corner of the room. The slick, sharp sound of metal on metal. I thought back to when I was peering into the room the other day and I couldn't see anything in my mind's eye except the three operating tables in the middle of the room.

I also remembered Oldman saying that the body chute opened up somewhere in the room. It was a long shot, and a fucking terrifying one, but if I could get to the chute and somehow get in it, it was at least a way out.

I swallowed hard, willing my eyes to adjust to the dark, but with the room having no windows and receiving no light from the outside, nothing happened. Everything in front of my eyes was just black on black on black.

I stepped away from the door and walked forward, taking slow, careful steps, my hands straight out in front of me in case I ran into something.

I walked in as much of a straight line as possible, trying to pull the layout of the room from my memory. I wished I had paid more attention at the time, but the truth was, even with Dex and Rebecca and Oldman at my side, I had been scared as hell. I would have done anything to have them at my side again.

And then there had been Dex, running away from me, the Dex who was never him at all. His doppelgänger. I could only hope that neither the real Dex nor Rebecca would run into the doubles of themselves—apparently if you do, you're supposed to die.

And I hope I don't run into myself, I thought, trying to imagine how surreal that was. Of course, in some ways it had happened before. Back in Red Fox, the skinwalkers took the shape of me, trying to lure Dex in with a kiss. That was as fucking trippy as it could get, not to mention aggravating, since Dex's first kiss with me wasn't with *me*.

The thought of him though, the thought of New Mexico and how far we'd come since that episode, gave me a new kind of strength. I'd been through so much already. We'd both fought against death and won. Now it was the last shoot of our last episode, and all I needed was just to come out of it alive. Fuck having the best episode—I just wanted to keep living my life.

I walked forward, determined to make it out.

I didn't make it far.

I walked straight into something cold and hard. I gasped from the pain, having hit my hands at an odd angle, and immediately felt along the chilled, slick surface, hoping it was a wall.

It wasn't. It was the corner of the body cooler. I nearly walked myself right into the morgue. I shuddered, my heart racing, my legs threatening to give out on me. I had to keep going; I had to get out of there.

I walked more carefully now, feeling my way along the edge of the cooler, when I felt something banging against it from the inside, a dull metal thud. I shrieked, taking a step back, the blackness disorienting. There was someone inside the body coolers. For a second I thought it could have been Dex, for a second I thought maybe I should make my way back to the doors and fumble through the dark to open one of the drawers.

But all it took was to hear silence—silence punctuated by a click and the slow, metal groan of one of the body cooler doors opening by itself—to know it wasn't Dex in there.

I waited, frozen on the spot, until I heard a dull slap. The sound of bare feet hitting the ground.

Someone coming out of the body cooler.

Someone dead.

I turned, and in my panic I started to run. I ran away from the sound, but only made it a few feet until I collided with the wall, biting my tongue as my head banged against it.

The world swirled in colors behind my lids then the colors were erased by a dull red.

I opened my eyes to see a light in the room, to see everything coming into focus.

The big, eye-shaped light above the operating table was turned on.

Beneath it was one of the tables, the one with the narrow moat around the edge.

The moat was red with a shiny river of blood. The young body on the table was pale as ice, its chest carved open like a turkey, flaps of skin out to the sides.

Standing in the shadows, a few feet behind the table, was a doctor. His eyes were cold and lifeless, and focused on me, his mouth and nose covered by a blood splattered mask. In his bloody, gloved hands he held a dull scalpel.

I didn't know if I could scream, if I should scream. I just stared at the sight, my eyes darting between the lifeless, massacred body on the table and the sadistic doctor standing above it, that sharp scalpel wielded in his hands like a weapon.

I heard the creak of one of the body cooler doors opening again and my eyes slid over to it just in time to see a young, naked boy stepping out of it, his chest exposed, balloons stuck inside him, expanding and deflating with each and every breath. When my eyes finally saw the big picture, saw what was really there in the room, I let out a pitiful cry.

The wall opposite me by the door I'd come through was lined with children. They were all naked or half-dressed, all of them sliced open for me to see. Their hearts pumped slowly, their lungs wheezed, the blood spilled out of them and onto the floor, creating a stream of blood that was slowly flowing toward me, pulsing with each ragged breath they all took.

When I looked back at the doctor, he was gone. In his place was the *bad thing*, standing upright on two legs and hunched over the patient, his/her heart dripping from the bad thing's razor-toothed mouth. The patient on the bed, a girl, slowly turned her head to look at me. Her mouth moved.

"Help me."

But I had to help myself.

I had to.

If it was the last thing I did.

Somehow I broke free of the terror, looking away just as the bad thing's white eyes sought me across the room. Using the light of the operating lamp, I ran my hand down the wall as I scurried alongside it, desperately searching for the door of the body chute.

I was almost at the far corner when I saw a small handle. I put my hands around it and tried to pull it open with all of my strength just as I heard a clatter behind me. It was probably a mistake to turn around and see what it was. But I did. It was the bad thing crawling across the room toward me, the dead, carved open children following it and coming for me with dead eyes and snapping mouths.

If I let the fear take over, I would have died right there and then. No question. Fear wanted me prisoner, for my limbs and organs and mind to just give up and give in.

But I couldn't.

I wouldn't.

I jerked the door toward me and it opened, assaulting me with a heavy gust of stale air. Wasting no time, I jumped inside, a sloping concrete incline leading from the room into the tunnel and quickly pulled the door shut behind me. It was pitch black inside the tunnel but it didn't matter, I couldn't think about it. I started running down the smooth walkway of the chute, my feet echoing as I ran. I didn't get far before I saw the fuzzy grains of light appearing around me and heard the sound of the door opening. I paused and looked behind me.

The door to the room of blood was opening, light spilling inside the passage and the shape of the doctor stepping into the tunnel. He shut the door behind him.

Everything went black again.

I was sealed in the tunnel with him.

I sucked in my breath, surviving only on instincts now, and I ran. I ran as fast as I could, occasionally tripping down the steps that were alongside the path, or bumping into the cold walls. I kept running despite the fact I had no idea where I was in the chute, no way to get out, no light to see by. I kept running because I could hear the quick footsteps of the doctor coming after me, hear his coat flapping as he hurried.

He was Shawna's father. I knew that now. Was he trying to appease her, to make amends for supposedly failing her, by trying to take my lungs? Was he really the bad thing now, something that would feed off the hate and fear in me?

Either way, I couldn't get caught. I had to keep going. I had to keep running.

Eventually though, when I felt I'd been going forever, the sound in the tunnel changed. The footsteps behind me had dropped off and the sound of my own body, of my stride, of my breath, became dull, almost muffled. By the time I was trying to figure out where I was, if I'd possibly run as far as the post office, I ran straight into something hard.

I cried out, nearly falling over, more from surprise than from pain. What the hell was this? I stuck my hands out and ran it up and down the barrier.

It wasn't really a wall; it felt more like a bunch of wood planks nailed together.

I heard a noise behind me, a scraping sound, and I knew that this was far from over. The sound continued, coming closer, like nails dragging across a rough surface.

The bad thing crawling on the cement ceiling.

And I was stuck. Trapped. It couldn't end like this.

Suddenly, a pair of tiny, cold hands grabbed my wrists and yanked me forward.

I cried out again, only this time I heard something in response.

"You're so close, so close, Perry."

It was Elliot. He tried pulling me further in, my arms disappearing through some of the barrier, the rest of me pushed up against it. It took me a while to realize that the whole thing wasn't solid. It must have been the thing that Oldman had been talking about when that teen went missing and they had to block off the tunnel in some way.

"Keep trying," Elliot yelled.

It was then I noticed the air around me had grown grainy and grey with the gradual increase of light. I still couldn't make out anything, but I knew that I had to start prying the boards away, that freedom lay on the other side.

I was so close, as Elliot said.

I began grabbing every edge I could find, pulling the planks toward me until they either gave away with the flying clank of nails hitting the ground or snapped in two, and more dull light began to fill the tunnel. I kept at it, my fingers raw and bleeding, all too conscious of the malevolence that was quickly closing in on me.

Finally, with Elliot's hand yanking me forward, I found the small opening I had created and dragged my body through it, landing on the other side of the wooden wall in a heap. Elliot's hands were at my arms, trying to get me to my feet. By the time I got up, I saw him running into the distance, toward the grey light, his silhouette disappearing.

I ran after him, my lungs filling with fresher air with every step I took, the light overtaking my eyes with hope until finally I burst out of the tunnel and into a dirty, abandoned room covered with empty shelves and mounds of dust, the late afternoon light coming in through the intact windows that shuddered with each blast of wind. I'd never been so happy to see daylight before, never been so happy to be inside an abandoned building.

Knowing I still wasn't one hundred percent safe, I closed the heavy door to the tunnel behind me, marveling as it camouflaged into the wood stylings of the wall, then turned back around, looking for the door out and looking for Elliot.

But while I could see the door in the corner, looking rusted beyond repair, I couldn't see Elliot anywhere.

I took a few steps forward into the middle of the room. I had to get out of there. I had to go back to the school and see if Dex and Rebecca were alright. I had to do all of that. But while I was crossing over to the door, I nearly stepped down into a hole.

I stumbled back, catching myself just in time, and looked down. A few of the floorboards were pried up. Maybe it wouldn't have normally been of importance, except that Elliot's hat was lying beside them.

I crouched down and picked it up, turning it over in my hands. Then I peered down into the space in the floor.

There was a large mail sack sitting in there. I frowned and reached my hands inside, hoping nothing was in there ready to bite them off. I pulled out the burlap sack and started rifling through it.

Inside there was nothing but letters upon letters upon letters. Curiously, every single one of them had already been opened, some ripped in two, some neatly sliced along the top.

I picked up a letter in an orange envelope, closest to the top, and turned it over in my hands. It was written in the faded scrawl of a child's writing and addressed to Mrs. Valerie Wolfe in Seattle, Washington, from Elliot Wolfe.

I opened up the letter and pulled the paper out.

It wasn't very long and seemed to be written in an ink that had almost all but faded, but I could still make out the gist of it.

Dear mommy,

I hope I can visit you sooner now. The doctors here say they are closer to a cure. We can't speak about it but we all know. My friends Sam and Phillip died the other day. I think they were left outside in the cold here for too long. It gets really cold at night. Please send me some slippers and socks. Love Elliot.

I blinked a few times, reading it over and over. I put it aside and picked up another letter. This was also from Elliot, addressed to his mother.

Dear mommy,

Please come get me. I am very scared. I think that nurse Amy wants to kill me. I think she killed Susan. I don't want to be here anymore. Everyone is scared that Amy will come after them next. She didn't let me eat dinner for all of last week until I started crying. Please come get me and take me home. I love you. Elliot.

I swallowed hard and brought out another letter from the bag. This one said Mildred Wachman from Gold Beach, Oregon on the envelope but had no return address. Inside the letter though, it was obvious who it was from.

Dear Aunt Mildred,

I keep writing you every day but I still haven't gotten a response. You never call or write or visit and I'm so scared. After father died, I've had no one to turn to and no one to talk to. We are not allowed to talk about death at Sea Crest, and yet that's all I see, all day long. The nurses promise me that I'll be allowed to go free, but the other day one of them told me that I would need to be moved up to the fourth floor in order to make room. I don't want to go up there, that's where the children go to die. I don't want to die, in fact I feel better each day. Oh, please come see me Aunt Mildred and take me out of here. You're all I have left.

Love, Shawna.

I exhaled slowly, trying to wrap my head around it all. My heart was still galloping from the escape, my nerves still buzzing along on adrenaline. And yet, the crazy thing was that the minute I found the bag, the fear seemed to blow away from me, like the wind that was howling at the windows. All these letters were from children pleading to be taken away, that they were in danger and scared for their lives, letters that were never mailed.

And souls that were never found.

CHAPTER SIXTEEN

I just couldn't believe it. I sat cross-legged on the floor and rifled through the rest of the bag but it was all the same. So much loss in one place.

Suddenly the door to the body chute swung open, snapping me back to the danger, to the fear, and I screamed as I tried to get to my feet, nearly falling into the hole.

"Perry!" Dex cried out as he appeared in the doorway, looking down at me in amazement, flashlight in hand. "Are you hurt? Oh, thank fuck you're here," he said as he took a step toward me.

"Get back!" I screeched, trying to get to my feet. I put my hands out in front of me. "Stay away from me!"

He looked absolutely bewildered, sticking the flashlight into his jacket pocket, but I wasn't buying it.

"Baby, it's me."

I narrowed my eyes at him, my heart getting another workout. "Yeah, well I thought it was you earlier too."

"I ran into Rebecca," he said. "She's gathering up our stuff and meeting us down here. She told me what you guys saw. You saw my doppelgänger."

"How do I know *you're* not the doppelgänger?"

He cocked his head and frowned. "Because, baby, I'm me. And I'm yours. Ask me anything if you have to. Or fuck, let me tell you a few things."

"Stay away, I'm warning you."

"You know, you're awfully cute when you get all threatening and stuff."

"I mean it." And I did. I think.

"That doesn't mean I won't start flapping my mouth. I *know* you, Perry Palomino."

He took two steps forward, eyes never leaving my face, and I staggered backward only to hit my back against a counter. He raised his palms at me. "I can tell you that you hum Twinkle, Twinkle Little Star to yourself as you brush your teeth and I think it's completely adorable. I can tell you that when you eat, you like to get equal amounts of each different food on your fork with every single bite. Drives me fucking crazy. I can tell you—or show you—exactly how you like to be kissed, how you like to be touched, what I do to make you come in five seconds flat."

With his palms still up, he came forward another step. "I can tell you that I'm head over heels in love with you. That this..." He paused and breathed in deeply, his eyes glittering. "What we have, it consumes me. It devours me. And it scares me more than anything we have ever encountered, because if I ever lost you, if I ever had to live without you, I wouldn't be whole. You, Perry, have my heart. You are my heart."

My breath hitched as I was lost in his words, lost in his eyes as they looked deeper into me than ever before.

"Do you still need convincing?" he asked in a low, husky voice, taking another step forward.

I didn't. I knew this was Dex. My man, right in front of me. Still, I could never pass up the opportunity to hear him say these wonderful words, to hear him speak from his soul.

So I nodded. I needed more convincing.

His mouth ticked up into a smile. "Well then..."

He briefly closed his eyes, exhaled through his nose, and shook out his limbs. If I didn't know any better, I'd say he was nervous as hell.

Then he got down on one knee.

For a moment I was completely puzzled, like what the fuck is he doing, why is getting on his knees? My first thought was that it was something sexual and kinky. My second thought was that something was scary and wrong. After all, we were in an abandoned post office; the door to the body chute was still open, and a storm was raging outside.

My third thought was...*holy shit. Holy shit! Is he proposing to me?*

"I was waiting for the right time," he said, staring intently at me, his voice shaking slightly, "but you're right—I do have shitty fucking timing. So I might as well embrace that. And so, here it goes."

He reached out for my left hand, never taking his eyes off me.

I felt like I was about to black out.

This couldn't be happening.

This had to a dream. A beautiful, crazy, amazing dream.

I needed him to pinch me.

Instead he said, "When I first met you, I knew, somehow, that you were going to change my life. I just didn't know in what way. I didn't know that you'd make me love you. And most importantly, I didn't know that you'd make me love *me*. Baby, you make me see the good in myself and the good in everything on this damn earth. You chase my ghosts away, and..." He cleared his throat, and to my surprise, I saw his eyes were watering.

Oh fuck. Please don't cry, Dex, cuz I will fucking lose it.

He swallowed hard, blinking tears back. "And you bring me peace. I can't thank you enough for being in my life. And I want you there for the whole journey. Through everything—the good and the bad, the batshit crazy and the sane, the scary and the sexy. Especially the sexy. Just you and me, baby, until death do us part."

Somehow I found my voice. "Even though we've only known each other for eight months?" I asked quietly, afraid of his answer.

But he just smiled up at me. "Time has no bearing on the truth. And what we have, that's true as fucking anything." He gave my hand a squeeze and reached into his pocket.

I sucked in my breath, feeling all my emotions flood me at once, and watched as he took out a beautiful, sparkling ring, and held it poised at my finger. He gazed at me, and it was like I saw every moment we had with each other captured in his eyes.

"Perry Palomino, kiddo, baby—will you be my wife?"

I didn't even have to think about it.

"Yes!" I blurted out in a sob as the tears started coming. I put my hand to my mouth, trying to control myself, but it was useless. I was a goner. "Yes, I will be your wife."

A single tear rolled down his cheek, which he didn't wipe away. His face broke out into the most breathtaking smile I had ever seen, a smile of absolute pure joy, the same joy that I felt bursting out of me like hot butterflies. He slid the ring onto my finger and it sat there perfectly, like it was custom made for me, vintage-style with shimmering stones that sparkled like heaven.

"It was meant for you," he said, voice still choked up. "Just like you were meant for me. My future wife." He got to his feet and cupped my face in his hands. "My god, I'm going to do whatever I can to make you happy."

I smiled, sniffling back the tears. "You can start by pinching me. This doesn't feel real."

He grinned cheekily. "Oh, I'll show you how real this is." He kissed me passionately, just the way I loved to be kissed, and reached around to grope my ass. He snuck in a pinch, a wonderfully sharp pain. Yup. That hurt. And *this* was real.

I buried my head into his neck as he held me close to him, our bodies melding into each other, giving each other support and strength.

Holy fuck. Oh my god. Dex just asked me to marry him.

I was going to be Mrs. Declan Foray.

Me.

Oh my god, oh my god, oh my god.

"How you feeling?" he murmured, pulling away and gazing down at me. He wiped the tears away from under my eyes.

"I feel like I'm going to die from excitement," I said. "I feel like I want to tell the whole world we're getting married." I pulled him close to me and kissed him. "I feel like I want you to show me that thing where you can make me come in five seconds flat."

He groaned lustfully. "My fiancé is a wild one." He slid his hands under my shirt, feeling my skin. "Unfortunately, I do think we should probably get the hell out of here."

I nodded. I'd been so over the moon, so crazy overwhelmed about his proposal that I had completely forgotten where we were. Damn fucking reality. I pulled away and looked over at the body chute's door. "How did you find me anyway?"

He glanced at it over his shoulder. "Rebecca told me that you disappeared into the autopsy room. I figured if you were going to find a way out, you would go through the chute. I went through on the first floor and just kept walking, calling for you."

My chest tightened at the memory of the doctor, the sounds that the *bad thing* was making in the tunnel. "Did you see anything?"

He shook his head and tucked a strand of my wayward hair behind my ears. "No, nothing. Then I came across the little woodpile in there, and it looked like you might have wormed your way through it."

"And Rebecca is back at the school alone?"

"She should be here any minute. As soon as I found you, I said we were getting the fuck out of there." He glanced down at the mailbag near the hole in the floor. "What's that?"

"Something *very* interesting," I informed him. I went over to it and bent over to pick it up. My ring gleamed on my finger as I did so and I did a whoop of joy inside my head.

I was engaged!

Oh man, it was going to take a long time for me to get used to that.

I brought the mailbag up for him to see. "This whole bag is filled with letters written by patients, letters that never made it to their final destination. In every one of these, a child is telling their loved ones that they are scared for their lives, and that abuse is happening in the hospital. Obviously, whoever was working here at the post office didn't want these letters to see the light of day. But now, they're going to have to."

He frowned, turning an envelope over in his hand. "What are you going to do?"

"We're going to take this down to the museum and give it to Gary Oldman and whoever else works there, and we're going to make sure that this comes to light. I want every single letter to be read and I want everyone to know the truth of what happened at Sea Crest."

"This is getting to be a very Scooby-Doo ending."

I shrugged. "Call it what you want, but there was a grave injustice done here. If we can expose this place, maybe then the haunting will stop. The demons, Shawna, the doctor, they all seem to be held here like they're bound by a grudge or revenge, eaten up by what happened. Even Shawna is keeping Elliot here, preventing him from moving on. I don't know, but I bet once these patients are recognized for what happened to them, the ghosts will leave. And people like Brenna and Jody, everyone in the school, they will be safe."

Dex smiled shrewdly.

I gave him an odd look. "What?"

“I think you found your calling, Mrs. Future Foray.”

I couldn’t help but grin at the way he addressed me. “What do you mean?”

“You know the story of the Warrens, don’t you? They were the couple—a married couple—who were responsible for investigating the Amityville case, the Perrons, the Smurl haunting. They founded the New England Society for Psychic Research. They didn’t just hunt ghosts; when they could, they banished them, like a mini exorcism, or something like it. Encountering a truth, figuring out the reason for the haunting, and then fixing it.”

“So you’re saying that could be us?”

Now it was his turn to shrug. “I don’t know. I’m just saying, if we aren’t going to be chasing ghosts for entertainment, maybe we can use our, um, abilities, for something good.”

“Meaningful.”

“That’s right,” he said with a nod and took the burlap bag from my hands. “And I think this is a good start.”

The sharp blast of a horn from outside startled the shit out of us. We looked out the window to see the Highlander running outside. Seconds later, Rebecca came running up to the door, pounding on it.

Dex swung the bag over his shoulder and we hurried over before Rebecca hurt herself trying to break it down. Unfortunately, the door was bolted shut.

Lucky for me, I was marrying an extremely strong man.

“Get back,” he yelled through the door before taking a step and kicking it off the hinges with one go. Fuck that was hot. Fuck, I was lucky.

Rebecca stared down at the splintered door that was lying beside her then snapped her gaze up to us, eyes wide. “Impressive, Dex.”

“Do you wanna know what else is impressive?” he asked as he grabbed my hand and led me out of the building toward her.

“I don’t want to know,” she said with a grimace.

“This!” he boasted, holding up my left hand and flashing the ring at her. “She said yes!”

It took a moment of shock before it hit her. “Bloody hell!” she exclaimed. “Congratulations!” She ran toward us with open arms, engulfing us both at once. She started jumping up and down, making us jiggle. “I’m so happy for you!” She squeezed us hard and then pulled back, her eyes moist. “I’m serious. This, this couldn’t have happened to better people than you two. You’re meant for each other.”

"Thank you, Rebecca," Dex said warmly. "And congratulations to you and Dean."

I raised my brows. Rebecca looked at me accusatorily even though I hadn't said a word to Dex about it.

"Don't worry," he assured her. "Perry didn't tell me anything. I don't have to be a genius to figure it out, either. I've seen the way you've been around him lately."

She bit her red lip. "How do you know I'm keeping it?"

He gestured to her face. "Because despite the fact that you're scared, you're glowing. You're also happy. You've wanted this for as long as I've known you."

"I don't know what Dean's going to say," she mumbled, looking away.

"I don't know either," he said. "But knowing Dean, he's going to be okay. You both are, no matter how this plays out for you. You're going to be a wonderful mom, you know." He pulled her closer to him and kissed the top of her head. Even after everything I'd learned, there was something pretty special about their relationship, and I could see now, it really was like they were brother and sister.

She looked at me and smiled shyly. "Let me see the ring again."

I held it out for her so she could ooh and ahh over it. Then we headed for the Highlander, mailbag in tow, and drove off down the road, away from the school and sanatorium, from the demons and the death.

I went there as Perry Palomino and I was leaving as the future Mrs. Declan P. Foray.

***

Even though it was after five in the evening and the storm had covered the town in a blustery shroud of wind and rain, there were still signs of life in the local museum. You could see Oldman working at his desk in the quaint wooden building with its blue seascape mural on the outside. We got out of the car and ignored the CLOSED sign, pounding on the doors until he opened them.

He invited us in for tea and some shortbread cookies while we told him what had happened to us at the sanatorium. I told him about my encounters with Shawna and the *bad thing* and Elliot, and when he seemed to have absorbed all of that, Dex plunked the mailbag down on his desk.

It was like it was fucking Christmas. Oldman was in historical heaven as he poured through all the envelopes, bringing out the letters and reading them. I could see he was crushed that the allegations of murder and abuse were true, even though they didn't seem to have happened when his grandmother was working there. Still, it was a tough truth to swallow.

The good thing was that Oldman was loyal to the truth and to the hidden events of history and promised us that he would keep us updated in the coming weeks as to whether the discovery of the letters would help to end the hauntings. He had a feeling they would, just as I felt the fear dissipate the moment I found them in the post office. He said he would make a formal announcement through the museum and the local paper, attributing the find to me and Dex. I didn't think it was necessary but I didn't protest either. For once, I wanted to be known publicly for something that didn't involve me screaming my head off on camera. I wanted to be known for something more respectable.

And, if I'm being honest here, I wanted something to impress my damn parents with.

Because, as we got back in the car and headed up to Seaside where we'd be spending the night in a hotel, I knew my parents weren't going to be very impressed with the fact that I was engaged.

They were going to be more upset than they were before.

And suddenly it all came back to the fact that after everything I'd been through so far, facing my parents was going to be the scariest thing of all.

CHAPTER SEVENTEEN

We woke up bright and early in Seaside, having gone to bed as soon as we checked in—Dex and I in one room and Rebecca in another. The sunshine was spilling out along the beach as the waves crashed on the shoreline. It was warm again and shaping up to be a beautiful near summer day. In some ways it felt like the sanatorium was just a distant memory, but I knew too well that it wasn't.

Besides, the ring on my finger was a constant reminder of what had changed. Dex and I drank mugs of steaming hot coffee on the balcony before crawling back into bed for another roll in the hay. I thought I'd done a lot with him, but sex as an engaged couple was something truly special. It added bliss on top of bliss.

When it came time to check-out, we met Rebecca in the lobby and headed out on the road, taking route 26 through the lush interior toward Portland. The music in the car was blaring (Metallica) and the sunny weather was holding up, the fresh forest air flowing in through the open windows. I was with two of my most favorite people, yet I got more and more nervous with each mile that brought us closer to my parents' house.

Unfortunately, it also was Friday, so even though I kept texting Ada to the point of getting car sick (and no, I hadn't told her about the engagement yet), she had to be at school until three, meaning there would probably be a good hour of just the three of us along with my parents. It was amazing how much I had depended on Ada as a buffer between them. Now I had to suck it up and deal with it alone.

Of course, I wasn't totally alone. Dex was with me, and I could tell from the way he kept glancing over at me as he drove, the way his eyes lit up when he saw the ring, that he would do what he could to stand up for me, to stand by me. I kept repeating that to myself, trying to quell my nerves.

Once we drove across the Skidmore Bridge and started heading further east, toward the airport, I was a mess, nervously chewing on my fingernails, my knee jumping.

"You'll be alright, Perry," Rebecca said, putting her hand on my shoulder. "It's just one night, and Dex and I will be here. Even if you don't get their approval, they will love the fact that they got to see you. You'll see."

Rebecca really didn't know shit about my family, but she'd soon see it wasn't going to be that easy.

Dex turned the car down our family street, and I was struck with a sharp pang of homesickness. I loved Seattle and all, but I missed the countryside, the wide, green lawns and wildflowers, the trees, and the invigorating smell of the Columbia River.

But as soon as we nosed into the driveway, I realized I did not miss living at home. At all.

"Honey, we're not home," Dex joked. I shot him a wide-eyed look. It wasn't funny. I was freaking.

He leaned over and gave me a soft peck on the lips. "Come on, kiddo. Let's go show them your ring."

That didn't get me moving either, so I sat there, frozen to the seat, until Dex and Rebecca got out of the car and opened my door for me. I could tell that I if I didn't step out on my own accord, they'd carry me.

“It’s going to be fine,” Dex said. “They’re just your parents. Appreciate them while they’re alive and not mental.”

I appraised him for a moment, thinking about how hard it must be sometimes for him, being more or less an orphan. Even his own brother, Michael, was like a mysterious stranger to him, wanting nothing to do with him, leaving Dex truly without any family. Now my parents were going to be his in-laws, whether they wanted to be or not. He had a lot riding on this as well.

I nodded. “Okay.”

The three of went up to the door, me in front, Rebecca and Dex to my side and slightly behind. I lifted my finger to ring the doorbell.

And the door flew open before I even had the chance.

It was my dad, looking as he always did with his round face, strong Italian nose, and rectangular reading glasses that he had to constantly adjust. Unlike his brother, he looked like he’d lost weight. He also looked really happy to see me.

“Perry!” he cried out, bringing me into a big hug. “It’s so good to see you, pumpkin.” He held me so tight that my own boobs were choking me. When he pulled back he stroked my face with his warm hand and gave me a squinty-eyed smile. “You’re looking beautiful.”

It's not that my dad never paid me compliments before because he was always the more vocal, warmer parent. But for some reason, it was surprising me now. Maybe I was actually believing it this time.

His eyes darted over to Dex and Rebecca behind me, and I could see from the way he was moving his jaw that he wasn't happy to see Dex, and Rebecca was throwing him for a loop. He addressed her first. "Hello, I'm Perry's father."

Rebecca smiled like a pin-up girl and gave his hand a hearty shake. She had dressed in a form-fitting grey retro skirt suit, complete with an hourglass inducing belt and kitten heels. I had wondered that morning why she was looking so professional, but now I was appreciating it—it made her look like the mature one, and one out of three wasn't bad.

"I'm Rebecca." She cocked her head at Dex. "And I believe you know Mr. Foray here."

A smile twitched on my lips. Somehow my dad had to be more polite now that Rebecca was doing the introduction.

"Yes of course," my dad said in a tight voice, offering his hand as he stared Dex down.

Dex stared right back with a stupid grin on his face and did the two-handed shake. This was like Uncle Al all over again, yet Dex seemed a million times more confident. I guess because he knew I was stuck with him now and so were they. “Mr. Palomino. Or can I call you Daniel?”

My dad’s smile froze momentarily. “You can call me Daniel,” he allowed.

“How about—“

“Dex!” I said sharply, afraid he was going to say something else that started with Da.

“Daniel,” I heard my mother’s voice from inside the house. “Stop standing out there and bring them inside.”

Oh boy. My mother. I took in a deep breath and stepped through the doorway.

My mother was standing in the middle of the hall, looking as if she was having the same anxiety attack that I was. Though she looked put together as always with a jeweled tunic and white capri pants, her gaudy bracelets jangled on her wrists because she kept nervously flapping them by her side. When did my mom turn into Lucille Bluth?

“Perry,” she said, once she saw me. She gave me the once over. And here it came, the look of disappointment, the remark about me gaining weight. Only she snapped her lips shut and forced a stiff smile on them. I wondered if my dad had said something to her about being nice. “Your face looks very pretty. New makeup?”

It was more about what she wasn't saying than what she was saying, but I'd take it.

"New eye shadow," I lied to her and she gave me a quick hug. She'd lost weight too and I could feel the bones in her back.

"Looks lovely," she said, as she inspected me closer, her strangely tired eyes going from my hair to my chin, to my shirt, to my arm, to my hand...and suddenly her eyes were light blue discs bulging out of their sockets. Realization was setting in. She looked up at me in some sort of shock or horror or I don't know what.

"What is this?" she asked as she picked up my left hand. She stared at the ring dumbfounded then looked to me for an explanation.

"I have some news," I said, trying to pretend this was all totally awesome.

She eyed my dad, still not acknowledging either Dex or Rebecca behind him. "Did you see this?"

My dad furrowed his brow and walked over. His mouth dropped once he saw the shiny piece of jewelry. "When did this happen? And to whom?"

I let out a small snort. My god, were they ever in denial about whom their daughter had been living with for the last two months. I stuck my thumb in Dex's direction. "That man, of course."

And here came the real horror. My mom and dad looked over at Dex who gave them a small wave. "Mom," he said with a crisp nod. "Dad."

That set them off, both of them battering me with questions and ridiculous statements.

"What the hell are you doing?"

"You're too young to get married!"

"This has to be a joke."

"You're wasting your life, Perry."

"You don't know him at all."

"Is that a tattoo?"

"I hope you said you'd think about it."

"Why do you have a tattoo?"

"This is ridiculous."

"An anchor, what are you, a sailor?"

"You better give that ring right back."

"Did Alberto know about this?"

"This guy asked you to marry him and you said yes?"

I folded my arms, ignoring them until they were done.

"He asked me to marry him yesterday," I said sternly. "I said yes. I love him. End of story."

My mom gave me a wave of disgust. "Love," she scoffed, "you're too young to know what that is, let alone get married."

My father turned to Dex who was still standing beside Rebecca and taking their comments in stride. "Didn't you know that it's customary to ask the father's permission before you propose to his daughter?"

"Well, I thought about it," Dex said slowly. "But I figured you'd say no."

"Damn right I'd say no!" he yelled at him, his face starting to go red. I really hoped this didn't start a major argument because as sharp-tongued as Dex was, my dad's temper was worse.

"Hey, dad," I said, pointing at him. "This little reaction right here? Maybe that's the reason I don't live here anymore."

"Oh, where did we go wrong?" my mom cried out dramatically. She turned away and started shuffling to the living room, probably to get the wine out. "It's our fault, Daniel," she muttered hopelessly as she went. "We pushed her away."

Well, she wasn't entirely wrong about that. I looked at my dad who wasn't too happy about me talking back to him. But you know what, fuck that. I just watched Dex—my fiancé—get verbally slaughtered by my parents and he just stood there, taking it and not backing down. I wasn't going to back down either.

"I'm sorry if you think I've made a mistake," I told him. "I'm sorry if you think he's not good enough for me or maybe I'm not good enough for him, or we're just not good enough for you. I'm sorry I moved out, and that I'm, once again, not living the life you wanted me to. I'm sorry I'm just a big disappointment to you and I'm making all the wrong choices. I'm sorry...actually, you know what, Dad, I'm not sorry about *any* of that."

His eyes grew larger behind his glasses.

I went on, pointing behind me at Dex. "I love that man and that man loves me. He loves me for who I am, no matter what I look like, what I do, how I act. He loves me and he understands me, and whatever he doesn't understand, he tries damn hard to. You and mom can disapprove of him all you want, and you can disapprove of me all you want, but I really don't give a shit anymore. I'm done trying to please you, to make you love me, to make you proud of me. I don't need any of that anymore because that man over there gives that to me and he gives it freely. I'm happy, okay, and once the two of you realize that, maybe the happier you will be. Because you're both looking pretty damn miserable with your lives."

I was breathless by the time I finished my speech, breathless and feeling high, and it was punctuated by the sound of breaking glass.

I turned my head to see my mother standing in the hall, a wine bottle smashed at her feet. Droplets of it had splattered on her pants, looking like blood.

"Oh," she said distantly, looking down at the floor in slow motion. "It's okay, I'll clean it up."

Suddenly Rebecca was jogging down the hall to help my mother, leading her into the kitchen. Whatever I said had just stung the hell out of her.

Good.

I looked back at my dad who was totally acting like my mom didn't just drop a whole bottle of wine. He was speechless. This was a first for him.

I felt Dex come up behind me, resting his hand on my shoulder as Rebecca came out of the kitchen with paper towels and started wiping up the floor.

"Mr. Palomino," he said, reverting back to being formal. "I love your daughter. I promise I'll keep loving her for as long as we're together. I know she's important to you, I know she's precious. And I know she can be a pain in the ass. But I just want you to know that I have her best interests—and your best interests—at heart."

My father slowly nodded, eyeing the both of us like he was unsure what we were going to say or do next. Having my father be afraid of me wasn't a new thing, but this time it felt good. I felt like he was respecting me. I felt like I got some power back.

He cleared his throat and straightened his shoulders. He gave us a smile that might have been forced, but it was still there and that's what counted.

"Well, I hope you both like roast. It's been in the slow cooker all day."

Then he turned and walked over to Rebecca, helping her clean up the floor.

I looked up at Dex and twisted my lips as if to say, *well that's that.*

He smiled warmly at me as if he were proud as fuck and kissed my forehead. That was that.

***

After the altercation, the rest of the evening went smoothly. Ada came home right after school and she burst into tears the minute she saw me, mascara running down her cheeks.

"You should have worn waterproof," I said to her as I held her in a tight hug and she sobbed into my shoulder.

"I tried a new brand," she said, pulling out a monogrammed handkerchief that was probably by some hip designer and dotted her cheeks with it. "It was too clumpy," she sobbed.

We went out to the car and moved our bags inside, including the camera with all our footage. Dex and I were taking over my old bedroom while Rebecca was sleeping on the pull-out couch in my father's den. While dinner was getting ready—my mom feeling more chipper despite the wine incident—we set up a makeshift studio in my room and invited Ada in to watch.

We went through all the footage together and even though it was hard to watch sometimes, reliving the fear that was stalking us just yesterday, it also felt good. Without any editing yet or music or anything to enhance it, we could tell we had made the best Experiment in Terror episode ever.

Ada leaned into me as we sat together on the bed, while Rebecca and Dex sat on the edge of it, staring up at the computer monitor on my desk. “Having second thoughts now?”

I smiled and shook my head. “Nope. I’m sad that it’s over but I know we’re doing the right thing. Going out with a bang.”

She brushed her blonde bangs out of her eyes and put her head on my shoulder. “I’m glad I don’t have to worry about you anymore.”

“I just hope I don’t have to worry about you,” I said.

She tensed up for a moment, and I waited for her to say something but she never did. I’d have to come back to that later. Finally she stuck out her long leg and tapped Dex on the back with her foot. “Hey, bro.”

Dex eyed her over his shoulder. “Hey watch it, Little Fifteen.”

“Well you’re my big brother now, aren’t you?”

"I will be," he said. "And when I am, you can expect fifteen years worth of wedgies and atomic wedgies and noogies until I'm all caught up."

She stuck her tongue out at him. "I turn sixteen next month."

"It gets even worse for you then," he said with a grin. "Too bad there is no song called Little Sixteen."

"I'm sure you'll think of something," I told him dryly.

I settled back into the pillows, and with my sister at my side and my fiancé and best friend in the same room with me, I was struck by how damn lucky I was. Maybe I was jobless, and maybe my parents would never understand me, but I had these people in my life who did.

I stared down at my ring.

I was the luckiest bitch in the world.

CHAPTER EIGHTEEN

After dinner, where my parents perfected the art of small talk and Dex and Ada argued over some film re-make, we all went our separate ways to digest the food, have some more wine, and talk. My parents told us they were going out to a friend's house. I'm thinking that was code for grab a drink somewhere and bitch about me and my poor life choices. The rest of us hunkered down in the TV room, hoping something good would come on HBO.

After my fifth glass of celebratory wine that evening though, I wasn't feeling the best. I pulled a bottle of water from the fridge and told everyone I was heading up to bed.

"I'll join you in a minute," Dex said.

I nodded, slugging back the liquid, and made my way upstairs to my parents' bedroom to fish out some of the Excedrin my mom often had lying around.

I went into their washroom and opened the medicine cabinet, going through their bottles of medication, but coming up empty for something that would stifle the headache that I knew was coming on. It was my fault for drinking so much red wine after a week of drinking Jack Daniels and beer, but once we started toasting to our engagement, I got carried away.

I gave up, shutting the cabinet door, and was about to leave the room when I decided to check my mother's bedside table. I opened up the drawer and saw the bottle of Excedrin in there. I snatched it up and saw a few prescription pill bottles underneath. I didn't think my mother was on any meds these days, and a naughty part of me was wondering if it was something fun and stronger, like the Vicodin I used to use as a teenager.

I picked up a few of the bottles, wondering why there were so many, and held them up to the light that was streaming in through the hall.

They were all prescribed from Dr. Freedman—my doctor, my old damn shrink—and had medical names I recognized. Though I couldn't be one hundred percent sure, I was fairly certain they were the same meds that Dex had been taking back in the day, the ones that kept him from seeing ghosts, the ones I hid on him in order to uncover the truth.

And now, it looked like my mother was taking the same medication.

With shaking hands, I stuck two of the bottles back in the drawer, along with the Excedrin, and sat down on the edge of their bed, rolling the other two bottles between my hands. I stayed like that for a few minutes, trying to make sense of it, trying to figure out what to do. When I heard the door to my bedroom close further down the hall, I got up and left the room, pills in my hands.

I couldn't believe I was doing this again.

I went to my bedroom and gently closed the door behind me. Dex was sitting up in bed, reading a copy of The Gunslinger which he must have pulled off my old bookshelf, looking totally immersed in it. I subtly put the pills into my purse, hiding them for now, then stripped and slipped on my sleep shirt.

"Baby?" I asked as I got under the covers.

"Mmmmm?" he said without looking up. He thumbed a page over.

"What was the name of the medication you used to be on, you know the ones that made you stop seeing the ghosts?"

"Clozaril, Zyprexa, to name a few," he said. He slowly put the book down and gave me a hard look. "Why? You're not thinking about going on them are you?"

I shook my head absently, totally focused on what he said. The same fucking pills that Dex had been taking to keep the ghosts at bay were the exact same ones my mother was taking. How was that possible? Why was my mother taking pills for people who hallucinated?

"Hello?" Dex asked, waving his hand in my face. I stared at him blankly. He shook his head. "Nevermind. It's like talking to a wall." His eyes rested on my chest. "With boobs."

"What were you saying?" I asked.

"I said why did you want to know?"

I shrugged as casually as I could. "No reason."

I wasn't about to tell him what I was doing; it ran a little too close to home for him. I didn't want to be known as the pill-switcher, but I had to know. I *had* to. My mother wasn't the type of person who would ever admit to anything like that, especially after what her own mother and daughter had gone through. Holy shit. Holy shit. The more I thought about it, the crazier the whole situation became, the more fucked up the implications were.

If my mom was taking pills because she was like me or Pippa, that meant this *entire time* she knew what I was going through. It meant she was in complete denial about our affliction, about every fucking thing.

I had to know if this was true—I deserved to know.

"Perry?"

I looked at him.

"What's going on in that head of yours?"

"I think we should stay here for the rest of the week."

He jerked his chin back. "Uh, what? How about no?"

"Come on, I think you'll make good progress with my parents."

"Baby, no. Maybe they'll come around, but as much as I'll keep trying to win them over, after some time you have to know it's out of our hands."

"Please, Dex."

"What about Fat Rabbit?"

"Call Ana Rita and tell her we'll be back later. Or see if Rebecca can take care of him. She might want the company while she deals with the Dean situation."

"How is she going to get back home if we have the car?"

I thought about that for a moment before I exclaimed, “She can take Putt-Putt! I need to get that bike to Seattle anyway.”

“I’m not sure if Rebecca knows how to ride a bike,” he said.

“She told me she used to have a Vespa in England. Same thing.”

He laughed. “Yeah, I’m sure tooling up I-5 on Putt-Putt is the same as popping over to some English pub on a Vespa.”

“She’ll do it,” I told him. “She’s always wanted to ride it, she told me that herself.”

He pursed his lips as he watched me closely for a few beats. “Okay. We’ll stay. Because if it’s important to you, it’s important to me.”

“I knew there was a reason I said yes to you,” I told him, kissing him quickly on the cheek.

He grinned, running his hands through my hair and leaning in closer. “Do you want me to show you all those other reasons?”

I closed my eyes into his kiss and buried the thought of what I was going to do in the back of my head. I would watch my mother for a few days and see what happened. If it seemed like a big mistake, I’d put the pills back. But if it seemed like she was like me, was like Pippa, was like Dex and Ada, then I was going to get to the bottom of it. I was going to let everyone know and I was going to confront her.

She didn't have to be alone in this. Not like I had to be.

I took the book off of Dex's chest and tossed it to the floor. He brought his head down between my legs and I let all the other reasons wash over me.

***

The next morning Rebecca agreed to take my bike back up to Seattle. Actually, she seemed kind of excited about it, although it led to her fretting over what to wear since she didn't really pack for that kind of excursion. Luckily, Ada came to the rescue and let her borrow her McQueen leather jacket and designer jeans for the ride. Turns out both of them could wear each other's clothes with ease. I pretended I didn't hate them for that.

After we said goodbye to Rebecca, who also assured us she would love to take care of Fat Rabbit, Dex and I went back to work on the footage for the show while Ada popped in and out, enjoying her weekend. My parents kept themselves scarce and decided to head into the city to do some shopping. I think I even heard the phrase, "I'll keep an eye on the bridal boutiques" come out of my mother's mouth, which both thrilled and horrified me. Thrilled me because it meant she was accepting I was getting married—not to mention it reminded me that, holy crap, I had a wedding to plan—and horrified me because clothes shopping with my mom was always a nightmare. I could only imagine how wedding dress shopping was going to go, let alone anything else that had to do with the wedding.

But we would cross that bridge when we came to it. For now, I was just going to enjoy being engaged, and when it came time to pick a date and plan a wedding, well then I'd jump right in with both feet.

We'd been inside my bedroom for hours, just editing and adding music and talking about how we were going to tell Jimmy that it was all over, when I'd had enough.

I got up off the bed, stretching as I went. "I'm going for a walk, you want to come with?" I asked Dex.

He shook his head. "You go ahead, kiddo. I'm so close to being done here."

"All right, be right back."

I was halfway out the door when he said, "I love you, baby."

"Love you too," I told him. I skipped down the stairs and called out for Ada. She came out of the TV room looking sweaty. "What are you doing?"

"Exercising," she said, wiping her sweat off her face. "Remember, I told you about it and stuff?"

"Right," I said, only then hearing the Jillian Michael's DVD that was playing on the TV. "Well, I'm going for a walk to the river if you want to come do exercise the healthy and natural way."

She put her hand on her hip and said, "Boring," in an exaggerated Valley Girl impression and bounded back into the room before Jillian could yell at her.

I left her to her sweat session and stepped outside. It was back to being cloudy again, although the air was warm and there was a nice breeze coming out of the north that smelled like sweet wildflowers. I breathed in deeply and walked off down our quiet street like I used to do all the time.

I made my way down to the river, following the winding path, and found a bench where I could stare at the far bank, the Washington side. I plopped myself down, bringing my knees up to my chest and breathed in deeply. It was crazy to sit here and think about how far I'd come, even from the last time I was here at this very same spot. My life had changed so quickly, and in the end, so brilliantly.

With the wind whipping up my hair and a bunch of ducks waddling ashore that made me giggle about "duck spunk," I sat there and let myself feel really, truly happy. I had no idea what the future held for us, but knowing Dex loved me, that I was going to marry him, that I'd be with him every step of the way—nothing seemed scary anymore.

I sighed and closed my eyes, leaning my head back on the bench.

"Hello there."

I abruptly sat up and looked behind me.

There was a man standing a few yards away, in the middle of the path and smiling at me. Though he was handsome with his sharp features, sandy brown hair, and blue suit, there was something both unsettling and familiar about him.

I think it was his eyes. They were set deep and very dark, framed by long lashes.

I didn't say hello back, just stared at him while all my warning bells were going off inside. It's not like Portland was the rapist capital of the world, and it was the early afternoon, but still. There was something about this man who made my heart race and my legs want to run.

Finally, after he didn't say anything else, just stared and smiled, I said, "Sorry, were you talking to me?"

He took two fluid steps forward and I noticed how shiny his wingtip shoes were. "Yes," he said simply. "Sorry if I startled you."

I forced a stiff smile. “That’s okay.” I immediately started thinking of plotting my way out of the situation. I could excuse myself and say I needed to get back somewhere. I could try walking past him, or I could try going further down the path. I looked over at the opposite riverbank, thinking maybe someone over there could help, but it was too far away.

“Don’t be alarmed,” he said, putting his hands behind his back and rocking on his feet. “I don’t mean any harm. I’m new in town and wanted to see the Columbia River.” He grinned at me and stroked his clean-shaven face, and again I was hit with a weird sense of déjà vu.

“Where did you move from?” I asked, trying out my parents’ art of small talk. I knew I was probably overreacting in every single way, but the more I knew about this man, the more I could use against him later.

You are being so paranoid, I chided myself. Still, I brought my phone out by my side, my fingers twitching to hit the emergency call button.

“I’m here from New York City,” he said with a touch of arrogance. “Manhattan. And I haven’t moved here, I’m just visiting. I heard my brother was in town.”

I nodded, trying to ignore the tightening in my chest. “Cool.”

"Yes," he said slowly. "Very cool. What's your name?"

I didn't say anything. I couldn't. My tongue felt especially thick.

He chuckled coldly. "Oh, don't worry. I'm sure I could guess your name if I tried."

I didn't smile. "I doubt it."

If that fucker made any kind of move, he was going to know just how hard I could fight back. My karate skills were rusty and my hamstrings were tight, but instinct always brought them out.

"Pam," he said. "No wait, Priscilla." He took another step forward, only ten feet away now. I flinched, my body ready to run. "Nah, Priscilla is too fancy for some like you. It starts with a P though, I can tell." He said the rest of that in a rich, velvety voice.

I found myself getting up, my thumb hovering above my phone. "Nice talking with you," I told him. "I have to go back home."

I started walking toward him, my body tensing as I went past, our shoulders almost touching because of the narrowness of the path.

"See you in New York then," he called after me. "Perry."

I stopped dead, my blood thumping through my head. I blinked stupidly and turned around to look at him.

He stood there looking like a cocky asshole. The stance was familiar; his eyes were familiar.

I felt like I couldn't breathe. "How did you know my name?"

He smiled and shook his head, strolling toward me. I tried to run, tried to move, but I couldn't do anything. I was stuck in place, paralyzed somehow. This wasn't just fear, this wasn't something on my end.

I couldn't fucking move.

And he was doing it.

He frowned at me as he came close. "You really are pretty, you know that. And young. So young. Young blood is the best. My brother has excellent taste."

No.

No.

Pippa's message from my dream came flying back into my head.

I think the problem is something you won't see coming. I think the problem will come in the form of someone who is trustworthy. And when I think he comes, he will bring you here. Where everything will end.

He tilted his head and watched me with a discerning eye, watching my face contort in horror. "He doesn't know I'm here, and I wanted to keep it that way. I already tried to call the other week, but you answered and well, that was probably a blessing. I could never convince him to talk to me over the phone. You see, I was rather a jerk to him after our mother died. And yet, now I need him. And I'm sure I'll need you. Perry."

He reached out and put his fingers into my hair, cupping the back of my head. I could only stand there and watch as he brought his face in closer. Though the deep, almost exotic shape of his brown eyes were so much like Dex's, this man lacked something that made him human, that made him real. As I stared into the black pupils, I could see a swirling vortex, a hole with nothing underneath.

No soul.

"I'll give Declan your regards," Dex's brother, Michael O' Shea, whispered before kissing me on the lips. I felt like a hand was reaching into my skull, into my brain and twisting it around until my world started turning black. "See you soon, princess."

I slumped to the ground.

And that was that.

THE END

Read more for an excerpt of **Donners of the Dead**

A Standalone Paranormal Romance coming February 2014

Jake McGraw was unlike anyone I'd ever known. He was brash, rude, unapologetic and arrogant; chauvinistic, close-minded, and terribly stubborn. He was built like a tree, tall with a hard chest and wide shoulders and hands that looked like they could wrestle a bear. He was a cigar-chomping, scruffy-faced, beast of a man. I was pretty sure I hated him. And I know he hated me. But among the flesh-eating monsters in these snow-capped mountains, he was the only thing keeping me alive.

The year is 1851 and pioneers in search of California gold are still afraid to travel on the same route as the tragic Donner party did years before. When the last wagon train to go into the Sierra Nevada Mountains fails to arrive at their destination, Eve Smith, an 18-year old half-native girl with immense tracking skills is brought along with the search party, headed by an enigmatic former Texas Ranger, Jake McGraw.

What they find deep in the dangerous snow-covered terrain is a terrifying consequence of cannibalism, giving new meaning to the term "monster." While the search party is slowly picked off, one by one, Eve must learn to trust Jake, who harbors more than a few secrets of his own, in order to survive and prevent the monstrosities from reaching civilization.

An Excerpt of Chapter One

The dream never starts the same, but it always ends the same.

In death.

My father's death.

Sometimes I am six years old again and playing in the Truckee River, throwing up the cold, mountain runoff with my tiny hands and shooting shy glances at him as he watches me, the smile spreading wide on his auburn face. Sometimes we are walking hand-in-hand down the dusty dirt road toward Mrs. Young's homestead where he'll leave me for a few hours to learn maths while he enquires at Barker's General Store whether there are any hunting requests for him. And sometimes we are just sitting on the rickety porch back at our old place, watching the insects gather around the lantern as he tells me the Washoe names for them. They always sounded so poetic coming from his Native tongue.

No matter how the dream starts though, how wonderful the memories are, I can never enjoy them. I know they are about to be ripped from my heart. In a matter of seconds, the picture changes. In the river, he jumps into the water to join me – but never surfaces again. On the road, he drops my hand and runs away into a cloud of dirt. The worst one is what happens to him while we spend the evening hours on the porch. A low, guttural growl emerges from the surrounding pines, as if the trees themselves have unfinished business with him. Pa gets to his feet slowly, hesitantly, and walks straight into the forest. He doesn't even send me a backwards glance. Then the pines shake, their silhouettes frenzied against the moon, and I hear him for the last time.

One final scream.

Like always, I woke up covered in a thin sheen of sweat.

As I poured my bedside water jug onto my rag and wet my face, the reality sinks back in. I'm alive, in my bed, but my father is not. He really is dead and the irony is that I sometimes wish those nightmares were real. At least then I would know what happened to him. Either he drowned, or ran away from me, or the trees ate him. I'd take any of those to at least have an answer of why he left on that tracking expedition and never came back.

This night though, I had no time to feel the heaviness in my heart. Far away hollering interrupted my sleep and brought myself to my feet without thinking. I fumbled to light the candle in my stall-sized bedroom then quickly slipped on my robe and opened the door into the main room. It was dark and no one else in my uncle's house was stirring.

I paused, feeling slightly foolish at my impulsiveness and listened for a few beats, trying to catch my ragged breath.

The hollering again, coming closer to us. My uncle's ranch was on the far outskirts of the settlement. Our closest neighbor was miles away. Whoever was out there was in serious trouble.

I gathered my robe closer to me and made my way to the front door, about to open it, when someone on the other side started pounding on it wildly. I nearly screamed. I waited for a break before I opened it and saw our neighbor, Ned Kincaid, on our porch, looking like he'd seen something worse than a ghost.

"Eve!" he managed to croak out before collapsing into a coughing fit. I put my arm around him and began to lead him inside the house. He shook his head and leaned against the doorframe. "No, it's still out there."

"What's still out there?" I looked past him but only saw darkness cloaking the nearby acres and the pinpricks of stars in the sky. There was a strange pounding noise though, faint but wicked, off in the distance. Like Ned had, it was also coming in our direction.

"Nero!" he yelled and glanced behind him, his eyes glowing white from fear.

Nero was Ned's horse. A magnificent coal-colored stallion that I'd often see trotting proudly in his pasture.

"What?"

"Evie, what are you doing, who is that?" my uncle Pat's voice boomed from behind me. He was standing at the foot of the stairs, lantern in hand, my frail Aunt June cowering behind him and holding onto his long johns.

Ned stepped clumsily into the house and looked at my uncle imploringly. "It's Nero. He's sick, Pat. He tried to kill us!"

The corner of my uncle's mouth turned up at Ned's outburst.

"Now, Ned, let's calm down a bit here before we –"

"I'm serious!" he screamed so sharply that Pat's mouth was replaced with a hard, thin line. I sucked in my breath and took another look outside.

"Perhaps we should close the door," I said quietly, reaching over for the handle. Whether Nero was actually trying to kill Ned or not, the late September night brought a chill with it.

"No," said Ned, turning around and placing a wet hand on mine. I looked down at it. He was covered in blood. "I need you to see this, I need you to believe me. Martha didn't, she didn't and now I don't know where she is, my God, I don't know..."

He trailed off. There was a loud, solid *thunk* on the porch, followed by another. The house shook slightly. I kept my eyes trained on the outside but couldn't see anything.

But I could smell it. And knowing my tracker skills, I should have smelled it before. It was blood and sweat and hay and horse and something unfathomable. Nero was here, a few feet away from us, hidden by the black night, half-way onto the porch.

A severe chill threaded down my back. My lungs refused to exhale.

I thought about throwing Ned's hand off mine and quickly shutting the door but everything happened so fast.

Nero snorted.

Ned gasped.

A flash of red eyes and the horse lunged forward towards the door, his long muzzle snapping at us like a wolf, all white, powerful teeth.

Uncle Pat dropped the candle in the surprise, and joined me at the door, trying to shut it on the horse who was trying wildly to fit inside the frame, his wide girth only allowing him to come in halfway.

Ned covered his eyes and shrank to the floor, while June scooped up the candle before it managed to catch on the nearby rug. Pat and I kept trying to slam the door in Nero's face, something that, naturally, only made him angrier.

The sides of the door frame began to crack under the horse's pressure, the wood splintering. Between my uncle's grunts, Ned's child-like wails and June's quiet repetition of the Lord's prayer, I kept focused on Nero's head. It should have bothered me to be beating a horse in such a way, but this was no horse. Its eyes were blood red and surrounded by yellow discharge, its mouth was a foaming, angry mess, and its only intent was to do what Ned had said. To kill him. To kill all of us. No, this was no horse. It barely even smelled like one. My father would have known what it was.

Finally, Pat and I did one powerful heave in unison and the result appeared to shatter the bones in Nero's once handsome head. He screamed, a mix of anguish and frustration and then retreated, almost taking the door with him as he went. We slammed it shut and locked it, as if that would prevent Nero from coming in again.

"June!" Pat yelled. "Go wake up Rose!"

"I'm already here," was his daughter's reply. I looked to see Rose standing beside June, staring at us in horror.

He nodded, both of us keeping our bodies against the door. "Good, now go get the piano and move it over here. We have to make sure he doesn't try and get in again."

June and Rose scampered over to the grand piano that rested in the corner of the room. Rose loved to practice on it after dinner in the evenings and you could see the reluctance on her fair face as she and her mother leaned against the piano and slowly pushed it toward us until it was in place.

We stepped back and looked watched the door carefully, our breaths held in our mouths, our fingers twitching nervously. The piano was barely moveable to June and Rose but they were both small women and Nero was a thousand pound animal. He could easily destroy it in a few seconds.

We waited for a good few minutes, all of our ears tuned carefully, none of us making a sound. Even Ned had stopped his blubbering and was listening in-between sniffs. Rose made her way to him and placed her arm gently around his shoulders. I breathed in deeply through my nose and closed my eyes, concentrating on the animal. I couldn't smell him anymore.

He was gone.

"I don't think he's coming back," I said quietly, my voice sounding deep in the stillness.

"How do you know that?" Pat asked scornfully. "Don't tell me it's your half-breed mumbo jumbo."

That *was* precisely why, but of course I didn't say that. I learned a long time ago that talking back to Uncle Pat got you nowhere, and if it did, it was usually a slap across the face.

Pat looked down at Ned on the floor, who was now staring mindlessly at his bloody hands, and calmly said, "Now Ned, let's start from the beginning."

"Yes," I said. "What on earth were you feeding that thing?"

ACKNOWLEDGEMENTS

I'm keeping it simple this time.

Thank you to my readers, my wonderfully loyal Experiment in Terror fans who love all things Team Derry. Your passion and devotion does not go unnoticed. Yes, I write for myself but I also write for *you*.

Simply put, you guys fucking rock.

30525726R00244

Made in the USA
Charleston, SC
18 June 2014